THE PURSUIT OF SAM BASS

Moore drew his pistol and, shouting at the store clerk to get down, began firing into the store. The interior was quickly filled with an acrid, blinding pall of gunsmoke. Moore dauntlessly moved into it. All the combatants could see of one another were dark shapes illuminated momentarily by muzzle flash. Bass felt his right hand go numb. He held it up close to his hand. His finger was still wrapped around the trigger of his six-shooter, but a bullet had sheared away his middle and ring fingers. He took the gun into his left hand and emptied it in the general direction of Moore, then stumbled toward the door. Frank Jackson grabbed him by the arm and led him out.

The outlaws were heading across the street toward the alleys where their horses were located, but as Moore watched, three Texas Rangers emerged from opposite ends of the street, blazing away. Moore reloaded his pistol and joined in—and for a moment Bass and his friends faltered in the middle of the street, fired on from all sides, and uncertain which way to go. . . .

THE OUTLAW TRAIL

JASON MANNING

St. Martin's Paperbacks

THE OUTLAW TRAIL

ISBN: 0-312-97569-4

Printed in the United States of America

St. Martin's Paperbacks edition / October 2000

St. Martin's Paperbacks are published by St. Martin's Press, 175 Fifth Avenue, New York, N.Y. 10010.

10 9 8 7 6 5 4 3 2 1

THE OUTLAW TRAIL

CHAPTER ONE

THE GOOD PEOPLE OF ROUND ROCK, TEXAS, SHOT SAM BASS to pieces because he came there to rob their bank.

Bass rode into town with Frank Jackson, Jim Murphy, and a hardcase named Seab Barnes. The latter took a bullet in the head, and Bass caught one in the hand that removed two fingers, and another one in the back. He figured the second one would kill him—it had entered about an inch to the left of his spine and emerged three inches left of his belly button. A gut-shot man can't do much for himself, and Bass would have remained in Round Rock permanently but for Frank Jackson—maybe dead that very same day and strapped to a board leaned up against a wall with rifle-toting locals posing for the local photographers on both sides of his carcass, and if not dead then wishing he were as he lay on a bloody table with a sawbones trying to keep him above snakes just so they could hang him all nice and proper.

But Jackson was as game as a rooster and loyal as a friend could be, and had gotten Bass out of there. Slinging lead at the citizens of Round Rock with a pistol in one hand, he helped Bass up on his horse; there was no way Bass could get into the saddle without assistance. They rode out of the dusty central Texas town with the bullets buzzing like bees around them, Jackson staying right alongside his wounded friend's horse and holding on to Bass so he didn't slide off. It wasn't the pain—that would come later—but the world had started to bob around Sam Bass. Everything turned blurry and twisted and unreal, the way it got when a man drank too much snakehead whiskey.

Bass endeavored to load his pistols as they rode out of Round Rock, but try as he might he couldn't seem to slip the beans into the cylinder. They paused at the bone orchard on the edge of town so that Jackson could retrieve the rifle he had stashed there that morning. An old black man was at the cemetery, holding some wildflowers in his hand. Bass reckoned he had come to pay his respects to a dearly departed someone. The man stood there gaping at the outlaws, slack-jawed and wide-eyed. Bass knew he was a sight to see, covered in blood and white as a ghost. He tried a brave smile on for size. Living was all in how you died, and Sam Bass understood the importance of dying well.

"We gave 'em hell," he told the old black man, "but they gave us some back."

The old man didn't say anything. He just stood there and stared at Bass with his sad, rheumy eyes, and Bass was thinking that maybe he ought to point out that he might be the last man to see the famous outlaw Sam Bass alive, since it might be of some profit to him, but Jackson had them on the move again before he could do anything of the sort.

They splashed across a creek and up a lane past a stone farmhouse, and a girl was sitting in the fork on a live oak tree. Jackson yelled at her to get into the house where it was safe. He assumed that a posse would be hot on their trail. And when you put guns into the hands of store clerks, innocent people sometimes got hurt. Jackson didn't want to see any harm come to the little girl.

Reaching the Georgetown road, they headed north. Bass had no concept of how long they spent in the saddle that day. The pain was catching up with him and it was all he could think about. At some point during the ordeal he looked up and realized that they weren't on the road any longer. Jackson had taken them into a thicket of live oaks.

It was about as far as Bass could go, and Jackson could tell as much. He helped Bass out of the saddle and started to lay him out on the ground, but Bass said no. He wasn't quite ready yet to lie down and die. So he had Jackson prop him up against the trunk of a tree. He tried to drink some water. His throat was very parched. But he could not keep the water down.

"How far did we get?" he asked Jackson.

"Three, maybe four miles, I reckon. Barnes is dead."

"Yeah, I know that. I saw him go down. Wonder what happened to Murphy."

Jackson shrugged. They'd left Jim Murphy at Old Town so that he could keep an eye out for the Texas Rangers. Those steel-eyed killers had been on the gang's heels for months, and they'd been spotted around Old Town just a day or two earlier.

"You get a move on," Bass told Jackson. "I'll just rest up here for a spell."

"Reckon not. I'll stick with you, Sam. I'm a match for any posse, as you well know." He grinned.

"No, Frank. I'm done for and we both know it's true."

Jackson's grin faded. He didn't say much of anything else. Tried to bind his friend's wounds with strips torn from an extra shirt he carried in his saddlebags. Tied Sam's horse nearby and made sure Sam's pistol and rifle were loaded and within reach, and left Bass his canteen. Bass watched him, knowing this would be the last time he'd see his saddle partner, and wondering how long it would be before Jackson ended up in the same condition as he was in now.

When he had done all he could for Bass, Jackson stood there for a minute, looking around and frowning as though he'd lost something but couldn't remember exactly what.

"Guess I always knew it would end up this way," he said finally. "Thought it was the way it *should* end for men like us. I know I said we never wanted to grow old. But hell, Sam, I kinda wish right now that you *were* gonna grow old and gray, after all."

Bass smiled at him. "You know, Frank, you talk too much. I think I've told you that before."

"I believe you have."

"And you're burning daylight, too."

"Yeah." Jackson went to his horse and climbed into the saddle. "I'll meet up with you later, Sam," he said, then disappeared into the drought-stunted and wind-twisted live oaks.

Bass lay there and watched the sky darken through a canopy of dusty gray leaves. When night came he made up his mind that he would not die in the dark, so he held on until daybreak. He felt weak, light-headed, and numb in both arms and legs. The pain wasn't too bad now, unless he moved. By midmorning he had drunk all the water in his canteen and Jackson's, too, and still had a raging thirst. So he crawled to the edge of the thicket, and a little while later saw a black man driving a wagon across the open pasture. Bass called to him, but the man took one look and spooked; he whipped that wagon right around and high-tailed it back the way he had come.

A couple of hours later Bass felt strong enough to walk, and he had to have water, so he left the thicket, using his rifle to keep him upright when he felt himself tilting too far one way or the other. He left his horse—there wasn't enough still in him to climb into a saddle and ride. He had to walk bent over—it caused him too much pain to straighten up—and stopped frequently to rest. He didn't think about much of anything except his next step, then the next, and then the one after that. Every step taken was a personal triumph. It was important to know that Sam Bass was not the kind of man who would just lay down and die. It didn't matter how many times you told yourself while you were alive and healthy that you would meet death bravely; you just never knew for sure how you would act until the time came, and it was a big relief when you realized you were not going to embarrass yourself unduly.

It seemed to him like he walked forever. But the sun was still high when he reached the new Georgetown spur

of the Great Northern Railroad. There was a crew working
on the iron road, and Bass settled down in the scrub about
fifty yards away and called to them, asking that someone
bring him water. Finally someone did.

"You're all shot to hell," observed the laborer, a craggy
and sun-dark man, burly and big-boned, with rough, blunt-
fingered hands—an honest and straightforward man, the
kind who would look you right in the eye because he had
nothing to be ashamed of, even though he had nothing to
show for a lifetime of toil. In his presence Bass felt like a
no-account, a shirker. He knew he was in the presence of
a better man than he had ever been. And Bass envied him—
envied him his clear conscience and honest convictions and
the fact that he wasn't going to die that day.

"I am a cattle buyer," lied Bass. "Got myself bush-
whacked up near Round Rock."

Bass could look into the railroad worker's eyes and see
that the man wasn't buying into that. "I'll fetch the crew
forcman," he said, and turned away. Bass waited until the
man had gotten back to the spur before struggling to his
feet and stumbling deeper into the brush. He didn't get far
before feeling the need to sit down, finding himself in some
trees at the edge of a pasture and knowing somehow that
this was as far as he was going to go.

He dozed off, and the whicker of a horse woke him a
short while later. Opening his eyes, he saw a half dozen
armed hombres looking down at him. Two were still in the
saddle. The rest had dismounted. And all but one were
pointing a long gun or pistol at him. Bass recognized Milt
Tucker, a deputy sheriff. The rest were Texas Rangers.

"Who are you?" asked Tucker.

"I'm the one you're looking for. Sam Bass."

"Keep him covered, boys," said Tucker. He knelt and
confiscated Sam's rifle, plucked the shooting iron from the
outlaw's belt, and handed both weapons to the nearest
Ranger.

"I think they want to shoot me, Sheriff," said Bass.

"Sure they do. You've given them a real run for their

money. But they won't shoot you unless you try something."

"I've got nothing left to try."

Tucker was inspecting his prisoner's wounds. "No, I'd say you surely didn't. I don't know how you made it this far, frankly."

"Where are you going to take me?"

"Back to Round Rock, I reckon."

"I'm not afraid of you or these Rangers, but I don't want to face a lynch mob."

"If you hang, Bass, it'll be done nice and proper, after you've had your day in court."

"Oh, I won't live long enough to hang the right way."

By the expression on his face Bass could see that Milt Tucker agreed with that assessment.

More riders appeared. They were Rangers, too, a Sergeant Neville and two others, accompanied by an old black man on a swayback mule. It was rare, mused Bass, to see so many Texas Rangers congregated in one place. The Ranger motto was, "One fight, one man." They figured that no matter what the trouble or how steep the odds, one Ranger was enough to handle any situation. Bass was flattered that they thought so highly of him; they'd sent a whole company to bring him in, dead or alive.

Neville started questioning him. The Ranger sergeant wanted to know where Sam's horse was. Once he had his bearings, Bass was able to tell him where he'd left the cayuse. Neville sent two Rangers off to fetch it. After all the walking he'd done, Bass was surprised to learn that he was only three-quarters of a mile from where Frank Jackson and he had parted company. Then Neville sent the black man into Round Rock to get a doctor. Milt Tucker rode back, too; he told Neville that he would send a wire to the state attorney general to inform him that the notorious Sam Bass had at last been captured.

"What brought you down here?" Neville asked Bass once Tucker and the black man had ridden away.

"Money. What else?"

"You thought the Round Rock bank would be easy pickings?"

"That's what I'd been told."

"Who told you such?"

It had been Jim Murphy, but Bass wasn't about to name names. "Doesn't matter now. Thing is, we thought we had a soft job, and it turned out pretty serious."

Neville nodded, looked Bass over with the same telltale expression Bass had seen on Milt Tucker's homely face. "I'd say. Very serious, indeed. How many rode with you?"

"There were four of us in all. Three of us meant business. The fourth lost interest."

Again Bass was thinking about Jim Murphy. Jim had seemed to lose his nerve the night before they were set to ride into Round Rock, and that was one reason Bass hadn't balked when Murphy had suggested he check at Old Town to see if any Texas Rangers had been seen lurking in those parts. He hadn't wanted Murphy to go with him into Round Rock if his heart wasn't in it.

Neville didn't ask for names. He knew Sam Bass well enough to know that he wouldn't get any.

The Rangers settled into a camp. The pair dispatched to recover Sam's horse returned, their mission accomplished. Neville gave Bass water and offered him a corn dodger, but Bass wasn't hungry. Just bone-tired. He went to sleep not knowing for certain if he would wake up, and too exhausted to care much. The return of Sheriff Tucker, with a Round Rock sawbones by the name of Cochran, woke him up. The afternoon shadows had lengthened—it looked to Bass like he was going to be facing another night to try to live through.

As Cochran checked his wounds, Bass listened to Tucker and Neville talking things over. Seemed that the big augurs in Austin didn't believe Sam Bass had finally been caught. They wanted the prisoner brought to the state capital. The doctor said Bass wouldn't make it as far as Austin, and maybe not even to Round Rock, which was four miles away. But they had to shoot for Round Rock, at least, because there was only so much he could do for a severely wounded man out in the scrub. They used a blanket to carry Bass to the doctor's hack, laid him out in the back, and got started. After a few hundred yards of being bumped and jostled, Bass was sure he would not live to see Round Rock. But he was wrong.

They rolled into town well after nightfall. The Rangers kept the curious at bay. Bass was placed on a cot in a small clapboard shanty behind Hart House. While Cochran and a fellow physician named Morris tended to his wounds, Rangers stood guard outside. A Major Jones of the Rangers showed up. He hired a black man called Jim to stay with Bass at all times and do what he could for the prisoner. A young black woman, Nancy Earl, who worked as a waitress at Hart House, brought Bass his meals, but he wasn't much interested in food.

On one occasion Nancy Earl brought Bass his supper and turned to go, only to swing back around and gaze intensely at the outlaw. "You're such a young man," she said.

"I don't feel young. I don't ever remember being young."

"But you are. Everybody is talking about you. You're all they talk about these days."

"They'll forget about me right quick when I'm gone."

"I don't think so," she said, and gave him a smile before leaving.

Bass had a visit from a correspondent writing for the *Galveston News*.

"Is this the end of the outlaw trail for you, Mr. Bass?" asked the reporter. "Or do you have some scheme in mind for an escape?"

He was a frail man with black hair slicked with pomade. He sported a gambler's rakish mustache, but it looked more foolish than rakish on him. Bass could smell the rye whiskey on the man's tweed suit. Here was a man who did not go to great lengths to stay sober. But he seemed sober enough at the moment.

Bass had to laugh, even though it hurt something fierce.

"No, I think I'm pretty well finished. There's no use denying it."

"Your intention was to rob the bank here, is that right?"

"That's right. Needed a grubstake, and then I was bound for Mexico. The Rangers were making things too hot for me here in Texas."

"Did you know that a man was killed in the shootout? A deputy sheriff named Grimes. Were you the one who killed him?"

"He asked me if I was heeled. I said yes I was, and then all three of us drew down and shot him. If I'm the one who killed Grimes, he was the first man I ever did kill."

"You said all three of you. Who else besides Seab Barnes?"

"I won't tell the Rangers, as bad as they want to know, so I sure as hell won't be telling you."

"You were born in Indiana, is that not true? Do you still have kin up that way?"

Bass said that he did, and told him about his brothers John and Dent and his four sisters, all of whom still lived in the vicinity of Mitchell, Indiana.

"How did you get started in a life of crime, Mr. Bass?"

"Call me Sam. Sporting on horses was the start of it, I reckon."

"How did you get from horse racing to bank robbery?"

"I got cheated out of the winnings I made on a racehorse. Took some ponies that rightfully belonged to me, but some folks saw it as stealing. Went to robbing stages in the Black Hills. Robbed seven in all. But they were slim pickings. So I moved on to trains."

"Many folks consider you a kind of frontier Robin Hood, Sam. Were you aware of that?"

"I've read something along those lines—in your newspaper, probably. Its on account of me taking on the railroads, I think. A lot of folks don't have a high opinion of the railroads, and I can't say as I blame them. The railroads cheat the common man six ways from Sunday."

"Is that why you started robbing trains?"

Bass chuckled. "Heck, no. I started robbing trains 'cause I needed money."

"Did you ever give some of your loot away to poor folks?"

"Maybe once or twice. But I didn't make a habit of it, no matter what people say. I didn't usually have enough to take care of myself, much less any extra to pass around."

"Do you believe in God, Sam?"

"I do. Though He and I ain't exactly on speaking terms. Never have been what you might call religious, though I may get that way real soon."

The reporter looked up from his notebook and smiled. "Think you'll go to heaven or hell?"

"Damned if I know. I thought you were a newspaperman, not a preacher man."

The reporter put the notebook in his pocket and sat there for a minute, looking at Bass and chewing on the tip of his stubby charcoal pencil.

"Got a proposition for you, Sam. How about if I write your life's story? What would you think of that?"

"I'd think you had waited until the last minute, Mr. . . ."

"Banks. Jed Banks. So what do you say?"

"I don't know. I'll think on it and let you know."

Banks nodded and stood to go. "Just don't wait too long."

"You know, there's an old saying—something about how good deeds are candles that light the darkness of the grave. Reckon it's gonna be pretty damned dark for me."

"Are you afraid of dying?"

"Why, yes, Jed. I sure am. Ain't everybody?"

"I'll be back in the morning."

Bass made it through another night. In the morning Dr. Cochran came in to check his pulse, feel his brow, and examine his wounds. Bass asked him to tell him the truth, straight out.

"To be honest," said Cochran bluntly, but not without compassion, "I'm surprised you're still among the living, Bass. But I, um . . . I would not count on that being the case much longer. Would you . . . would you like for me to send for a preacher?"

"No, thanks, Doc. I've got other company coming."

When Banks showed up, Bass told him he was game. "Hope you can write fast," he said. "Don't think we have a lot of time. Last night the world started bobbing."

"Bobbing? How so?"

"Moving around real funny. Nothing seemed to be standing still. Scared me some, I admit. So where do you want me to start?"

"Let's start back in Indiana," said Banks, taking out his notebook and sitting down.

CHAPTER TWO

*I THINK IT ALL STARTED WITH THE AUCTION, BECAUSE
everything that happened in the thirteen years of my life
that came before that day seemed like just a dream. But
when they put my folks' belongings on the auction block,
life became awful real to me all of a sudden. My mother
had come down with child-bed fever giving birth to my
baby brother Denton, and not too long after that my father
caught pneumonia and died without leaving a will. It was
Wednesday, March 30, 1864, and my Uncle Solomon,
whose farm was just west down the Bedford Road, had been
appointed administrator of the estate. I didn't know what
that meant, exactly, but it clearly gave Uncle Sol the right
to sell off all my father's things and rent the house and the
one hundred and eighty acres it stood on. . . .*

It was the only home that Sam Bass had ever known,
and witnessing it being parceled away, he figured he should
have felt sad. But he was too numb to feel much of anything as he sat on the corner of the weather-warped porch,
cold March winds cutting right through him. They auc-
tioned off 124 items, from hoes to plows, an iron kettle and
a grindstone, the bedstead and the log sled, candlesticks and
a rifle, the one Sam's father had used to teach him how to
shoot. Sam's grandfather was present, and no one had the
gall to bid against old John Bass on the things he wanted—

a wagon, a bottle of good whiskey, and a gold watch belonging to Sam's father. The horses were sold to the highest bidder. So were the hogs and the cows. Ben Blackwell bought a Spanish saddle for thirteen dollars. It was then that Sam had a sudden urge to do some bidding himself. He hunted up his other uncle, Dave Sheeks, the one who had agreed to take him in, and asked him for the loan of some money.

"What do you need money for, Sam?"

"I want to buy my pa's other saddle."

"You have no earthly use for a saddle, boy."

Sam had never been one to take no for an answer. "I'll pay you back. I got money coming from the farm, don't I?"

"That's true. But most if not all of it will have to come to me for your upkeep, you understand."

"You can have most of it. All I want is ten dollars. That's all."

"We're farmin' folk, Sam. Don't need a saddle. You ain't got a horse to put a saddle on. I don't know why your father bought that fancy Spanish rig in the first place."

"Ain't the Spanish rig I want. Besides, Mr. Blackwell just bought that."

"You're missing my point. You got no use for a saddle."

Sam didn't bother telling Uncle Dave that he *would* have a horse one day. And not just any old horse. No, his horse would be the fastest hay-eater on either side of the Mississippi. And he had no intentions of living and dying a farmer, either. He had watched his father grow old before his time trying to make a go of the farm. It was like the land had sucked the life right out of his body. Sam had already decided that he was going to seek his fame and fortune out West. He didn't know exactly what he would do once he got out there, but whatever it was would be a long sight better than being a farmer in Indiana.

But Sam couldn't tell Uncle Dave any of that. He wouldn't have liked it, not one bit. He had taken Sam on because he needed help with his own farm, about two miles away, at the east fork of the White River. His two sons were off fighting the Rebs, just like Sam's older brother George had done. George had served with the Sixteenth Indiana Volunteers and died in battle two years ago. Uncle Dave had told the rest of the family that he would take care of Sam and raise him proper, though not necessarily like one of his own. He wasn't a bad man, Dave Sheeks. Just practical to a fault. Not only was he getting free labor, but had the prospect of making a tidy profit off Sam, pocketing the boy's share of the lease on his father's farm.

"I just wanted something of my pa's," said Sam forlornly. "Something that meant a lot to him. Something to remember him by."

"Oh, David," said Sam's Aunt Susan, who stood nearby, "give him the money."

Uncle Dave didn't want to come across as too much the hard-hearted miser, figured Sam, because he gave in and reluctantly handed over ten dollars. He looked like it pained him something fierce to part with the money.

Sam had four dollars in his pocket—his life's savings— and with that and the ten-dollar loan he bought his father's other saddle. It cost him seven bucks. The saddle wasn't as fancy as the Spanish rig, but it was pretty new. That left Sam with enough money to buy a bull calf. He didn't have enough cash to purchase one of the horses, and he had no desire to anyway. They were plow mares, and nothing like what he had in mind to put under his saddle. He bought the bull calf out of pure sentiment. He had raised it as his own from the day it had been born, and had in mind that one day he would own thousands of cattle on a big spread out West somewhere, and every last one of them would wear his own brand. So it was never too early to get started as a cattleman, and a bull calf was as good a place to start as any.

That bull calf and saddle were just about all Sam Bass took with him when he went to live with his Uncle Dave. His brothers John and Dent came along, too, as did three of his sisters—Clarissa, Mary, and Sally. His older sister,

Euphemia, being sixteen, refused to go and took off on her own. Before long Sam couldn't wait to do likewise.

Uncle Dave had nine children of his own, including two by Aunt Susan, his second wife, and all but three—a married daughter and the two boys off fighting what Sam's uncle, a diehard Democrat, bitterly called Abe Lincoln's war—still lived on the farm. That meant there was a passel of kids under one roof, and the first order of business was to build an extension onto the Sheeks house, a three-room cabin made of poplar logs. From the long porch on the north side of the house a person could look out past the orchard at the valley of the White River's east fork—a handsome view. Not that Sam ever had much leisure time to enjoy the scenery.

Being a man of considerable importance in the Mitchell township, Uncle Dave had a lot of land—better land than the stubborn clay soil Sam's father had wrestled with for so many difficult years. Sheeks raised corn, oats, wheat, barley, and flax. He owned the only threshing machine in the area, so in addition to working his fields Sam sometimes found himself loaned out with the thresher to reap the fields of total strangers. Uncle Dave made a tidy profit off the threshing machine—and off the sweat of his nephew's brow. Sam learned to hate that god-awful contraption with a passion; they called it a labor-saving device, but it didn't save him any labor.

Once the threshing was all done, there were apples and peaches to pick. When winter came, it was time to move on to cutting timber. Sheeks owned a sawmill in Juliet and had a thriving lumber business. During the winter months Sam was supposed to attend school, too, but he played hooky a lot. Dent and his sisters were very apt students, but Sam lacked the patience that scholarship required. So he could not read nor write worth a damn—and couldn't have cared less. The only books he had any interest in were the novels Aunt Susan liked to read aloud as all the kids gathered around the fireplace in the evenings. Exciting tales of pirates and knights and daring frontiersmen fascinated

Sam. His favorite was the story of Daniel Boone. Fighting savage Shawnee Indians and tangling with bears and blazing trails across the Kentucky wilderness—Boone seemed to have lived a life that was chock-full of splendid adventure. That was the kind of life Sam wanted to lead—wanted so bad that he lay awake at night imagining all sorts of heroic deeds he would perform. Why, there would probably be a book about Sam Bass one day, and maybe even a song, and in the future kids would sit with eyes wide and filled with wonder as they listened to his many glorious escapades.

Usually, Sam did not have to work on Sundays. It wasn't that Uncle Dave was much of a religious man. They seldom went to church, and that suited Sam just fine. He didn't want to spend his Sunday mornings on a hard wooden pew listening to the preacher spouting his fire and brimstone. Instead, he spent most of his free time fishing and swimming in the White River. Every now and then there was a dance, most of the time held in someone's barn. It turned out that Sam had two left feet when it came to dancing. And while he never had trouble making friends with other boys, he was terribly bashful around the girls.

Uncle Dave was very active in local politics and always had visitors at the farm, some of them important people. While Sam could not make heads nor tails of the *Cincinnati Enquirer,* the newspaper that came once a week with the mail, he heard all about the big doings just by listening to Uncle Dave and his company converse. That was how Sam found out about Lee's surrender at Appomattox, and the killing of the president at Ford's Theater in Washington. But none of that really mattered much to Sam. He was far more interested in the exploits of the notorious Reno brothers.

The Reno Gang was the first bunch of scofflaws ever to take to robbing trains in the United States. There were five brothers and a sister, but one of the brothers stayed on the right side of the law. They called him "Honest" Reno to set him apart from the rest of the brood. Folks claimed that the sister was as daring and bad as her brothers, that she could ride and shoot and cuss right along with the rest.

Immediately after the war, the Reno Gang began making a name for themselves. They boarded an Ohio & Mississippi Railroad passenger train at Seymour, Indiana, and, as soon as the train had begun to move, entered the passenger car and held up their fellow travelers. They also hit the mail car and used the messenger's keys to open the safe. Word had it that they got away with thirteen thousand dollars that day. The robbers wore masks, but everybody assumed that the Renos were the culprits, so two of the brothers, John and Simon, were arrested and indicted. They never went to trial, though. According to Uncle Dave, the Renos were savvy enough to spend some of their ill-gotten gains in the form of bribes to make sure they had free rein to continue their criminal careers. It got so that the railroad detectives finally resorted to kidnapping John Reno and hustling him off to Missouri, where he was sentenced to twenty-five years in prison. The railroads knew that the Renos would never be brought to justice in an Indiana courtroom.

The Renos robbed banks and trains for several years, and the biggest job they ever pulled off was the holdup of a Jefferson, Madison & Indianapolis train which netted them ninety thousand dollars. But that was their high watermark. A messenger was thrown from the train during the robbery and died of his injuries. The three remaining Reno brothers decided it was time to look for greener pastures— by this time the sister had forsaken a life of crime, and nobody wanted to prosecute a woman anyway. The Reno brothers were captured before they could get out of Indiana, and were held in a New Albany jail which was supposed to be escape-proof. It might have been capable of keeping prisoners in, but it didn't keep a mob of masked vigilantes out. The vigilantes arrived aboard a train in the middle of the night, got the drop on the sheriff, and used three Reno necks to stretch hemp.

"That's the fate deserved by those who do not abide by

the rules," Uncle Dave said, well satisfied with the work of the vigilantes. Sam figured his uncle could tell that he had been intrigued by the careers of the Reno brothers. And he just could not stop wondering how much money ninety thousand dollars really was! There was no telling what a person could buy with that kind of money. One thing was certain—a fellow with ninety thousand dollars in his pocket would not have to work from sunup till sundown behind a middle buster.

Sam had been in Uncle Dave's keeping for three years when he heard one of the many visitors to the farm speak of Texas. It seemed that now that the war was over the East had worked up a mighty big appetite for Texas beef, and some enterprising men were making fast fortunes driving longhorns to railheads, from whence the cattle were shipped to eastern markets. From what Sam heard, driving cattle was an adventurous undertaking, with Indians and flooded rivers and cow thieves and stampedes being only a few of the challenges cowpunchers faced. But many a young man was living a wild, free life as a Texas cowboy. Girls swooned when they caught sight of these devil-may-care knights of the open plains with their long jingling spurs and fancy sombreros. It didn't take much to convince Sam that this was the kind of life he had been born to lead. He was sick and tired of working his fingers to the bone, and, to make matters worse, his uncle wasn't even giving him his share of the rent money from the leasing of his father's farm. Uncle Dave was keeping it all for himself, and when Sam got mad enough to call him on it, Sheeks told him that he was putting his share in a safe place so that when the time came for Sam to go off on his own he would have a grubstake—or, better yet, enough money to buy his own plot of Indiana dirt to work. Sam didn't believe his uncle for a minute. He figured Uncle Dave was keeping every last dime for himself. And the last thing Sam wanted to do was to buy 160 acres and a mule just so he could bleed his life into the ground like his father had done. There was no way he would stay here and work like a slave for Uncle Dave until he reached his majority.

But it wasn't the money that triggered the big ruckus Sam Bass had with his uncle. It was all about gambling.

Uncle Dave called him into the common room early one evening and asked him point-blank if it was true what he had heard—that Sam had been betting on horses and playing cards at the Juliet sawmill. Naturally, Sam's first reaction was to insist on knowing who had ratted on him.

"That isn't important," said Uncle Dave righteously. "Answer me at once, Sam. Have you or have you not been gambling?"

"I have, and what of it?"

Sam's defiance angered Sheeks. "Don't you dare use that tone of voice with me, young man. You know full well that I forbade you to gamble, and you have willfully disobeyed me. This only demonstrates that I was right not to give you the money you say belongs to you, or to pay you wages for the work you do here to earn your keep, as you continually insist that I do. You would just squander it away."

"Earn my keep? You get plenty of money to pay for my keep. I shouldn't have to earn it! As much as you profit off me I ought to be able to spend my days sitting on the porch with my feet propped up."

"Yes, that would suit you, wouldn't it?" sneered Sheeks. "You are the laziest person I believe I have ever laid eyes on."

"Lazy?" Sam had to laugh at that. "I've worked as hard or harder than anyone else around here for three years. But I ain't gonna do a lick of work from here on in unless you pay me what I'm due."

"Pay you? Pay you what you're due?" Uncle Dave's cheeks were beet-red. "So you can fritter it all away on nags and pasteboards? Never!"

"Then you'll have to find somebody else to work like a dog,'cause I'm done."

"By God, you're an insolent little runt!" And with that

Sheeks picked up a chair and appeared to be ready to smash it into kindling—on top of Sam's head.

Sam wasn't afraid of his uncle, but he was kin, still and all, and Sam wasn't about to fight him. So he cussed Uncle Dave instead—and then took off running out the front door and down into the orchard, where he hid until later that night, at which time he snuck back to the barn to get his father's saddle. His mind was made up. He'd had his fill of Indiana and his uncle and farm work. He was going to Texas, and all he was taking was a saddle and the clothes on his back.

Then Sam got to thinking about just how far Texas was from the Sheeks Farm. He wasn't sure exactly how far, but the way people talked it was a good piece, a long way down at the other end of the Mississippi River, and folks said the mighty Mississippi was the longest river in the world. And even if a person could get to the end of that long river, he still had to strike out to the west and travel God only knew how far to finally get to Texas. Clear as mother's milk, that was too far to walk with a saddle on your back. The only thing to do was put the saddle on something that could do the walking for you. So that was what Sam did, choosing a mule named Hannibal for his traveling companion. It didn't really bother him that Hannibal was Uncle Dave's mule and not his—he figured all the money that Sheeks had stolen from him would more than pay for a knobhead mule. Fair was fair, after all.

Sam rode all that night, falling asleep in the saddle from time to time, jerking awake just in time to catch himself from sliding off the plodding mule. Old Hannibal would have kept going, leaving him in the dust. There was a train from Mitchell to St. Louis, and Sam counted that to be his best bet to get to the Mississippi River. The fare on that westbound train turned out to be ten dollars. That was all the money Sam had to his name—all his winnings from the gambling that had set his uncle off. He thought about trying to sell Hannibal, but just about everybody in the Mitchell township would be able to figure out that the mule belonged to Uncle Dave. So Sam just tied Hannibal to a post, stripped off his saddle, and bade the mule farewell. Hannibal looked at him like he was a rank fool and flicked an ear at him in curt dismissal. Sam wasn't going to miss the knobhead much, either.

The train trip was a long one, all the way across Indiana and Illinois, across the Wabash at Vincennes, and then through that part of southern Illinois they called Little Egypt, though Sam couldn't figure out why they called it that. He wasn't certain of his facts, but he thought Egypt was nothing but desert, sand, and rock, and the part of Illinois he saw was rolling farmland and forest. The corn stood high and golden in the sun.

When they got to the Mississippi, Sam switched from the train to a ferry. The river was an awesome sight. He'd had no idea a river could be so wide. It was the biggest body of water Sam had ever seen, full of boats of every description—from paddle wheelers belching black smoke from twin stacks to canoes, keelboats, bullboats, broadhorns, skiffs, and rafts. But even more impressive to Sam was what lay on the far side of the river: the city of St. Louis.

The gateway to the wild frontier.

CHAPTER THREE

SAM DIDN'T SPEND MUCH TIME IN ST. LOUIS. IT WAS AN UN-friendly city for a poor country boy, and he was in a hurry to get to Texas anyway. The problem was in finding passage down the mighty Mississippi. Sam didn't have the money to pay for even deck passage on one of the riverboats. So he lingered around the wharves, looking for his chance and wondering if it would come before he starved to death. Finally he got the break he was looking for—passage on a barge laden with the produce of midwestern farms and bound for Natchez and points south. All he had to do was learn how to measure the depth of the river with a plumb line and shout his findings to the pilot up in the wheelhouse. It was not that difficult a job, and Bass soon had the hang of it. In return he got two square meals a day. And best of all, he was headed in the right direction to get to Texas.

By the time the barge had passed Cairo, Sam had had the opportunity to talk to the pilot, whose name was Ben Simms, and Simms had convinced him to alter his plans. The pilot took an avuncular interest in young Sam and was genuinely concerned for the boy's welfare. Dave Sheeks had made Sam a little suspicious of people who appeared to have his best interests at heart, so one day he asked

Simms why it mattered to him whether an Indiana farm boy made it to Texas or not.

"Because I was just like you once, lad," replied Simms. His voice was rough and booming; the result, Sam assumed, of a lifetime of yelling at deckhands over the constant voice of the river. "I wasn't an orphan, the way you are, but I might as well have been. I ran away from home when I was about your age, maybe even a little younger. Always knew I wanted to be a pilot. But I learned quick enough that I had to earn the right. So I got what work I could, in the dockyards back at St. Lou. From there I went to being a keelboat man. Then got work on a sternwheeler. I learned this river inside and out. Finally wrangled my way into becoming a pilot's apprentice. Now here I am, doing what I always wanted to do."

Sam puzzled over the significance of the pilot's narrative. "Well," he said, "all I want to be is a cowboy. How does a feller work his way up to being one of those? No such thing as an apprentice cowboy, far as I know."

"Nope. But you need a good horse, for one thing. And you need boots and spurs and a lariat and all the other accouterments of a cowboy. You think a cattleman is going to hire some backfoot country boy to push his cows? Maybe to shovel horseshit out of the barn, but not to drive cattle up the trail to Kansas."

"I ain't got the money for those accouter—whatever you call 'em. But I do have a saddle."

"You're going to need a better saddle," advised Simms. "A double-cinch roping saddle."

"How do you know so much about Texas cowboys?"

"I have been to Texas. I have been all over. I have seen the elephant, as they say. Trust me, Sam, I know what I'm talking about."

"So what am I supposed to do?"

"Get yourself a paying job. Save every penny. Save up enough money to buy yourself a good cow pony and everything else you'll need. Oh, and you'll be in need of a pistol, as well. Nobody goes around Texas without a shooting iron. It just isn't healthy."

"Sounds to me like I would have to work for a good long while to make enough money to buy all those things," said Sam, dismayed. "I have it in mind to get where I'm going now, and not when I'm old."

"You're young and impetuous, that's your biggest problem. You have to learn patience, Sam. Do a thing right and you'll go places. Get in a rush and you'll make mistakes and land flat on your face."

"I know one thing—I ain't gonna lay my hand on another plow as long as I live."

"What else do you know how to do, boy?"

"Well, I do know my way around a sawmill."

"That's it, then. I happen to know a man in Rosedale, Mississippi, who owns a lumber business. I'm thinking I could put in a good word for you with him."

"You would do that for me?"

"I would—on one condition. That you do not betray my faith in you. You put in a decent day's work and you don't let Texas lure you away until you've got what you need to make a proper go of it there. Texas is a cruel mistress. I've seen her lure many a young man into her arms. But I've also seen many of them come back whipped by a frontier life they weren't prepared for. I don't want to see that happen to you. Texas, she has a lot to offer a man, but he has to pay for it."

"I'll do right by you, sir. You've got no reason to worry on that score."

"Fair enough."

When they reached Rosedale and moored there overnight to take on wood, Simms talked to the sawmill owner, and the next day Sam started to work there. He didn't mind the work at all, especially since he was getting a decent wage for his labor—for the first time in his life. Keeping in mind what Ben Simms had told him, Sam saved nearly everything he made. And he tried to keep his impatience in check. Simms had known what he was talking about;

Texas was calling to Sam and it was all he could do to keep from running to her. But he had given his word to the pilot, and so he stuck it out in Rosedale for the better part of a year.

Like the rest of the South, Mississippi was in the harsh grip of Reconstruction, and feelings ran high and hot against Yankees, who were blamed for the fact that blacks were elected to the state legislatures, some of whom were lording it over their former masters. Things turned ugly when a group called the Ku Klux Klan came into the picture. Those white-hooded hellions claimed they were defending the southern way of life, not to mention the honor and virtue of southern womenfolk, and they used harsh measures to get the job done. Being from Indiana and a family that had supplied the Union cause with several soldiers, Sam just tried to keep a low profile and do his job. He rarely went into town and even managed to refrain from gambling, though there always seemed to be a card game going at the sawmill, and he was always tempted to play. But as soon as he started thinking about how he might be able to double his wages with a good run of luck on the pasteboards, he reminded himself that he could also lose everything in a heartbeat, and he would ask himself if he really wanted to spend the rest of his life working at a Rosedale sawmill. The answer, of course, was no, so Sam rarely risked a dollar of his grubstake all the time he was there.

It was the summer of 1870, and Sam had just turned nineteen when he decided it was time to go to Texas. He had the money to buy a good horse and a double-cinch saddle, as well as a set of spurs and a six-shooter. It so happened that he met a family heading west—Robert Mayes and his wife and sons. The oldest son, Scott, was Sam's age, and they hit it off. Robert Mayes had been to Texas before, opening a hotel and livery stable in a town called Denton, and he had come back to Mississippi to get his family and take them to their new home, now that he had established himself on the frontier. Sam had heard of

Denton, since the town had been named after an Indiana man, John Denton, who'd gone to Texas before the Civil War and earned a reputation as a fierce Indian fighter.

The Mayes family made Sam feel welcome to ride along with them, and since Mr. Mayes had spent some time in Texas, Sam was able to learn a lot about his future home from him.

Texas, Mayes told him, was a land of unlimited opportunity. But it was also a wild and untamed land. Many of the men who had gone there were running from something—debts, a crime, a broken heart. There were plenty of thieves and killers and all manner of desperadoes operating in Texas. You had to be prepared to fight for what you wanted, and to keep what you already had. General Phil Sheridan had said that if he owned Texas and hell, he would rent out Texas and live in hell. Life was cheap there, but so was the land, and if a man was tough enough and was on good terms with Lady Luck and the God Almighty, he could get away with making big dreams come true.

From what Mayes said, it sounded to Sam as though Texas was still fighting the Civil War. A lot of Texans refused to accept that Lee's surrender at Appomattox Courthouse way up in Virginia applied to them. Union men were being harassed, and freed blacks, too—and sometimes killed. Martial law was still in force in parts of Texas, and the harsh tactics of the Reconstruction governor, a man by the name of Davis, just made matters worse. The harder you pushed a Texan, the harder he pushed back. Sooner or later, though, predicted Mayes, the carpetbaggers would leave and tempers would cool. Texans were beginning to realize that they had bigger problems to deal with—the infestation of desperadoes from Mexico to the south and the lawless Indian Territory to the north, as well as the hostile Indians who were raiding along the frontier.

Six weeks after leaving Mississippi, they reached the Arkansas town of Hot Springs, nestled in the wooded Ozarks, and spent a couple of days there to rest and stock up on provisions for the last leg of the trek. Then they headed south by west and two weeks later crossed the Red River—a body of water that was aptly named, since it looked like liquid clay, and tasted like it, too. Crossing the shallow Red was no hill for a stepper, and once they were on the other side Sam had to cut loose with a whoop of pure joy. He was in Texas at last! He felt free and full of life. It was the best day of his life because he had been carrying some of those big dreams that Mayes had talked about, and he aimed to make them come true.

The land here was flat and arid, filled with mesquite trees and big patches of prickly pear cactus. When they reached Denton, Sam took his leave of the Mayes family. They told him that their home would always be open to him, and he and Scott vowed to stay in touch. Sam rode west, looking for work as a cowboy, and hit pay dirt fifteen miles out of town at the ranch owned by a man named Bob Carruth, who needed a hand, no questions asked. Sam took the job without a second thought. Though he might have looked like a cowboy enough to suit Ben Simms, there were still plenty of things he needed to learn about his chosen trade, and the Carruth spread looked to be as good a place as any to serve an apprenticeship.

He stayed on through the spring of 1871, and by the end of his stint riding for the Carruth brand he was a fair hand with a lariat, could ride as well as most, and had learned the art of the branding iron. Such lessons were not nearly as easy as he had expected them to be, but he worked hard and because of that Carruth proved to be a patient tutor. But in spite of all that he learned, Sam didn't have the experience to go on a cattle push that spring.

"Another year, two at the outside, and you'll have what it takes to get picked for the big push," Carruth explained to him. "As it stands now, you're still a little green. I reckon that isn't what you want to hear, Sam, but it's how I see things."

Carruth was right—it was not good news. Doing his part on a cattle drive was every cowboy's dream—it set a man apart from the rest. It was a real accomplishment, one that proved your mettle, and gave you the right to strut up and down those trail-town boardwalks with a look-at-me gait. Missing out on that opportunity soured Sam some on cowboying, so when he heard that several men were getting together to ride west into the Llano Estacado and hunt buffalo, he made up his mind to give that a try. Buffalo hides were bringing two dollars apiece, and they said there were so many shaggies out on the Staked Plains that a man might have to sit and wait two or three days for a middle-sized herd to pass by him. You could just pick your spot and shoot until you had spent all your cartridges and account for a buffalo with every shot, and for a couple months of work you would make more than a cowboy put in his pocket all year. All Sam had to do was kill a dozen buffalo and sell their hides and make what Bob Carruth paid him for a month's work.

Carruth tried to talk Sam out of going. "A buffalo runner's life is a damned hard one," said the rancher. "I know. I tried my hand at it. And buffalo runners are prime targets for Injuns. There's not much an Injun hates worse than a buffalo runner, because they depend on the buffalo for their very existence, and so don't take too kindly to white men cutting down their shaggies by the hundreds."

"Injuns don't worry me none," Sam replied, with all the bravado that he could muster—and that was a lot.

"That's on account of you don't know any better. And because you haven't crossed paths with the Comanches yet. They are not to be trifled with, the Comanches."

Sam Bass soon had proof of that. Late that spring a raiding party of Comanches and Kiowas ambushed a United States Army supply column on the Salt Creek Prairie less than a day's ride from Carruth's spread. Every last man in the column was killed. A number were captured alive and tortured to death. Sam rode out with a bunch of men from the Denton area and viewed the gruesome scene firsthand. Some of the teamsters had been burned to death over slow fires. Others had been castrated, while still others had been cut open so that their insides spilled out all over the ground. There had been some bold talk among the men Sam rode with that they would pursue the hostiles and exact a terrible vengeance for this atrocity. But the vision that greeted them at the site of the massacre put a halt to such reckless boasts. Besides, the sign they found made it plain that over a hundred warriors had ridden against the supply train, so the Indians outnumbered the Denton posse three to one. The new consensus was that they ought to let the army handle it.

The massacre at Salt Creek Prairie also put a stop to the plans to embark on a buffalo-hunting expedition. All of a sudden many of the men who had said they were going, come hell or high water, remembered they had other obligations. Sam was keenly disappointed. It seemed to him that the Comanches would be more likely to strike at an isolated farm or a small frontier town or, at worst, a poorly guarded supply column than to take on a large group of well-armed men. But after the massacre spooked his would-be companions there weren't enough brave men left to make up a poker game.

Since he had already said so long to Bob Carruth, Sam found himself at loose ends. While Carruth might have taken him back on the payroll, Sam didn't test those waters. Cowboying hadn't been what he'd expected it to be, so he drifted into Denton instead. It was good to see Scott Mayes again. The Mayes hotel was thriving on account of all the new people pouring into Texas, but they could not give Sam work, so he took a job at another hotel, the Lacy House, run by a widow woman and by all accounts the best accommodations the town could offer. Sam stayed with that for a spell, and his principal responsibility was taking care of the guests' horses. Mrs. Lacy treated him well and he did as good a job as he could for her, but soon grew tired of shoveling manure and grooming nags.

It was through Mrs. Lacy that Sam met Sheriff Egan. The sheriff's wife was friends with the widow woman. Egan had been sheriff of the county for quite some time, having settled near Denton before the war. He had fought for the Confederacy and prospered after the war, buying and selling land and getting into the freight business. That was a profitable business to get into, since goods had to be hauled to Denton from the railhead in Dallas, about fifty miles to the south.

The sheriff's wife, Dillie, was always bright and lively, always smiling, and always very nice to Sam on the occasions that she dropped by to see Mrs. Lacy. She never failed to ask him how he was and what he was doing. There wasn't much to tell her as far as his doings were concerned. But he didn't complain about his work—complaining had never helped matters at all. But somehow Dillie Egan knew that he wasn't content with his lot—which was why she talked her husband into going to see the widow's hired hand.

Sam had no way of knowing that was why Sheriff Egan had come to see him, and when he saw the badge-toter coming toward him, it gave him pause to wonder what he had done wrong.

Egan showed up early one morning at the Lacy barn. Sam was cleaning out the empty stalls and didn't hear him approach—just happened to look up and see a stocky figure silhouetted in the doorway against the bright morning sunlight.

"You be Sam Bass?"

"I am."

Egan stepped forward and a streak of dusty sunlight slipping past a loose roof shingle flashed across the surface of the tin star pinned to his frock coat. The sheriff had dark curly hair, a trimmed beard, and piercing pale blue eyes beneath stern brows.

"I reckon you know who I am," said Egan.

"Yes, sir," said Bass, getting a little tight in the throat and trying not to betray his nervousness.

"I've been asking around about you. Bob Carruth and my friend Mayes have told me what they know. And my wife has spoken of you, too."

"Why are you asking about me, Sheriff? I ain't done nothing wrong that I know of."

Sam wasn't certain, but he thought he glimpsed the barest flicker of humor in those icy blue eyes.

"You haven't? Well, then, that makes you the only bona fide saint residing in Denton, Texas." Egan glanced around at the interior of the barn. "How long you been working for Mrs. Lacy? Four or five months?"

"That sounds about right, yes, sir."

"And you don't like the work? How come? You too good for it?"

"It ain't that. But this ain't what I want to do for the rest of my life, either."

"The same go for cowboying? Is that why you up and quit Bob Carruth?"

"I had it in mind to try my hand at buffalo hunting."

"So you're looking to get rich quick, I take it. With a little adventure thrown in for good measure. That sound about right?"

"Maybe so. Anything wrong with that?"

"Mayes and Carruth tell me you're a fair hand with rifle and short gun. That you can handle a horse and a team of mules well enough, too."

"They told you true, sir."

Egan nodded. "Well, I'm in need of a good man to drive a wagon for my freighting business. Think you could handle that?"

Sam's face lit up. "I sure could!"

"You'll be on your own most of the time. Have to be able to deal with anything that might arise. Have to keep your eyes peeled for trouble, and be ready for it when it comes."

"Just give me a chance, Sheriff. You won't regret it."

"I'll pay you sixty dollars a month. That's a good wage, but you won't get rich anytime soon."

"It's twice what I would make punching cows."

Again Egan nodded. He pursed his lips. Sam had a hunch he wasn't too sure about offering the job, but he was going to go through with it—and Sam figured then that he probably had Dillie Egan to thank for that.

"Well, you'll start as soon as Mrs. Lacy finds a boy to take over your chores here. That's only fair to her. She can't handle all this by herself."

"Yes, sir! Thank you!"

Egan started to turn away, but a late thought stopped him and he fixed a steely gaze on Sam again.

"You do what I tell you and we'll get along. But don't ever let me down, Sam. And don't cross me. I ain't one to forgive or forget. You do me wrong or ever step across the line into lawlessness, and you'll rue the day you ever set foot in Texas."

CHAPTER FOUR

JED BANKS REACHED OUT AND TENTATIVELY TOUCHED THE *wounded outlaw's shoulder.*

"You still with me, Sam?"

Bass opened his eyes and managed a wan smile. "Yeah. Sorry. The world started to bob a bit there."

"We can stop, and you can rest—"

"No. No, better not. Got a lot more to tell."

The newspaperman settled back in his chair, charcoal pencil poised over the notebook laid against his knee....

THE NEXT YEAR and a half went all right for me. I had a good job, made some good friends, and earned good money for a change. "Dad" Egan—that's what they called him, Dad, though I'm not sure why, he wasn't all that old— found out that he could trust me. The sheriff gave me expense money when I freighted a long haul and I made sure to keep a careful and honest accounting of what I spent on myself and the horses or the mules that made up the team I was driving. Although I didn't always travel alone—some jobs required more than one wagon on account of all the freight we had to haul—I liked it best when I was on my own. I liked the freedom, too, knowing that I had only myself to rely on if some mishap should occur. There were bandits to look out for, and you never knew when the Co-

manches might show up with mischief on their minds. Then there were the hazards of nature to contend with—and Texas was Mother Nature's favorite place to romp; flooded rivers, quicksand, tornadoes, dust storms, and blue northers that could lay a thick sheet of ice on everything in no time at all.

I was lucky in that I never ran afoul of Comanches, but I did have one or two brushes with road agents. I was in my night camp on the way back from Dallas with a wagonload of coffee, corsets, and cloth when two men appeared out of the night shadow, walking their horses. They pulled up short when I reached for the scattergun I carried, and said they were out-of-work cowpokes just looking for a cup of the java I was brewing on the fire. I had never seen cowboys with eyes that looked haunted like the eyes of this pair, but it was considered bad manners to turn a man away from your fire, so I told them to help themselves. They seemed mighty interested in the freight and the team of horses, but they didn't make a play. I don't know if it was the sawed-off shotgun or the news that I worked for the sheriff of Denton County that gave them cold feet, but after they'd drunk my coffee they took their leave. I wasted no time in killing the fire and slipping off a little ways into the night so that I could watch my camp just in case they decided to come back. They didn't, but I never regretted that all-night vigil. I figure losing a little sleep beats a throat cut ear to ear any day of the week. . . .

Sam Bass spent most of his free time in Denton. Apart from Scott Mayes, he took to hanging around with Frank Jackson, who worked for his brother-in-law Ben Key, who was a metalsmith. He also befriended Jim Murphy, whose father, Henderson Murphy, had built Denton's Transcontinental Hotel and was part owner of the Parlor Saloon. Like Dad Egan, Henderson owned a lot of land and was an important man in the county. Jim had never gotten along with his father, and for a good while would not tell Sam why that was. Then one day the two of them got their hands on a bottle of whiskey and found a nice quiet alley in which to share it. Jim Murphy's share loosened up his tongue. When Sam commented that Henderson Murphy would skin them both alive if he caught them, Jim just snorted.

"I would like to see him try! He's raised his hand against me for the last time. I won't take anything more like that from him."

"How come he does you that way, Jim?"

"Because I don't live up to his expectations. He says I'm always letting him down. Says I'm spoiled, and it's on account of my mother, how she pampered me when she was alive."

"You don't strike me as spoiled, Jim. Maybe a little on the lazy side." Sam grinned. He was just ribbing his friend, trying to lighten the mood. But Murphy didn't think it was funny.

"Yeah, well, that's what he tells me all the time. Says I don't know what hard work is. That I haven't done an honest day's work in my life. And that's not true. I've worked for him, at all kinds of jobs. Did the best I could, but my best was never good enough. Why should I work twice as hard as anybody else does, just because I'm his son? That's not fair, now, is it?"

"No, it ain't fair," allowed Sam.

"No. Fact is, I shouldn't have to work if I don't want to. My father is probably the richest man in the county. He's got more money than you can shake a stick at. If he lived to be as old as Methuselah he wouldn't be able to spend it all. But does he give me any? No, not one red dime. Says I need to make my own way in the world. That he won't give me nothing, and that it's for my own good."

"They always say that," remarked Sam, remembering his Uncle Dave.

"Yeah, they do, and it's horse puckey. That's what it is. So I've just about had all I can take of the high and mighty Henderson Murphy. How does he expect me to make my own fortune when he's got me working for him for no pay?"

"There's got to be a way to make a fortune out here,"

said Sam. "Looks like everybody else is doing okay, so why not us?"

Sam made another friend in a farm boy by the name of Charley Brim, whose folks owned a piece of land near the Egan farm. Charley was a good bit younger than Sam, but he could read and write very well. That caused Sam some embarrassment at first, but Charley wasn't the type to josh him about his shortcomings, so the two got along well. They worked out an arrangement by which Sam taught Charley how to play poker in return for Charley writing Sam's letters to Uncle Dave and his sister Sally back in Indiana. Charley also read the letters that came to Sam. As it happened, the court declared that Uncle Dave was no longer Sam's legal guardian, so he had no excuse for keeping the money due Sam from the lease of his father's farm. As a consequence, Sam got three hundred dollars one day. Sam was astonished when he opened the packet and saw all that money. It was more than he had ever had at one time. And he knew exactly what to do with it. He figured that three hundred dollars was his ticket to fame and fortune.

Every Sunday when the weather held, a horse race took place near Denton. It was just about the only excitement in town unless one went to the local bordello, and the way Sam saw it a fellow could only lose money at a cathouse, never make any. This wasn't true with the horses. Sam seemed to have a knack for picking winners at the scrub races. Other folks looked at a racing pony's legs, or ran their hands over the nag's withers to feel the lay of the muscle. Sam looked into the animal's eyes. He had to see a certain something in the eyes or he wouldn't put his money down. It was something like a wildfire, something hot and smoky and glowing.

The Denton track was a quarter of a mile long through the scrub at the edge of town. Nearly every Texas town of any consequence had its own scrub races, and there were men from as far away as Tennessee and Kentucky who would bring bluegrass thoroughbreds down and go from one frontier community to the next, making a profit off the locals, who would usually bet on the county champion.

Sam had spent nearly every Sunday for a year at the Denton track by the time he got the money from Uncle Dave, so there was no question in his mind how to put this unexpected windfall to good use. But he didn't want to bet his money on any old nag. He wanted to run his own hay-eater in the scrub matches. He had a horse in mind—he had seen her run and he had seen that wildfire in her eyes, too. What he needed was a partner, though, someone to throw in with him and match him dollar for dollar, because three hundred simoleons wasn't going to buy that particular horse.

The partner he found happened to be Dad Egan's younger brother, Armstrong. Folks called him Army. He was the black sheep of the Egan family. Sam thought maybe that was why he and Army got along so well. Army wasn't too fired up about the idea of owning a racing pony, though.

"I dunno, Sam. Where racehorses are concerned, I don't know a durned thing."

"Yeah, but I do. Mose Taylor over in Hilltown owns this chestnut mare. She's got one white foot, and you know what they say about that."

Army pulled on his chin. "No, I don't know. What do they say?"

"That it's the mark of a horse that's plenty fast, of course."

"They say that, do they?"

"That's right. They also say this mare has Kentucky blood in her, that she was sired by none other than Steel Dust."

Army Egan scratched his head. "Steel Dust? Don't seem to recollect ever hearing that name."

"Why, sure you have. You live in Texas and you ain't dead or deaf, so you've for certain heard of old Steel Dust. Back before the war that horse could outrun every thoroughbred and quarterhorse matched against him. I'm telling you, Army, for five hundred dollars we could own a horse out of Steel Dust, and she's guaranteed to make us rich men. Why, with any luck at all, you'll be rich enough to buy and sell your brother several times over."

"My brother won't like this, not one bit."

"Then don't tell him anything. I sure don't aim to, myself."

Army went along, finally, and they bought the chestnut mare from Mose Taylor, and when they ran her the first time, Army got more interested in a big hurry. But Sam didn't have a partner for long. Dad Egan found out that his little brother had bought a racer, as Sam had known he would all along. What Sam hadn't counted on was that no matter what Army and he said, the sheriff had made up his mind that no Egan would own a horse that was used for anything besides work. He was so dead set against what Army had done that he loaned Sam the money to buy Army out. That was how Sam Bass got to be the sole proprietor of a fast-as-the-wind mare with a single white stocking. He named her Jenny because he couldn't come up with a fancy name like all those Kentucky thoroughbreds had, no matter how hard he concentrated.

The sheriff wasn't too happy that Sam was involved in the sport of kings, either. He bluntly warned Sam that delving into horse racing would bring him into contact with the wrong kinds of people—people with low morals and shifty characters. But Sam wasn't Dad Egan's kid brother, so he wasn't going to let the sheriff talk him out of his plan, and Egan couldn't stop him, either. Sam was convinced that Jenny was his ticket to fame and fortune.

His next order of business was to find a jockey, and he picked a featherweight black fellow named Charley Tucker. Charley and Jenny hit it off immediately. They both soon learned to know what to expect from the other. Jenny ran several scrub matches at the Denton track and won every one of them. Folks began to say that she was the fastest horse in north Texas. And they started to think highly of Charley, too, though in the beginning many of them had just made fun of him because instead of using a saddle he would ride Jenny bareback, smearing some molasses on her to help make him stick.

Before long the reputation of Sam's horse, the "Denton Mare," spread far and wide, and men were bringing their racing ponies from all over to try Jenny on for size. A lot of people would show up at the track when Jenny was set to run, and those who bet on her were guaranteed a winner. Sam was making more money then he knew what to do with, sometimes as much as five hundred dollars a race. He would always pay Charley Tucker at least a hundred bucks every time, and sometimes more. There were occasions when others would try to lure Charley away, wanting him to ride for them, but Charley stayed loyal to Sam, and to Jenny. And Sam learned the hard way that Jenny just wasn't the same horse without Charley on her back. One time a man named Buck Tomlin brought his famous horse Rattler to challenge Jenny. Tomlin refused to race against a "nigger," so Sam replaced Charley with another jockey, confident that Jenny would win, and wanting Tomlin's money something fierce. But this time Jenny didn't win. From then on Charley was the only jockey for Sam Bass.

One day Dad Egan came to Sam and told him that he had to make a choice—either give up his gambling ways or quit working for the freight outfit. He collared Sam just as the latter was about to enter one of Denton's saloons, where he was planning to sit in on a poker game. Egan loomed over him, a stern eminence. Sam had a roll of greenbacks in his pocket, so he was feeling a little cocky. Looking back on the confrontation later, Sam reckoned he said some things he shouldn't have said, but he didn't cotton to being lectured on a public street. He wasn't a wet-behind-the-ears kid any longer.

"How come I have to quit freighting for you?" he asked, indignantly. "I've always done my job, haven't I? I never let you down, did I?"

"No, you didn't," acknowledged the lawman. "You're a hard worker, Sam. Honest and conscientious when you want to be. You could make something of yourself, no doubt. But you will come to regret it if you keep hanging around with the likes of Hank Underwood."

Sam bristled at that. Henry Underwood was from Indiana, too, though a few years older—old enough to have fought on the Union side during the war. He had shown up in Denton a year before Sam, bringing a woman along that he had married in Kansas. Underwood made a living hauling wood into town, but what he really liked were cards, racehorses, whiskey, and women. Underwood reminded Sam of his older brother George, who had died wearing Union blue. Sam figured he was a lot like George would have been had he survived.

"Hank ain't done nothing wrong," retorted Sam. "He's not a bad man."

"He hasn't done anything that he has to answer to me for—yet. But he'll come to a bad end, mark my words."

"How can you judge a man like that? There's no way you can be sure of that."

"I have spent a lifetime reading people, Sam. I know what kind Underwood is, and I also know what happens to them."

"Well, then I guess you know how I'll end up, too."

Dad Egan's voice softened noticeably. "I know how you will end up if you keep down the road you're traveling, Sam. I hope to God you see the error of your ways before it's too late. Because if you don't, then one day you will have a reckoning with the law." Egan thumbed the tin star pinned to his frock coat.

Sam was in no mood to listen to reason and he had no intention of giving up the easy money he was making. So he told Dad Egan he didn't need his freighting job, that he could do a lot better for himself without it, and that he would pay the sheriff back in full the loan he'd given Sam to buy Army's share of Jenny. Sam's only problem there was that though he did make a lot of money off the Denton Mare, he never could seem to keep much of it for very long. He spent it as soon as he made it—on whiskey, cards, and women. There didn't seem to be any harm to doing that, since he was bound to make a lot more.

Some of the money went to one woman in particular. She called herself Delia, though Sam was pretty sure that wasn't her real name. She wouldn't tell him anything at all about her past, or how she had come to be one of the girls at a bordello in a place called Rockbottom, located on the road between Denton and Dallas. Sam first met her on a freight run and there was something about her that intrigued him mightily. He had never had much luck with women, being entirely too shy to get very far with them, but Delia was different somehow. He felt at ease with her right from the start.

Sam never forgot his first look at her, pulling the wagon up in front of a weathered two-story clapboard house in the hopes of getting some water for his team. It was one of those hellish Texas summer days, and at first Sam thought maybe that was why the willowy woman with the curly auburn hair hanging in fetching disarray about her shoulders was wearing next to nothing as she sat in a creaky rocking chair on the front gallery. The only thing she had on was a thin peach-colored wrapper and Sam knew that because she had one leg raised, the heel of her foot hooked on the edge of the chair's seat, and she was paring her toenails with a clasp knife. The wrapper was loosely tied at the waist and had fallen away from the raised leg, to expose an alabaster-white thigh and more. She wasn't the least bit concerned about this immodest display. She just glanced up idly and brushed tendrils of reddish curl away from her eyes and smiled at the expression on Sam's face as he sat there gaping at her.

"What's the matter, handsome?" she asked. "Haven't you ever seen a woman's leg before?"

It wasn't just her leg that Sam had been admiring, so he stammered and stumbled over his words and finally managed to make clear that he had come to see about getting some water for his overheated horses.

"Water," she said, and her voice was smoky, soft, and seemed to set all the blood in his veins on fire. "I think you might be as overheated as the horses. Are you sure water is all you want?"

Sam's cheeks felt like they were on fire. "Well, um, I . . . that's all I have time for."

"That's too bad, because I have plenty of time on my hands. Especially for a good-looking man like you."

Sam figured he was pretty slow to catch most of the time, but he had already figured out what kind of place this was, and right then an older woman came out of the house. She wore a long scarlet robe unlike anything Sam had ever seen, for it was elaborately adorned with golden dragons. Her black hair, streaked heavily with gray, was long and straight and hung down to the small of her back. She wore more paint on her face than a Quohadi Comanche on the warpath. This was her brothel, and her name, she said, was China Blue. That was Miss Blue to Sam, she added, and he was more than welcome to the water in her well. The water was free. He was also welcome to anything else that might strike his fancy. But it would probably not be free. Sam looked at Delia and the smile on her slightly parted lips took his breath away, so all he could do was gasp and gulp his answer—that all he needed was water for the horses, which of course was a bald-faced lie. What he really wanted—needed—was Delia. He needed her more than he had ever needed anything in his whole life.

But he was on the job, and due back at Denton by nightfall, and if he was late getting in, Dad Egan would come looking for him, thinking that he had fallen victim to foul play. So Sam left Rockbottom with his virtue intact. But he didn't want it to stay intact, so he got himself back to that old house as soon as he was able. Delia wasn't waiting on the porch that time. Sam had to bide his time in a downstairs parlor because Delia was entertaining what China Blue called a "male friend." Miss Blue had three other girls in her employ—she preferred to think of them as under her wing. One was an Indian, another a quadroon straight from New Orleans (or so she claimed), and the third was a plump white woman. But Sam had no interest in any of them.

He got a look at Delia's male friend when the latter was on his way out—a tall dark fellow with a scar across his chin, who dressed like a riverboat gambler. Sam took an immediate and strong dislike to the man.

Delia came downstairs a little while later and the way she smiled at Sam made him forget all about the man, and everything else in the world, too. He gave Miss Blue two dollars and accompanied Delia up to her room. In the months to follow he spent as much time as he could in that room, since his favorite place to be was that four-poster bed with Delia's long slender legs wrapped tightly around him. At night the moonlight would slip through the sheer curtains on the window and fall upon her skin, making it look like cool white marble. Sam decided that he was in love with her, and told his friend Hank Underwood as much. Underwood had a good laugh, thinking Sam a fool for carrying on with a whore. He got an even bigger laugh when Sam announced that Delia loved him in return. Hank replied that if she had said such a thing she was lying. In fact she *had* said it, and Sam believed it, and refused to be swayed. He avoided further embarrassment by keeping his true feelings about Delia to himself from then on.

He wanted Delia to leave China Blue, and he promised her that he would take care of her if she would only come to Denton and be with him. He tried to convince her that he had the wherewithal to do that. She kept putting him off, telling him that maybe someday she would do as he wished. Sam learned from Miss Blue that the man with the scar on his chin, whose name was Penrose, was also trying to lure Delia away, and so far had met with no more success than Sam. She was trying to make Sam feel better, but somehow the news didn't sit well with him. After quitting Dad Egan, Sam spent as much time as he could with Delia, bringing her presents designed to show her that he had the money to guarantee that she would live in high style if only she would choose him over Penrose. He was spending so much time in Rockbottom that all his friends eventually figured out what was going on. Neither Frank Jackson nor

Jim Murphy laughed at him the way Hank Underwood had, but they both thought Delia was going to be trouble. They didn't have to say it—Sam knew where they stood on the matter.

And then one day he went to the Rockbottom bordello and found Delia with bruises on her face and a swollen eye—Penrose's handiwork. She told him that Penrose had promised her a horse, and had finally brought one to her—only to attach a condition to the gift: that she leave with him. Her refusal infuriated him, and he had hit her, several times.

"He'll be sorry he ever laid a hand on you," Sam swore, so mad he was shaking.

"No, Sam, don't tangle with him. He is a dangerous man. He would end up killing you."

"I ain't afraid of him."

"I know you aren't. But I *am* afraid. Afraid for you. I couldn't live with myself if you got killed on my account."

It rankled that she would assume he had no chance against Penrose—even though, upon further reflection, he calculated that she was probably right.

"But I've got to do something," he protested. "I can't let him get away with treating you this way."

"This is what we'll do," she said. "If you'll help me get that horse he promised me, I'll go away with you. But we will have to go very far away. We could not stay in Texas. He would find us for sure if we did."

"I'll go anywhere you want," said Sam, breathless. "Don't care where I am, as long as I'm with you."

She smiled—a smile that was somehow both sweet and salacious. "And it's not like we would be horse thieves. He did promise me that mare."

This was the same reasoning Sam used on Hank Underwood when he asked the older man for help. By then he had come around to Delia's way of thinking about tangling with Penrose on his own. The issue of who the horse rightfully belonged to did not matter to Underwood. He took issue with Penrose, sight unseen, for an entirely different reason.

"I think a man who hits a woman—even a whore—ought to be gelded," he said savagely, " 'Cause he ain't no real man."

So Sam went after Penrose, accompanied by Underwood. In the months to come he would look back and wonder if it was right then and there that he had proceeded too far down the road Dad Egan had warned him about—too far to ever turn back.

CHAPTER FIVE

PENROSE WAS A GAMBLER SO HE TRAVELED A LOT, BUT DELIA told Sam that he was most often found in Dallas, that he kept a room there in one of the better hotels, so Sam and Hank Underwood headed in that direction, stopping off at Rockbottom so that he could see Delia. Underwood got his first look at her, and Sam was worried that, because Underwood had thought his love affair with a fallen angel was so amusing, his friend would do or say something that might offend her. But Underwood was on his best behavior, treating Delia like a lady—before going upstairs with the quadroon beauty

Delia wanted to go with Sam and Underwood when they went after Penrose, but Sam didn't cotton to that idea. It was too dangerous, and he had enough to worry about as it was. She told him that she was worried about him, and he told her not to.

"I'm glad you brought your friend along," she said, as they lay together in her bed, her body pressed against his side, an arm and leg thrown over him in careless abandon. "I don't know if you could handle Penrose on your own. No offense, darlin'."

"I'm not offended." That was a lie. It bothered Sam that she thought Penrose was a better man. He even toyed with the idea of sending Underwood back to Denton and taking care of things himself, just to prove himself to her. But his desire to survive overpowered foolish pride.

"I just mean that your friend, well, he's different from you," she said. "He's a—a killer. You can see it. It's written all over him."

"He was in the war, so I reckon he killed a few men. But nobody's going to get killed on this trip, Delia."

"Sure. I hope not." She was silent for a moment, then reached up to touch his face with her cool fingertips. "I'm glad you're not like your friend, Sam. You're very brave, but I don't think you could ever kill anyone."

"Suppose I could if I had to."

She moved her hand down over his chest, and lower, and her warm breath caressed his neck as she nuzzled closer, licking his jawline. "Oh, I think you're a much better lover than you are a fighter," she whispered huskily, and then she rolled over on top of him, her hands on his shoulders, smiling down at him through a veil of unruly auburn hair. Sam figured she wanted to change the subject—and she knew a surefire way to do it, too.

Sam rode out at daybreak with Underwood, promising Delia that he would be back in a few days with her horse, and then they would leave Texas. "You figure out where you want to go," he said, "and be ready to go there."

They got to Dallas late that day. A dusty little cow town only a few years earlier, Dallas had boomed since the arrival of the railroad. Next to St. Louis it was the biggest city Sam had seen. When they found the Palace Hotel, the place that Penrose called home, Underwood asked Sam for the first time how he wanted to play it. He acted like he really didn't care one way or the other. Talk or bullets, either way.

"Well," said Sam, "seeing as how they've been known to hang horse thieves in these parts, I figured we might ought to try and talk this hombre into doing the right thing."

"So you're aiming to try to reason with the man that beat up on that pretty gal of yours." Underwood sounded skeptical. "You always were a good talker, Sam, I'll grant you. But if you can't pull it off this time, there are other ways." He pulled his coat back just enough so Sam could see the butt of the Remington Army revolver shoved under his belt.

"They hang people for murder, too."

"Murder is one thing," said Underwood complacently. "Self-defense is another."

They walked into the hotel. Sam had never seen anything quite like it—big sofas and armchairs of shiny black horsehair, potted plants and thick rugs and portraits of fancy-dressed folks, and a crystal chandelier the size of a buckboard hanging from the ceiling. The clerk behind the polished counter was duded up like he was on his way to a high-society ball. While Underwood hung back, Sam went right up to the clerk like he owned the place and asked if Mr. Penrose was in.

The clerk leaned over the counter and gave Sam the once-over, not bothering to hide his contempt. Sam had been on the trail all day and was covered with dust, and besides that he had never been one to worry about the cut of the clothes he wore.

"What business do you have with Mr. Penrose?" asked the clerk, as though he couldn't imagine there would be anything that Sam could have to say that would be of the slightest interest to anyone who resided at the Palace Hotel.

Sam smoothed his hackles down, realizing that what he wanted to tell this pompous jackass wouldn't get him anywhere.

"I have a very important letter for Mr. Penrose," he said.

"Then give it to me and I will see that he gets it."

"I can't do that. I have to deliver it to him myself. I gave my word."

The clerk grimaced. "Mr. Penrose is not here at present. He left a few hours ago."

"Do you know where he went?"

"I believe he was taking a horse to Waco. A gift for a lady friend, or so he said."

"A lady friend. In Waco."

"That's what I said. Are you hard of hearing?"

Sam forced a smile. "Just a little slow sometimes, or so I'm told."

There was only an hour of daylight left, but he and Underwood pushed their tired horses down the road to Waco. Sam didn't figure Penrose would ride through the night, but would instead camp somewhere along the way. And that, as it happened, was just what Penrose did. Four hours out of Dallas they spotted a campfire flickering in a grove of oaks just off the road. Dismounting, they crept closer, quiet as Comanches. Penrose was sitting on a blanket, leaning back against his saddle, watching the campfire's flames dance as he sipped from a silver whiskey flask. Two horses were tethered and hobbled nearby. One was a blaze-faced sorrel, the other a coyote dun. Sam knew the first had to be the horse Delia had described to him, the one Penrose had promised to her—the same horse Penrose was now taking to another woman in Waco, since Delia had turned him down. Obviously Penrose didn't really give a damn about Delia, and that was a relief to Sam. All he wanted was a woman to own, one that he could buy and that would look good on his arm as he sashayed through the lobby of that fancy hotel back in Dallas. Knowing that Penrose was bent on giving the horse to someone else angered Sam. He was sure right then and there that he was doing the right thing.

"I'll circle around to the other side," whispered Underwood. "Wait until I call out to him, then move in."

Sam nodded, willing to leave the strategy to Hank, who had, after all, a lot more experience than he did when it came to closing in on the enemy.

Underwood started moving away, paused, and turned back to Sam. "When you move in, do it with your pistol in your hand."

Sam nodded. His mouth was drier than cotton, his heart beating like a triphammer.

It seemed to take Underwood forever to get into position. Sam kept an anxious eye on Penrose, expecting at any moment that he would realize he was no longer alone in the grove of oak trees. If he had time to kick the campfire out it would become black as pitch under the trees, and Sam didn't want to have to grope around in the darkness wondering where he was. But the gambler didn't move—he appeared lost in thought as he watched the flickering flames and the curl of smoke that rose into the branches overhead.

Penrose heard Underwood at the same time that Sam saw his friend emerge from the night, and the gambler was on his feet in a flash, whirling, pistol in hand. Sam crashed through the brush and into the clearing, yanking his own gun clear of his belt. He thought Penrose was a second away from shooting it out with Underwood—until he heard all the noise Sam made. Then he realized that he was boxed in. That made him think twice about gunplay, and by the time he'd done that it was too late for him. He lowered his pistol, but didn't drop it, took a look at Sam, then a longer one, and Sam could tell that he'd been recognized.

"I know you," drawled Penrose, his accent a thick southern one. "You're Delia's little Yankee stud."

"Guess I don't need to tell you why I'm here, then," replied Sam. Now that he'd made his play, he felt much better about things. His nerves had settled down. Both his voice and gun hand were steady.

"You've come a long way for nothing. You can have her. I'm done with her. Moving on to better things."

"You're free to move on—but without that blazed sorrel mare. You promised that horse to Delia and I'm going to see that you keep your promise."

Penrose bristled. "I told her she could have the horse if she came away with me. She chose not to."

"That's not her story—and I believe her over you."

Penrose gave him a crooked smile. "Well, of course you do, boy. You probably believe every damn thing she tells you. You're too wet behind the ears to know any better."

"He's just trying to bait you, Sam," said Underwood. "Let's get on with it." He was edging closer to Penrose while the gambler focused his attention on Sam.

"You're going to give over ownership of that horse to Delia," said Sam, "and sign your name to a paper saying that it's all nice and legal, too."

"The hell you say," rasped Penrose. "That horse cost me a lot of money."

"You had better let go of that pistol, mister," warned Underwood.

Penrose began to turn back toward Underwood—with the thumb-buster still in his grasp—and suddenly Sam could see just how this was going to turn out, and he didn't like what he saw. But before he could shout at Underwood not to, Hank had pulled the trigger. The gunshot was so loud in Sam's ear that he figured they could hear it all the way back in Dallas. Penrose went down. Underwood rushed in and kicked the pistol out of the fallen man's hand. Cursing, Sam moved in, too, thinking that Underwood had killed the gambler. But Penrose was clutching his right knee. His fingers were dark with his own blood. Underwood bent over and put the barrel of his pistol to the gambler's head and thumbed the hammer back.

"Now, are you going to do what my friend told you to do?" he asked quietly.

"Not if you're going to kill me anyway, I'm not," said Penrose through teeth clenched against the pain.

"We're not killers," said Sam. "All we want is the horse."

"I'll sign your paper, you little bastard."

Sam had already asked Underwood to write it out, since he couldn't spell worth a damn, so all Penrose had to do was sign it with the stub of a charcoal pencil that Sam produced. He got some blood on the paper, but there was no way to avoid that. When he was done he threw the pencil at Sam. Sam retrieved it, the paper, and then the mare.

"Reckon we don't have any more business with you," he told Penrose.

"That's what you think. You'll see me once more, you son of a bitch."

Sam didn't bother telling him that he and Delia were going to make tracks out of Texas. Penrose would find that out soon enough. With a bullet-shattered knee he would be a long while recovering enough to start looking. By then the trail would be cold. Sam didn't think it was likely he would ever see the gambler again.

"Come on, Hank," he told Underwood. "We're done here."

He turned away as Underwood stepped over Penrose to follow.

The second gunshot spun Sam around like a puppet on a string. He saw Underwood standing over Penrose, still aiming the pistol at him, a wisp of gunsmoke escaping the barrel. The gambler was dead—Sam could see that in a glance.

"Goddamn it, Hank!" Sam breathed. His whole body had gone numb.

"He would have come after us, Sam."

"I didn't care about that! Christ!"

"I cared about it. I don't aim to live the rest of my life looking over my shoulder."

"But you will now. We both will. You just guaranteed that." Sam cussed some more, feeling sick to his stomach.

"Don't worry. Nobody is going to connect us to this."

"Nobody? You're a gold-plated fool, Hank, that's what you are. Should we go back to Dallas and shoot that hotel clerk now?"

Underwood stared at him, and Sam couldn't read his expression. Then Underwood knelt and searched Penrose, coming up with a wad of money and the silver-scrolled whiskey flask.

"What the hell do you think you're doing?" Sam asked.

"Better make it look like he was robbed. We'll take his horse and saddle, too."

"The hell you say. If you take anything, you won't be riding with me."

Underwood looked at Sam with that flat, unreadable expression on his face again, and for a fleeting instant Sam wondered if his own life was in danger. Delia had been right—Hank Underwood was a killer. Sam was furious at him for gunning down Penrose. But at the same time he knew that if Underwood hadn't come along, Delia wouldn't have gotten the blazed sorrel that had belonged to her. And that meant he wouldn't have gotten Delia. So as much as Sam wanted to walk away from Underwood, he couldn't. In a bizarre way he was obligated to the man who had just turned him into an accomplice to murder.

Underwood tossed the money into the fire, and they watched the flames consume the bank notes. Then he went to Penrose's horse and used a clasp knife to cut the hobbles and the tether. By that time Sam had stomped the fire down to smoldering orange coals, and they made their way back to the trees to their own ponies, with Sam leading the sorrel mare. They rode a half dozen miles down the road before making a cold camp, and not a word passed between the two of them the whole time. Sam was bone-tired but he could not sleep. Underwood slept, though. He slept like a baby after a few swigs from the silver pocket flask. Too disgusted to say anything, Sam rolled up in his blanket and pretended to go to sleep.

The following day they stayed off the road, bypassing Dallas and reaching Rockbottom well into the night. When Underwood announced that he was riding straight through to Denton, Sam was surprised, but he got the feeling that Underwood wanted to be shed of his company. They said their so-longs and Underwood rode off into the night.

The look on Delia's face when she saw the sorrel mare warmed Sam's heart. He had never seen anyone so happy before. She promised him a night to remember, but Sam was so bushed he fell fast asleep as soon as he stretched out on her four-poster bed. He figured there would be plenty of nights with her to remember. She didn't ask him a single question about how he had gotten the horse away from Penrose, and Sam was heartily glad for her discretion.

The next morning he told her he would ride to Denton, get Jenny and his belongings, and be back in Rockbottom that night. He asked her if she had made up her mind where she wanted to go.

"California," she said, with conviction. "I want to live by the sea. Is that too much to ask, Sam?"

"Nah. Whatever you want, Delia, that's what we'll do. Be ready to go when I get back."

She told him that she would be.

When Sam returned from Denton that evening, Delia was gone.

"She lit out this morning, right after you left," China Blue told him. "Took that horse you brought her and rode off like the hounds of hell were hot on her heels."

Sam felt like he had been poleaxed. He sat on the porch in the same rocking chair Delia had been sitting in when he'd first laid eyes on her, and he stared off at nothing, trying to figure out why this had happened to him. China Blue took pity on him; eventually she came out and asked if he wanted anything to eat or drink. Sam said no thanks— he doubted if he would ever eat or drink anything again. She went back inside and later came back out and stood there with her hands planted on her beefy hips and looked at him. He didn't want to see the sympathy in her eyes so he avoided her gaze.

"Mark it down to one of life's lessons, honey," she said. "Delia liked you, but she wasn't ever in love with you. She might've taken Penrose up on his offer had he not told her that if she didn't come with him he knew another woman who would. That really made Delia mad. She used you to get back at Penrose, I reckon. Hell hath no fury like a woman scorned, like somebody—I forget who—once said."

"Did she go to California?"

"I have no idea where she was headed, and you shouldn't care."

Riding back to Denton, Sam tried not to. He was so wrapped up in his misery over Delia that he didn't give much thought to the fact that he had been party to a cold-blooded killing that had put him on the wrong side of the law—so far on the wrong side that he would never get back.

CHAPTER SIX

IT'S FUNNY HOW LIFE CAN THROW YOU. JUST WHEN YOU think you have got it all figured out so that the future is looking bright, all your plans go haywire. Before that business with Delia and Penrose I'd had everything right here in the palm of my hand. Afterwards, every last thing I tried to do went sour. I felt a lot older all of a sudden—and a little wiser, too.

My meal ticket, the mare named Jenny, had such a reputation by now that matches in the Denton area were hard to scare up. Charley Tucker, my jockey, pulled up stakes, said he was going home. I had no idea where home was for Charley, but I wished him well. His replacement was a rail-thin cowpoke name of Johnny Hudson, and it was Johnny who came up with the idea of taking Jenny into the Indian Territory. He claimed the "tame redskins" who lived up there in the Nations would be easy pickings, gullible as children. I wasn't too sure about that myself, but I went along with it, as I had nothing much to lose.

Hank Underwood rode with us. He and I never discussed the killing of Penrose. We both understood that our friendship depended on avoiding that topic at all costs. He was right about one thing—nobody connected us with the shooting. After all, Penrose had been a gambler. Had he pursued a more respectable living, people might have gone to some

trouble to track down his killers. As it stood, no one both-
ered much about it. The consensus was that he had run
afoul of some road agents who'd made off with his money,
horse, and saddle and left his carcass to the turkey vultures.
Being accomplices in the dirty deed seemed to cement a
bond between Hank and me. . . .

It turned out that the Indians in the Territory were anything but easy pickings for Sam Bass. They did not hesitate
to bet heavily on the horses they matched Jenny. But when
they lost, as they inevitably did, and the time came to pay
up, then the trouble started. And Bass found out that he
could not count on the tribal court or police to acknowledge
the justice of his claims.

A Choctaw village put up ten of their best horses as a
bet against Jenny, but when the Denton Mare won the race,
the local judge agreed with his brethren that Jenny had
jumped the starting gun, and would have lost save for that
early start. Bass offered a rematch—and this time Jenny's
challenger could have a head start, as long as the length of
the race was extended from a quarter mile to a half mile.
The Choctaws went along with that condition. Right before
the race started, Bass went up to Johnny Holden and told
the jockey that after he won he was to keep riding until he
got clear across the Red River.

"What about you and Hank?" he asked.

"I don't trust these Choctaws," said Bass, looking
around at the crowd of Indians that had gathered to watch
the race. "They didn't pay up the first time and I don't
expect them to this time, either."

"Then why are we running this show again?"

"Because I don't like being cheated."

"But what if we lose? You can be damned sure they'll
expect you to honor your wager."

"Jenny won't lose. Now, once you get across the Red,
you wait for us. We'll be along shortly."

"Maybe you will and maybe you won't. Your scalp
might just wind up on a Choctaw lodgepole."

Bass laughed. "The Choctaws are one of the Civilized

Tribes, Johnny. They don't scalp people anymore. They live in houses, too, not lodges."

He was trying to joke with Hudson, because obviously the jockey was nervous. But Johnny was doubtful that he would ever see either one of his companions alive again, and the furrows of concern in his brow just deepened.

"Civilized or not," he said solemnly, "they are still Indians."

The Denton mare won the race handily, even with the delayed start, and as Bass had predicted the Choctaws decided not to pay up. There were too many of them to quarrel with, so he and Underwood departed without the ten horses. But they didn't go far. That night they slipped back into the village and took the ponies and rode all night for the Texas border, crossing the Red just as dawn began to light up the sky. Reunited with Hudson and the mare, they figured they were safe in Texas. But the next day a United States marshal and three men he had deputized caught up with them. The marshal's name was Lane, and he looked tougher than old whang leather.

"I'm afraid you boys are going to have to hand over those Choctaw ponies," he said.

"They're not Choctaw ponies, not anymore," replied Bass. "We won 'em in a fair-and-square wager. The Indians tried to cheat us."

Lane nodded. He was a broad-shouldered, rangy man with steel-cast gray eyes and a sweeping tawny mustache. "I reckon that could be true," he allowed. "But the Choctaws have raised an unholy ruckus and I have been ordered by a federal judge to get those ponies back to them."

Bass looked at Underwood, and could see that Hank was ready to fight. They stood to make good money selling the Indian ponies—there wasn't a single nag in the bunch—and Underwood wasn't all that impressed by the marshal's badge pinned to Lane's shirt and glinting red as blood in the dawn light. He wasn't worried about the three deputies who rode with Lane, either; they looked like cowboys the marshal had dragooned out of the nearest saloon. Most cowboys were long on gumption but woefully short on gun experience. In fact, a cowpoke was more likely to use his hogleg to hammer a nail into a post than anything else. It was four against three, though Bass wasn't sure Johnny Hudson would be of much use in a scrape.

"These ponies are our winnings," Bass told Lane. "You'll have a fight on your hands if you aim to take them."

Lane just stared at him for a long minute. Then he said, "I think I had better know your name."

"Sam Bass is my name."

The marshal nodded. "You're in the right this time, Bass. But one day you won't be, and then we might meet again. I kind of hope so."

He turned his horse around sharply and rode away, followed by his posse—who to a man looked much relieved that there would be no gunplay after all.

"Well, I'll be," said Underwood in disbelief. "I never thought I would see the day when a United States marshal backed down."

"He wouldn't have," said Bass, "except he knew he was in the wrong. He wasn't scared of us, Hank. So there's no point in crowing about the way this turned out."

The incident with the Choctaws convinced Bass that he had made just about all the money he was going to make off the now-famous Denton Mare, so he sold Jenny, and paid Dad Egan the money he owed him. With the profit from the sale of the Choctaw ponies in their pockets, he and Underwood headed for San Antonio. Bass had no definite plans for the future. His experience with Delia had taught him not to make plans too far in advance. Like China Blue had said, lessons had to be learned. San Antonio was reputedly a wild and woolly place where a fellow with money could get anything he wanted. Bass wasn't too sure what it was that he wanted, but he did feel a powerful urge to get away from Denton for a spell.

It was in San Antonio that he made the acquaintance of Joel Collins, who owned a saloon that Bass and Underwood came to frequent. Collins had been a cowboy all his life, and a very enterprising one at that. He had built quite a reputation for himself as a drover, taking charge of herds of longhorns and pushing them north to the Kansas railheads. He had been doing this for three years running, and split the profits with the ranchers who put him in charge of their cattle. Moving a couple thousand ornery beeves up a seven-hundred-mile trail beset with hazards of every description was no easy task, but Collins had proven himself to be one of the premiere trail bosses. He wasn't a man to be trifled with, either. He had once been charged with the murder of a Mexican named Rosales, but a jury of his peers acquitted him. Turning himself in after the killing, Collins had been playing the odds, betting it was unlikely that an Anglo would hang for blowing out some Mex's candle. And he'd been altogether right about that.

The Panic of 1874 had temporarily brought the Texas cattle trade to a halt; that was why Collins was in the saloon business. He was in it, but he didn't like it. The panic, though severe, was short-lived, and Collins wanted to go back to doing what he did best and liked most—pushing cattle north to Kansas.

Bass was never too sure why Collins wanted him for a partner. Collins claimed it was because Bass looked like a man who knew his way around cattle, and one who would stick to it when the going got rough, which it surely would at some point. But Bass had a hunch it was mostly because he had some money to invest.

"We'll get at least ten, twelve dollars a head in the Abilene market," Collins told Bass one night as Bass was bellied up to his bar to polish off a few shots of whiskey. "We can buy them down here for five dollars a head, six dollars at the most. That's a hundred percent profit for three or four months of work. That strike your fancy at all, Sam?"

"Sure," said Bass, "but I ain't got enough money to my name to buy more than fifty, sixty head at that rate."

"No, we don't have to buy them like that. We give the ranchers a note with our signatures on it, redeemable when we've sold the herd. What we need cash for is supplies for the big push. We'll sign for about a thousand head. We'll only need three or four other hands to help us move that many north. And it won't be a problem there—I know where to find good men, men who have been up the trail before. Figure it out for yourself, Sam. We sell a thousand head at twelve dollars per. Take out what we need to redeem our notes and pay plus bonus for the hired help, and you're looking at at least two thousand dollars profit, free and clear. That's for each of us."

It all sounded mighty good to Bass. And besides, he would finally be making a dream of his come true. He would be an honest-to-God cowboy. After making a big push to Kansas, nobody would be able to say otherwise about him.

The profits were good, but the risks were high—that was why many ranchers settled for the five dollars a head a drover would guarantee them, easy money if ever there was any, over getting twice that much in Dodge City. If the herd was lost, Bass knew that he and Joel would be in big trouble. There would be no getting out of redeeming the notes held by Texas ranchers.

As for the risks—cattle rustlers, stampedes, flooded rivers, and Kansas farmers were just some of the problems that might arise. You had to give the Indian Territory tribes *wohaw,* or tribute, in the form of cattle or hard money, in return for passage across their lands. And a push in late summer like the one Collins proposed might find a shortage of good graze along the trail that numerous herds had already used that season.

Of all these possible perils, Collins was concerned most of all about the Kansas plow pushers. They didn't much care for Texas cattle or the Texas cowboys who drove them, and they used quarantine laws and barbed wire to discourage the cattle trade.

Collins made clear to Bass all of the problems they might face, but Bass threw in with him just the same. Hank Underwood did not, however. Underwood had a whirl in

San Antonio and then went back home to Denton. Collins had no trouble finding a thousand head of cattle; there were plenty of ranchers who were aware of his reputation and were willing to accept a note with his signature on it. Bass made his mark on the note, too. They bought a chuck wagon, stocked it with provisions, signed on three cowpunchers Collins knew personally, and were on their way up the Western Trail by the end of August in the year 1876. Bass said so long to Texas, figuring to be back by the end of the year with his pockets full of money and well established in the cattle business.

Seeing as how in the past his plans had never worked out the way he had expected them to, Sam Bass should have known better.

To his surprise, they met with hardly any trouble at all on the trail. Pushing cows was hard work, the day beginning well before sunrise and ending long after sundown. There were only six of them, not counting the Mexican that Collins had hired on as a cook, so two nights out of every three Sam spent four more hours in the saddle doing night guard duty. As the weeks turned into months and they got farther north, the nights grew colder, too. Making a living off a racehorse was a lot easier, but Bass really didn't mind the hardships, since he knew there was a good payoff at the end of it. And best of all, he was too tired to lay awake at night thinking about Delia. Somehow or other his broken heart was mended by the time they had reached trail's end at Dodge City.

As it turned out, theirs was one of the last herds to come up the trail that year. What that meant was that Bass had just enough time for one drink in the Long Branch Saloon before Collins informed him that they were going to push on to Ogallala, Nebraska. They would get a much better price for their beeves there. A couple of the hands grumbled a bit—they had been looking forward to a wild time in Dodge City, a wide-open town that offered everything a cowboy could want and then some. Going on to Ogallala just meant another month's wages to them. But the way

Collins had it figured, selling their cows in Ogallala added another one thousand dollars at least for he and Bass to split up. When he heard that, Bass knocked back the single whiskey and told Collins that they were burning daylight.

At Ogallala they found a ready buyer for the herd. They congratulated themselves on losing less than fifty head on the long push, and for getting top dollar. Paying off the hands, Collins and Bass decided to paint the town red. The topic of every conversation in every watering hole in Ogallala was the fate met by General Armstrong Custer and his Seventh Cavalry at the Little Bighorn last June. Bass had already heard about the battle, but now he found out that the United States Army was planning a massive campaign to crush the loose alliance of northern tribes, led by Sitting Bull and Crazy Horse, that had been responsible for Custer's glorious defeat. Custer had found gold in the Black Hills, and once the hostiles were dealt with there would be a gold rush in the Dakota Territory to rival the one in California nearly thirty years before.

A good many brave—one might even say reckless— souls had not waited for the army to deal a final crushing blow to the northern plains tribes. A town called Deadwood had sprung up in the Black Hills. Rumor had it that Deadwood was the wooliest town in the whole Wild West. The famous Wild Bill Hickok had recently been gunned down in a Deadwood saloon, shot in the back by a cross-eyed coward named Jack McCall. Life was almighty cheap in Deadwood; that young community's boot hill was said to be filling up very quickly.

Bass and Collins talked it over. New gold strikes were reported in the Wolf Mountains and Beaver Gulch, and that convinced them that they would be fools not to try for their share of the riches. Neither one of them had any intention of wrapping a hand around pick or shovel, or staking a claim on a piece of rocky ground in the hopes it might contain the mother lode. No, there was a much easier way to get rich in a gold strike. Let the miners do all the hard work and then take the gold off them when they visited Deadwood.

So they rode north in high spirits, figuring they couldn't lose, that they would parlay their profits from the sale of the herd into fortunes off which they would live like Arab potentates for the rest of their natural lives. Bass considered himself a better than fair hand at poker, certainly wily enough with the pasteboards to empty a miner's poke in short order.

There was snow on the ground when they reached Deadwood, and more fell the first three days they were there. The town was a collection of tent-cabins and clapboard buildings thrown up in a big hurry and wedged carelessly into a gulch between two rocky ridges from which most of the timber had been cleared and used for construction. The deep snow hid some of the boomtown's ugliness, but with the snow came a bone-aching cold unlike anything Bass had ever experienced, even during the worst Indiana winter. His first week in Deadwood he found a man frozen to death, sitting his horse in the middle of the street. The assumption was that this unfortunate soul had imbibed a little too much who-hit-john, mounted up to ride home, and dozed off before he could get there.

Deadwood existed to separate the gold seeker from his gold. It was as simple as that. There were more than fifty saloons and gambling halls in full swing every night, and it seemed like a new one opened up every other day. Bass decided that just about every cardsharp west of the Mississippi had set up shop, and damn near all the calico queens, too. The most notorious fallen angel at the time was Kitty LeRoy. She performed at the Gem Theater and ran a gambling den called the Mint. A voluptuous woman who always went about in public bedecked with diamonds, she carried an army revolver and a Bowie knife with her, and knew how to use both to lethal effect. She could emasculate a man—or make him wish he had been. Her game was to marry men who struck a rich vein; after squandering their riches, she would move on to the next candidate, who would prove quite willing to dispose of the previous husband in exchange for exclusive rights to Kitty's abundant charms.

Another woman with a colorful past resided in Deadwood when Bass was there. Her name was Martha Jane Canary, better known as Calamity Jane. She wore buckskins, sported pistols and a bullwhacker's blacksnake whip, and was rumored to have been Wild Bill's amour. She had been a teamster in her time, an Indian fighter, and an army scout, as well. They said she was reputedly a real wildcat in bed, but Bass opted to take their word for that; he saw her once and she looked and acted too much like a man to suit him.

Besides the miners and the gamblers and the prostitutes and the saloonkeepers, Deadwood had its fair share of soldiers and bushwhackers. So it was a pretty rough crowd. The only preacher who'd dared to try the town on for size had been slain the summer before. Some wit had remarked that this was probably just as well, since the Bible thumper would have died from sheer exhaustion anyway, trying to save all the sinners who congregated in Deadwood.

Bass and Collins had come to use their skills at poker to relieve the miners of some of their gold dust. As it turned out, though, the professional cardsharps ended up cleaning their plows. Then they were offered the chance to buy into a quartz mine. It seemed like a surefire winner, so they pooled the money they had left and bought in. The ink was no sooner dry on the deed than they learned that the mine was a worthless hole. They had been flamboozled by a slick confidence man, and lost just about everything but their horses and saddles. And it appeared they might have to part with those just to pay for their board and bar tabs.

That was when Jack Davis showed up. Bass was sitting in Kitty LeRoy's Mint Saloon, morosely trying to drown his sorrow in a bottle of cheap rotgut that he could hardly afford, and wondering what he had done to deserve such awful luck, when Joel Collins brought Davis in to meet him. Davis was a tall, dark, smooth-talking hombre with an easy smile, but just beneath that friendly exterior was a hard edge.

"Joel here tells me you two have come upon hard times," said Davis. "Well, you aren't the only ones. I've been trying to make a go as a freighter here and lost my shirt."

"All I know is, if we don't get a break pretty soon we're going to be sleeping in a snowbank," said Collins.

"No, it's worse than that," said Bass. "We lost all the money we owe those Texas ranchers, Joel."

"I heard about that, too," said Davis. "You boys got snookered, no question."

"So what the hell are we supposed to do?" asked Bass in desperation.

"Well, Jack has an interesting idea," said Collins. "Hear him out."

Davis looked around to make sure no one was close enough to overhear, then leaned forward and lowered his voice.

"There is a lot of gold rolling out of Deadwood," he said. "Just about every eastbound stage carries a small fortune."

He stopped right there and looked at Bass.

"You mean rob a stage," said Bass.

Davis nodded. "Most of the gold shipments come from the big mining combines like Homestake. The men who own those mines are so damned rich they won't hardly miss what little we make off with."

"Still, I reckon they will object to our taking it without asking," said Bass wryly. "Are you for this, Joel?"

Collins shrugged. "We're in a real bad spot, Sam. We have to do something, now, don't we? Jack has had some experience in this sort of thing."

Davis nodded again. "I had me a gang around Virginia City, Nevada, some years back. We held up a few stage-coaches. Would have done all right, I figure—except we made the mistake of trying to rob a Central Pacific train, too."

"What happened?"

"We got caught. Shot all to hell. I spent two years in the penitentiary. When I was walking out the gate a free man, the warden, damn his black soul, asked me if I had learned anything from my experience. I said, 'Hell, yes, Warden. I have learned to stick to robbin' stagecoaches!' "

Davis laughed. Collins felt obliged to chuckle, though his heart wasn't in it. Bass managed a halfhearted smile.

"Thing is," continued Davis, "I knew how to pull that job off. The secret is to ride with plenty of men. Six or eight men, so the guards who watch over those gold shipments can see right off how foolish it would be to try and keep us from taking the goods. Now, I've got five men willing to throw in with me. The two of you sign on, that makes eight. Then we're in business."

Bass exchanged a look with Collins, who said, "I don't see as how we have much choice, Sam. In a way we're already wanted men. If we don't redeem those notes down in Texas you know there will be hell to pay. Men will come hunting us. How else are we going to get our hands on that kind of money?"

Bass knew he was right. There was no use denying it. They were boxed in and there was only one way out.

"Okay," he said. "You can count me in."

CHAPTER SEVEN

Aside from Jack Davis and Joel Collins, the gang Sam Bass rode with included a freckle-faced Missouri kid named Jim Berry, a fellow from up Canada way who called himself Tom Nixon, and another named Bill Heffridge, who claimed he had two wives, one in Kansas and the other in Pennsylvania—which as far as Bass was concerned said something for Heffridge's stamina if not for his intelligence. There were two other hardcases, as well, Frank Towle and John Reddy. Bass thought they made a pretty salty-looking bunch of desperadoes.

Davis said he had it on good authority that a stage out of Deadwood would more than likely have at least ten thousand dollars in gold dust aboard, and probably a lot more than that. He claimed that only recently a single eastbound stage had carried more than *one hundred thousand dollars'* worth of gold. Bass told Collins that he was going to stick with the gang only as long as it took him to get enough money together to redeem those Texas notes. Collins assured him that this was also his intention.

The first stage they stopped was bound for Cheyenne, and they waylaid it in Whitewood Canyon, as likely a looking place for a holdup as one could find in the area. Like the others, Bass wore a bandanna pulled up over his nose to conceal his features, and a long duster so that no one could provide a good description of his build or the clothes he wore. This had been on the advice of Jack Davis, and Bass thought it was a damn fine idea. They had made an agreement—no one would shoot except in self-defense. All of them except maybe Towle and Reddy were determined to avoid a killing—and the hangman's rope. Those two, it seemed to Bass, had been riding the outlaw trail too long to care who they killed or when they died.

It was late at night and the stage to Cheyenne was running behind schedule, and Towle and Reddy had brought some whiskey along to steady their nerves during the long wait. Bass thought that was asking for trouble, and believed Jack Davis was making a mistake by not putting a stop to all the drinking. Since Davis was the one who had put the gang together and knew everyone, they had all agreed he would be the leader. But he didn't say anything about the drinking and neither did Bass, though he turned down the liquid bravemaker when it was offered to him and was glad to see that Joel had the good sense to do the same.

When they heard the stage coming—the rattle of trace chains and the hoof thunder of the six-horse hitch—they spread out, still mounted, across the road. The coach trundled into view and Sam could tell that the reinsman was trying to stop the team, climbing the leathers and leaning back in the box, but the offside leader spooked and veered off the road and the other leader went that way, too. Reddy raised his scattergun and fired, killing the jehu, who went flying off the stage. The man who had been riding in the box with him was just about to cut loose with his own sawed-off shotgun, but when the driver went over the side, he dropped his weapon and grabbed the reins and urged the wild-eyed team on. The stage went right around the bandits and rolled on down the road, leaving them in the dust on milling ponies.

Jack Davis got his horse under control and dismounted and went to the fallen driver. Bass could not see much in the darkness, but he could hear Davis cussing like a madman.

"Goddamn it! Reddy, you stupid son of a bitch! You know what you've done? Jesus Christ, you sorry bastard, you killed Johnny Slaughter."

"Who you calling stupid?" asked Reddy defensively.

"Who's Johnny Slaughter, anyway?" asked Joel.

"Just one of the best-liked men in Deadwood, that's all. Damn you, Reddy, we agreed—no shooting!"

"I thought he was trying to go right through us," said Reddy.

Davis went to Reddy's horse, reached up, and pulled the man out of the saddle, hurling him to the ground. Before Reddy could recover, Davis had his pistol drawn and aimed at Reddy's head.

"I ought to blow your goddamned brains out," growled Davis.

By then Bass was out of the saddle and jumped between Davis and the man on the ground. "That won't do any good now, Jack."

"No, but it will make me feel a whole lot better," rasped Davis. "This son of a bitch just signed our death warrants, Sam."

"They have to find out who we are first. Then they have to catch us." Bass turned to Reddy. "You've got one chance, John, and that's to leave the Black Hills. In a hurry. Go and don't come back."

Of course Reddy jumped at the chance.

A five-hundred-dollar reward was offered for the killer or killers of Johnny Slaughter, dead or alive. Frank Towle was taken into custody by Sheriff Seth Bullock, but Bullock didn't have any solid evidence that Towle had been involved in the attempted holdup. He just knew Towle as a hardcase who was capable of such a crime, and hoped he might be persuaded to talk. Towle didn't talk, though, and was eventually released. He didn't stay with the gang for long. When their second holdup attempt netted them a grand total of eleven dollars, Towle bade them farewell and joined up with the Hat Creek Gang that was operating down around Cheyenne.

The Hat Creek boys had a lot better luck than Bass and his companions. Or maybe, thought Bass, they were just better road agents. They found out that the stage Johnny Slaughter had been driving carried fifteen thousand dollars' worth of gold. That was the closest they ever got to a big payoff. In fact, the only loot they took away from one robbery was a sack of peaches. The next stage they stopped was full of passengers, but they only had thirty dollars between them. That infuriated Jack Davis.

"You people have got no damned business traveling if this is all the money you've got," he rebuked them. "By God, we're going to starve to death if you don't start doing better!"

"We'll be the ones starving," said one of the passengers. "My belt buckle is rubbing against my backbone and I was sure looking forward to a big breakfast at the next station. The driver told me the lady there makes the best sourdough biscuits north of the Cimarron. But she charges a dollar for a meal. You could at least leave us enough for breakfast."

"I agree with him," said Bass. "I don't want a man to go hungry on my account."

Davis stared at Bass. "Are you pulling my leg? We only got thirty dollars."

"So? Give them each a dollar and we'll have twenty-three dollars. Seven dollars isn't going to break us."

"What the hell," said Davis in disgust, and told Bass to give each of the passengers a dollar for breakfast.

They robbed seven stagecoaches in the Black Hills that winter—and not a single one was found to be carrying any gold whatsoever. In hindsight, Sam figured that was a good thing—the law did not take them too seriously and concentrated instead of catching the Hat Creek bunch. This they soon accomplished. Frank Towle was gunned down and his head taken to Cheyenne in a gunnysack by the man who killed him as proof to collect the reward.

That was the last straw—Bass and his saddle partners agreed that the Black Hills were no good for them, and that if they stayed much longer their bad luck would just turn worse.

It was Joel Collins who came up with the idea of heading down to Ogallala and trying their hand at train robbery. He reminded the others that Frank and Jesse James were meeting with great success in robbing trains. Gold shipments were always passing through Ogallala, eastbound from California on the rails of the Union Pacific. And trains usually carried a larger quantity of loot than stagecoaches. Bass was all for it, as were the others, with the exception of Jack Davis, as his only experience with train holdups had landed him in prison. But in the end he threw in with the rest, and in the summer of 1877 they rode south out of the Dakota Territory. None of them was sorry to say goodbye to the Black Hills.

TWENTY MILES UP the South Platte from Ogallala was a place called Big Springs, where the Union Pacific maintained a watering station. The town—if you could call it that—consisted of a small station house, a section house, and two shanties, plus the water tower. Shortly after sundown on a Tuesday evening in mid-September, Bass rode into Big Springs in the company of Joel Collins, Jack Davis, Jim Berry, Bill Heffridge, and Tom Nixon. The Number Four Express was due in at eleven that night and they intended to rob it.

They saw a light on in the station, so they swung a wide loop around the structure and dismounted. Leaving Nixon in charge of the horses, they pulled red bandannas over their faces, drew their pistols, buttoned up their dusters, and went inside.

A man was sitting behind a low railing at the telegraph desk, his feet propped up, his nose buried in a week-old San Francisco newspaper. When the outlaws barged in he was so startled that he tipped over backward in his chair, crashing to the floor. Collins stepped nimbly over the rail and loomed over him.

"That's a good place for you to stay," said Collins,

reaching out to disconnect the telegraph relay and put it in the pocket of his duster. "Is there anybody else around?"

"Just my wife and son," said the Union Pacific man, his voice shaky with fear. "Please don't hurt 'em, mister. . . ."

"We won't," said Bass. "What's your name?"

"George. George Barnhart."

"You just do what we tell you, George, and no harm will come to you or yours," said Collins.

"I'll do whatever you say."

"We want you to put out the red signal lantern and stop that eastbound express."

Barnhart nodded, and Bass could tell by the look on his face that he would cooperate completely.

They all knew what to do—there was no need for a last-minute review, but Collins insisted they have one anyway. Since the train robbing was his idea, they now looked to him as the leader. That suited Davis just fine. He was quite willing to relinquish command of the gang. Bass judged that his friend Joel was a little nervous and wanted to make sure the rest of them knew their assigned tasks. While Bass and Davis waited in the station, keeping an eye on Barnhart, the others would conceal themselves under the station platform until the train came to a halt. Then Collins and Heffridge would take care of the engineer and fireman in the locomotive, while Berry and Nixon would corral the conductor. Then Bass and Davis, with Barnhart's assistance if necessary, would gain access to the express car. The horses were taken to a ravine about a hundred yards due north of Big Springs and securely tethered, far enough from the tracks so that the iron horse would not spook them when it came.

The hardest part was the waiting. After Barnhart put out the red signal lantern, Bass and Davis took him back inside the station and they all sat down on the floor so that no one could spot them through the windows.

When they finally heard the train whistle off in the distance, Jack Davis nearly jumped out of his skin.

"What time is it?" Bass asked Barnhart, as he had noticed the watch chain arching across his vest.

The UP man fished the watch out of its pocket and consulted it. "Four minutes past eleven o'clock."

"Only a few minutes behind schedule," remarked Bass. "That's not bad. You work for an efficient bunch, Mr. Barnhart."

"That's a mighty handsome watch," said Davis, an avaricious gleam in his eye.

"You'll be able to buy a better watch than that one when we're done here," Bass told him. "Let ol' George keep his timepiece. It's probably a family heirloom or something."

"Well, no," said Barnhart, flustered. "I'm afraid it isn't. I bought it only last month."

Bass laughed. "It will be a family heirloom when you hand it down to your boy, then, won't it?"

They could hear the train coming closer, that iron horse huffing and puffing like a giant beast. Davis gave Bass a funny look.

"You're an awful cool one," he said. "My hands are sweating."

"Why worry?" Bass asked him. "Whatever happens will happen, whether you fret about it or not."

When the train had come to a complete stop, Bass put out the kerosene lamp and plunged the station into darkness. Davis threw open the door. They escorted Barnhart out onto the platform. The locomotive was to their right, and behind it the coal car, followed by two closed cars and two passenger cars, one of these a sleeper. Bass saw Collins and Heffridge hauling the engineer and fireman down off the mogul. He glanced up and saw the red sparks rising in the black plume of smoke coming out of the locomotive's stack. Then the conductor stepped down off the passenger car a few feet to their left. He looked at the knot of men on the station platform, peering hard into the darkness. "Is that you, George?" he asked. Berry and Nixon appeared behind him and hustled him on down the platform past Bass, moving toward the front of the train.

The door of the closed car directly in front of Bass slid

open, silhouetting a man against the light from within.

"This the baggage or the express car?" Bass asked him.

"Baggage."

"Then close your door and keep quiet."

The man hastily shut the door. Bass and Davis moved to the other closed car, bringing Barnhart along with them. Using the barrel of his pistol, Bass rapped on the door.

"What do you want?" came a nervous voice from inside.

"I have some freight for you," said Barnhart.

The door opened slowly, a few inches. Bass shoved it all the way open and jumped inside, knocking the express messenger down. Having left the engineer and fireman in the custody of Berry and Nixon, Collins and Heffridge entered the express car, too. Bass opened the safe with keys he had taken from the messenger. Inside he found nearly five hundred dollars in paper money.

"What about this safe?" asked Collins, motioning to a bigger combination box.

"That's the express safe," said the messenger. "It's on a time lock, set in San Francisco, and it can't be opened until we get to Omaha."

Heffridge menaced the UP man with his pistol. "You're a sorry liar. There ain't no such thing."

"I'm telling you the truth," insisted the messenger. "I—I have papers to prove it."

"There *is* a such thing," said Collins quietly, eyeing the big safe. "What's inside here?"

"I have no idea," said the messenger.

"He's lying," insisted Heffridge.

Bass didn't see much use in standing around arguing about whether the messenger was telling the truth or not—it was clear as mother's milk that they were not going to get into the big safe. He knew that because he took an ax and started hacking away at the combination dial—and hardly made a dent for his efforts. Giving up on that, he began to search the express car, and that was how he found three small wooden boxes, sealed with wax and covered with a tarpaulin.

"What's in these boxes?" he asked the messenger.

"I'm sure he doesn't have any idea," said Heffridge sarcastically.

"That's right, I don't," said the UP man.

Bass pushed the top box off the other two. It hit the floor and the lid came off and twenty-dollar gold pieces, freshly minted in San Francisco, rolled out on the floor.

Collins let out a low whistle. "Must be—I don't know—ten thousand dollars in each box!"

"Twenty thousand in each one," sighed the messenger. "Bound for Wells, Fargo & Company in New York City."

Bass stared at Collins and Collins stared right back. Sixty thousand dollars! That was ten thousand dollars for each member of the gang. And that meant they could pay off the Texas cattle notes and have some money left over. They had finally hit the jackpot.

"To hell with whatever is in that safe," said Bass. "This is enough for us."

They stacked the boxes on the station platform. Jack Davis insisted that they rob the passengers, too. Bass thought that was asking for trouble, but the others backed Davis and Collins didn't object. So Bass accompanied Davis into the passenger car. They harvested over twelve hundred dollars and gold watches from the travelers within. "Guess I won't have to buy a timepiece after all," Davis told Bass, and Bass knew he was grinning underneath his red bandanna. He was still in a good humor when, a moment later, Bass objected to his taking twenty dollars from a man with an empty sleeve. Bass told him to give the money back.

"Now, why would I want to do that?" asked Davis.

"Because he's only got the one arm."

Davis stared blankly at Bass, who expected him to ask what was wrong with robbing a one-armed man. Bass figured he would have a tough time trying to make Davis understand why it rubbed against the grain. But Davis didn't ask. Bass assumed he decided it just wasn't worth the effort. He returned the twenty dollars to the man with one arm and moved on to his next victim.

Collins came into the passenger car to tell them to hurry up. He looked apprehensive. Bass thought it was probably because they had been in Big Springs too long. They seemed to be taking their own sweet time with the holdup. As he and Davis finished up and left the car—warning the passengers of the dire fate that would befall the man who stuck his head out before they were gone—they heard a distant train's whistle.

"That would be the Number Ten freight train," said Collins.

The conductor, engineer, and fireman were put into the express car. "Don't open this door," Collins warned them as he rolled the door shut, "if you value your lives." Bass took one last look at the Union Pacific men and felt pretty confident that they wouldn't try anything. Then he turned to the station agent, Barnhart.

"Better grab a signal lantern and get on down the tracks to stop that westbound freight," advised Bass. "They aren't expecting a train to be stopped here."

Barnhart paled. He was in enough hot water with the robbery. The last thing he needed was a collision in Big Springs in which people would be guaranteed to lose life and limb. He hurried into the station, grabbed a signal lantern, and disappeared into the night.

Heffridge, Berry, and Nixon had emptied some canvas mail pouches. Breaking open the Wells Fargo boxes, they transferred the gold pieces to the pouches. That done, the bandits left the station, making haste to the ravine where their horses were located.

As they mounted up, Collins turned to Bass and said, "Andy Riley was on that train."'

"Who's might that be, Joel?"

"A friend of mine. We rode together for about a year, pushing cows to Kansas. I think he recognized me."

"Oh, that's just great," said Davis, who had overheard the exchange.

"Don't worry about it," said Bass.

"You don't worry about anything, do you?" replied Davis. He was no longer in a good mood. "But you may start after you've spent a little time in prison."

They rode north and made a clean getaway. Burying the gold-heavy mail pouches near the South Platte, Berry and Nixon and Heffridge accompanied Bass into Ogallala, while Davis stayed with Collins in an isolated camp. Full of brass as always, Jim Berry offered to join the posse that was quickly forming to track down the desperadoes who had robbed the Number Four express. A reward of ten thousand dollars for the capture of the bandits had been offered by Wells, Fargo & Company. After a day in Ogallala, Bass and his companions slipped away and rejoined Collins and Davis.

"Ten thousand dollars' reward!" exclaimed Davis. "Boys, we're in the big time now."

"Did you hear my name mentioned?" Collins asked Bass.

"Nope. But I did hear that there was two hundred and fifty thousand dollars' worth of California gold in that big safe we couldn't get open."

Davis cussed, using every word in the book.

"It doesn't matter," said Collins, looking a little sick. "We came away with ten thousand dollars apiece. I'd say it was time we split up."

And that was what they did. Berry went home to his wife and kids in Missouri. Nixon rode along with him. Heffridge opted to go to San Antonio with Collins, and Davis said he would ride with Bass as far as Denton. Bass gave Collins enough of his share of the loot to pay for half of the cattle notes they owed, and he and Joel agreed to meet up again in a few months. None of them was worried much about the Ogallala posse, and as it turned out they were right not to—that bunch of shop clerks rode around in circles for a few days and then went home.

On the Red River ferry a fortnight later, crossing over to Texas, Bass heard someone comment on the robbing of the Union Pacific train at Big Springs. Word was that the James Gang might have done the deed. Stepping foot on Texas soil, Bass breathed a heartfelt sigh of relief, feeling confident that he had gotten away clean. He had six thousand dollars—that meant he could end his career as a road agent and start off right in a new vocation. As soon as he figured out what that might be.

Bass couldn't have been more wrong about everything. He had not gotten clean away, and his time on the outlaw trail had only just begun.

CHAPTER EIGHT

"IN A WAY," BASS TOLD JED BANKS, "EVERYTHING THAT happened after that was on account of Andy Riley identifying Joel as one of the men who held up that train."

"How is that?" asked the newspaperman.

'Get me some water and I'll tell you," said Bass.

Banks got the water and Bass drank a little, but promptly spit it up, and the reporter noticed some bright red blood came up, too. Bass noticed it, as well, and smiled ruefully.

"Guess I better get to the telling," he said . . .

Since Joel Collins had been recognized on the UP train by his old friend, I guess we should have figured out that John Law would consider the possibility of our heading for Texas. After all, Joel called Texas home, and he was fairly well-known as a Texas drover throughout Kansas and Nebraska. Badge toters weren't the only folks we had to keep a lookout for—soldiers, railroad detectives, and bounty hunters were on the prowl for us, too.

Joel never made it home. He and Bill Heffridge stashed their share of the gold in a pair of old pants, which was then strapped to a pack mule and covered with a blanket. After crossing the Republican River they came to a station house on the Kansas Pacific Railroad. Riding in a heavy

*fog, they had lost their way, and asked the station agent
where they were. . . .*

"This here is Buffalo Station," said the station agent.
"You're about a hundred miles from nowhere."

"You run a store here?" asked Collins.

"Nope. But the section man, Jim Thompson, keeps a
stock of goods at his house, which is right over yonder."

Collins peered through the fog in the direction the station agent had gestured—and couldn't see a thing.

"Jim's gone to Saline, but his hired girl is here and she
can help you out," said the Kansas Pacific man.

Collins nodded. Dismounting, he handed his reins to
Heffridge.

"We'll find some graze for the horses, build us a fire,
Bill. I'm bone-tired. But first let me get some grub."

Following the station agent, Joel spotted a row of tents,
a picket line of horses, and man-shapes gathered around a
campfire.

"Who are those men?" he asked.

"Soldiers out of Fort Hayes. A squad of them, along with
a sheriff from Ellis County. They're looking for train robbers, I believe."

Reaching the section house, Collins prevailed on the
hired girl to sell him some provisions. She took him down
into the storm cellar where the supplies were kept. The
station agent tagged along. He was sitting on a barrel when
Collins pulled a wallet out of his coat pocket, and he saw
an envelope fall to the ground. Saw, too, the name "Joel
Collins" on the envelope.

"I better get back to the station," he said, casually standing up and turning for the storm cellar steps. "Got a train
due through here any minute now."

As soon as he was out of the cellar, the station agent
took off running to the soldiers' encampment. He woke the
lawman and told him what had happened. The fog was
slowly thinning out, and the sheriff saw Collins emerge
from the storm cellar out behind the section house and walk
over to where Heffridge was holding his horse. By the time

the troopers were saddled and mounted, Collins and his partner were riding away from Buffalo Station. The sheriff and the soldiers set off in pursuit. Collins knew by this time that something was wrong, but he didn't make a run for it. When the sheriff stopped him, Collins just smiled pleasantly and asked what the problem was.

"Are you Joel Collins?" asked the sheriff.

"I might be."

"I think you are. And you two fit the descriptions of some of the train robbers we're looking for. You'll have to come back to the station with me."

"Afraid you've made a mistake. We haven't robbed any trains."

"If you're innocent you have nothing to worry about."

Collins laughed. "Innocent men have been hanged before."

"You two are coming back with me," said the sheriff, hard-eyed. "One way or the other."

"Well, there's no use arguing," said Collins, surveying the ten blue-coated troopers arrayed on either side of him and Heffridge. "But this is a case of mistaken identity, Sheriff. We're just a couple of Texas cowboys headed home."

He turned his horse around and Heffridge did likewise, trailing the pack mule carrying the twenty thousand dollars in double eagles. Collins knew they would be searched, and once the gold was found it would seal his fate. Halfway back to Buffalo Station he turned to a pale and tight-lipped Bill Heffridge.

"We might as well die game, Bill."

No sooner had he said this than Heffridge was reaching for his pistol. Collins did the same. Heffridge spurred his horse straight ahead while Collins turned to face the enemy. He didn't get off a single shot, while Heffridge only had time to pull the trigger once. Riddled with bullets, both men were dead before they hit the ground.

*   *   *

JIM BERRY DIDN'T get away, either.

Accompanied by Tom Nixon, Berry got home to Mexico, Missouri, traveling the last stretch by train. From there Nixon headed for Canada with his share of the loot, riding on the Chicago & Alton Railroad. There were three banks in Mexico, and Berry went to each one, exchanging nine thousand dollars' worth of double eagles for paper money. He bought some new clothes, including a suit he ordered special. At the general store and mercantile he purchased several hundred dollars' worth of provisions and paid to have them delivered to his wife, who lived on a small farm in the next county, about twenty miles away. Then Berry made the rounds of the saloons, buying drinks all around and proclaiming that he had struck it rich prospecting in the Black Hills. Late that night he slipped quietly out of town.

Several days later the Mexico banks were informed that the gold Berry had sold them was part of the Wells, Fargo shipment stolen from a UP express in Nebraska. Railroad detectives arrived in town on the following day. They got word that Berry had been spotted in a nearby town, buying a brand-new saddle and a handsome gray thoroughbred horse. By the time the detectives got there, though, Berry was gone. They went next to the Berry farm, where his wife admitted that he had been home, but had gone after a couple of days without telling her where he was going. Posses scoured the countryside but could find no sign of him.

Berry might have gotten away except he had to have that new suit he had ordered. He wasn't fool enough to go back into Mexico to get the suit himself. Instead, he sent a friend by the name of Kasey, who told the clothing store owner that Berry had left the state, but not before giving him the order form and telling him he could have the suit. The storekeeper sent his boy out the back door to fetch Mexico's sheriff. When Kasey emerged from the store with the suit, Sheriff Glascock was hiding behind the corner of a building across the street. The lawman followed Kasey to the livery stable and waited until the man had one foot in the stirrup, preparing to mount his horse, before closing in. Glascock put a pistol to Kasey's head.

"Don't even breathe hard, friend," advised the tin star.

"I haven't done anything," protested Kasey.

"You got the wrong kind of friend in Jim Berry."

"Jim is long gone."

"Yeah, well, we'll see about that."

Glascock hauled Kasey to the local jail and locked him up long enough to gather four reliable men, all armed with shotguns.

"You're going to take us to wherever Berry is hiding out," Glascock informed his prisoner.

"I'm telling you, Jim Berry rode out a week ago. I'd bet he isn't even in Missouri anymore."

"No, I'm betting he's hiding out at your place. Take us there."

"I'll take you there, but that won't do you any good. Jim Berry is gone, I say."

They rode out of Mexico and reached the next county by late afternoon. Kasey, as it turned out, lived but a few miles from the Berry homestead. A half mile from their destination, Glascock called a halt. Kasey was hauled down out of his saddle and tied up. The sheriff left one man to watch over him and pressed on with the other three. Reaching the Kasey place after dark, Glascock positioned two of his men in back of the house.

"Boys," he said, "I've been manhunting for many a year and my instincts tell me that the feller we're after is around here close. My instincts are usually true. If you see him, stop him. If he shows fight, gun him down. Do whatever you have to do. Just don't let the slippery son of a bitch get away."

Glascock took the third man with him, circling around to a vantage point in a brush-choked ravine from which he could watch the front of Kasey's house and the adjacent barn.

They waited, and watched all night. Just before daybreak

a horse in Kasey's barn whinnied—and was answered by another horse, this one back in the woods west of the place. Glascock and his deputy moved down the creek through the timber and found fresh horse tracks. They heard the horse again, about a hundred yards to their right. Glascock motioned for his companion to stay put and crept through the brush toward the sound. Just as he spotted the tethered horse, he saw Jim Berry roll out of his blankets, stand up, and stretch. The sheriff stepped boldly into the desperado's camp, a shotgun held at hip level.

"Just keep those hands up, Berry."

Berry bolted, hoping to dodge into a thicket, but Glascock fired one barrel and the buckshot knocked the outlaw's legs out from under him. Berry groped for a pistol under his coat and just about had a hand on it when the lawman came up and slammed the shotgun stock against his skull, knocking him out cold.

Calling his posse in, Glascock had the unconscious man carried to the Kasey house. He sent one man after a doctor and another out to bring Kasey home, and asked Mrs. Kasey if she minded cooking everybody some breakfast. She minded, but did it anyway. The sheriff found that his prisoner had a load of buckshot in one leg and twenty-three hundred dollars in paper money in his pockets.

The doctor arrived, dressed Berry's wounds, and had him transported to Mexico in a wagon. Gangrene set in, and when it was clear that Berry would die, Sheriff Glascock had his prisoner's wife brought to town. She arrived a few hours too late to say her good-byes to her husband.

When Sam Bass reached Fort Worth he learned that three of the five men who had been with him on the Union Pacific robbery were dead. Jack Davis made up his mind to go east.

"Think I'll see what New Orleans is like," he told Bass. "I hear the women are pretty and the whiskey is good and you can find a card game every time you turn around. I don't know that I will ever come back west of the Mississippi again, to be honest."

Bass shook the man's hand. "Good luck to you, Jack."

"What are you aiming to do, Sam?"

"I'm going to stay right here in Texas, I reckon."

News of the fate met by Collins, Heffridge, and Berry rattled Bass some, and he decided it would be smart to lay low for a spell. He made camp in a place called Cove Hollow, a canyon filled with timber and brush, its limestone walls sporting plenty of caves. A day's ride from Denton, it was the wildest, roughest country around, and Bass felt safe there.

But he couldn't stay hidden forever. He had money to burn and he had friends in the area that he wanted to see. So he rode into Denton under cover of darkness and hunted up Hank Underwood. Underwood was happy to see him. They sat on the porch of Underwood's modest clapboard house and shared a bottle. Hank's Kansas-born wife, though, was barely civil—she didn't say two words to Bass all night, and turned in early.

"Your wife doesn't cotton to me, Hank," said Bass. "I better get going. I don't want to make problems for you."

"To hell with her. Keep your butt planted in that chair, Sam, and help me finish off this bottle. She just thinks you'll lead me astray, that's all." Underwood laughed. "Funny thing is, I've been in more trouble since you've been gone than I ever got into when you were around." Lifting his shirt, he proudly displayed a bullet hole in his side.

"That must have hurt," remarked Bass.

"It smarted some, I'll admit. I rode down around the Concho River to buy some cattle. Ran afoul of some vigilantes who were on the lookout for rustlers. Me being a stranger in that country and all, they gave me a hard look. So I gave 'em hell one night in a saloon. Three of 'em walked in and told me to shut my mouth. I cast aspersions on their pedigree, don't ya know. One of 'em slapped iron, and when the smoke cleared I had shot two men and been plugged right here in return."

"Sounds like a clear-cut case of self-defense to me, Hank."

"Sure, that's exactly what it was. But the two men I shot were important men from around those parts. So I knew it wouldn't matter who had drawn first—I was going to get the short end of that particular stick. I got out of town in a hurry. Hid in the brush. But didn't hide good enough, I guess, because they found me, and put me in a boarding-house under guard. The bullet passed clean through, but I had lost a lot of blood, and there for a spell the sawbones wasn't sure if I would live or die. Well, I wasn't near ready to cash in, but there was no harm done in letting them think that I was. One day the guards never showed up, figuring they didn't need to bother watching over a man who was never gonna get out of bed again. I got clean away."

"You always were a lucky cuss, Hank," Bass said with a laugh.

Underwood snorted. "Lucky, hell. I know when my chance comes and I never fail to grab aholt of it. But, you know, I was hardly home long enough to take my boots off when the courthouse burned right down to the ground. Guess who they thought did it."

"Now, why would they think you'd burn down the courthouse?"

"The talk was that the fire was started by a man hired by a bunch of cattle thieves who were about to go to trial. A lot of evidence in that case went up in smoke. So Dad Egan must have figured that I was the most likely candidate. I spent one hundred damn days in jail. They finally had to admit to having not one single shred of evidence against me—and let me go."

"They ever find the man who did burn it down?"

"Nope, never did." Underwood took a long pull on the whiskey bottle—and chuckled to himself—which gave Bass pause to wonder if maybe Dad Egan hadn't arrested the right man after all. "Anyway, what have you been up to, Sam?"

Bass shrugged. "Joel Collins and I pushed some cattle

up to Nebraska. Then I heard about the gold in the Black
Hills. Wandered up that way and got lucky. I struck it rich,
Hank."

"Did you, now." Underwood smirked and handed over
the bottle of who-hit-john. "Really, Sam, you're the worst
damn liar I think I've ever met." And he busted out laugh-
ing.

"Well, okay. You're right. I did strike it rich, but not in
the Black Hills."

"I hear Joel Collins got killed by a posse looking for a
gang of train robbers."

Bass nodded, the smile fading from his sun-dark face as
he remembered the good times he and Joel had had.

Underwood clapped him on the back. "Don't none of us
live forever, Sam. It's just a shame Collins got killed before
he could enjoy spending any of that gold. If you got it you
might as well spend it, because you sure as hell can't take
it with you."

"I got me an urge to go down to San Antonio and live
high off the hog for a spell," said Bass. "I'd like for you
to come along, Hank. Except I don't think your wife will
approve."

"Lucky for me, I don't need her approval. But I'm as
poor as a priest, Sam."

"I've got more than enough money for the both of us."

"Well, then, in that case, I'm game."

Underwood was so eager to get away from Denton—
and his nagging wife—that he stayed in the Cove Hollow
camp for a few days. Bass told him that he wanted to see
if a couple of others would ride with them, and with that
in mind he returned to Denton, again under cover of night,
and located Frank Jackson, who still worked at the tin shop.
The shop's owner, Ben Key, had gone for the night. Jackson was working late when Bass walked in. When they
were finished greeting each other like long-lost brothers,
Bass tossed his saddlebags on a table, unstrapped one side,
and let gold double eagles spill out.

"Damn," breathed Jackson, his eyes getting wide. "What did you do, Sam? Rob a bank?"

Bass laughed. "Struck gold in the Black Hills. I have a hankering to go to San Antone and live it up, and I want you to come with me, Frank." He grabbed some of the twenty-dollar gold pieces and offered them to Jackson. "Here, take this. Hell, take it all. There's plenty more where that came from."

Jackson gave Bass a long look, then solemnly shook his head. "I don't think so, Sam."

"Don't tell me you want to work here for the rest of your life. Ol' Ben doesn't pay you enough to stay alive. If you come with me, I'll see to it that you get a hundred dollars a month."

"It's true, I don't make much money," agreed Jackson. "But I don't plan to become an outlaw."

"Who said anything about becoming an outlaw?"

"I may not be very smart, and I ain't half as clever as you, Sam. But I got a hunch you didn't get this gold sweating over a Black Hills claim. Rumors are that since you rode north with Joel Collins you might have been in on that train robbery he led."

Bass wasn't sure whether he could trust Frank Jackson with the truth the way he had with Hank Underwood. Frank was a good friend, but he was an honest man, one who had never been in any trouble to speak of.

"I didn't have anything to do with that," lied Bass. "I met with good fortune up north and would just like to share it with my friends, that's all."

"I'm surprised Sheriff Egan hasn't had a talk with you."

"Well, he'll have a hell of a time finding me. Look, Frank, I'm keeping my head down around here because I figure John Law has the same suspicions as you. Joel was my saddle partner, and now here I am with more gold than I know what to do with, and even though I come by it honestly, I've heard of men being hanged on less evidence. If you don't want to ride with me, that's okay. But just don't tell anyone you saw me here. And if you do come along, I'd advise you not to mention where we're headed."

Jackson said he would think about going. Bass lingered in his Cove Hollow hideout for a few more days. He woke up one morning to find Frank Jackson building up last night's fire.

"Reckon I'll go along after all," said Jackson.

"You won't regret it," replied Bass, delighted.

"We'll see about that."

Hank Underwood stirred in his blankets. "I guess this means we can finally get going?"

CHAPTER NINE

DAD EGAN WAS SITTING IN HIS OFFICE AT THE DENTON JAIL-house when two men came in to talk to him about Sam Bass.

Egan's deputy, Tom Gerren, was also there—the two of them were sorting through a stack of wanted posters that had just arrived. At such times Egan wondered if the day might ever come that law and order would prevail in Texas. Seemed sometimes as though half the male population of the state was engaged in some kind of criminal enterprise. When the two men walked in, Egan knew right away that they were lawmen, though he had never seen either one of them before. A cold blast of air came into the office with them; it was early December and a blue norther had just roared across the Texas plains.

"Sheriff Egan?" asked one of the men.

"That would be me. Who are you?"

"Bill Everheart. Sheriff from up Grayson County way."

Egan nodded. "Yeah, I've heard of you."

Everheart gestured at his companion. "This here is Tooney Waits. He's a Pinkerton man."

"Don't get too many Pinkertons down this way. Help yourself to the java, boys."

The pair shucked their gloves and overcoats and grate-fully poured themselves some coffee, lingering around the stove to partake of the warmth it provided. Everheart was tall man with a deeply creased face and hair the color of gunmetal. Tooney Waits was a stocky, red-bearded fellow clad in a travel-worn tweed suit. Egan knew Everheart by reputation—he had been a badge toter in the county north of Denton for a long time and was known as a savvy and hard-as-nails lawman. As for Waits, the fact that he was a Pinkerton spoke to his skill as a professional manhunter.

"What brings you down here?" Egan asked Everheart.

"Sam Bass. Hear he used to live in Denton."

"Yes, he did. As a matter of fact, he used to work for me, driving a freight wagon."

"Seen him lately?" asked Waits.

Egan noticed that the Pinkerton detective had washed-out blue eyes that were as cold as the winter sky outside. They were the eyes of a mankiller.

"No, I haven't. But he has been here recently."

"Are you sure?" asked Waits.

Egan smiled thinly. "You're from up north, aren't you, Mr. Waits?"

"Pennsylvania. What does that have to do with anything?"

"Your manners," said Everheart. "Or lack of 'em."

"All I asked was if he was sure Bass had been around here."

"He said so, so he's sure," explained Everheart.

"I never saw him personally," said Egan. "But a few others claim they did. And his friends Henry Underwood and Frank Jackson have up and disappeared."

"Where do you reckon the three of them went off to?" asked Everheart.

Egan shrugged. "There's no telling. But Bass bought two horses from Jim Murphy. He paid for them in gold double eagles."

"That gold," said Waits, "belongs to Wells Fargo. Bass was involved in the robbery of the Union Pacific Express Number Four in Big Springs, Nebraska, about four months ago."

"There were six robbers, according to reliable accounts," added Everheart. "Three of them are dead."

"We figure Bass and one other man, whose identity we don't have yet, made it to Texas," said Waits. "Could that other man be Underwood or Jackson, you think?"

"Nope," said Egan. "Frank Jackson was here four months ago—and Henry Underwood was sitting right here in this jail when that UP train was held up."

Waits glanced at Everheart. "Sounds to me like Sam Bass is getting a new gang together."

Everheart shrugged. "Maybe. How well do you know him?" he asked Egan. "You say he worked for you."

"He's a smart kid," said Egan, "even though he's had no book-learning to speak of. Clever. If he says he'll do something, you can consider it done. And he's nobody's fool."

"You think pretty highly of him, then," said Waits.

"Well, I don't underestimate him. He could have made something of himself, I know that much. But he's the kind of man who wants success, yet isn't willing to work hard for it. He hangs around with the wrong people. I once told him that if he wasn't careful, he would have a reckoning with the law one day. Looks to me like that day is on its way."

"Yes, it is," said Waits. "My job is to bring Sam Bass in. You consider that done, too."

"The Union Pacific hired the Pinkerton Agency? I thought the railroad had its own men for this kind of work."

Waits sipped his coffee and did not respond.

"As for me," said Everheart with a self-effacing smile, "I'm just tagging along to make sure Mr. Waits here don't get lost. Texas is an awful big place, you know."

"Big, maybe," allowed Waits. "But not big enough for Bass to hide in."

"I wouldn't sell him short, were I you," advised Egan.

"Since you know him so well, why don't you come along?" Waits asked the Denton County sheriff.

"No. I reckon he'll be back up this way before too long.

Him and Underwood and Jackson, they all call Denton home. But I tell you what I will do. I'll send my deputy here along with you. He knows all three men by sight. Are you game, Tom?"

Gerren nodded. "If that's the way you want it, Dad."

"Question remains, where did Bass and his two friends go?" asked Waits.

"Well," said Gerren, "if I had money to burn, I'd burn it in San Antonio. I know that Sam Bass and Joel Collins spent some time down there."

"San Antonio," said Everheart, and nodded. "Yeah, that's as good a place as any to start."

WHEN HANK UNDERWOOD strolled into San Antonio's Palace Saloon and Dance Hall and found out from one of the bartenders working there that three men toting tin stars had just been in asking about him and Sam Bass, Underwood wasted no time in seeking out Bass. He found his friend in a high-stakes poker game at another of San Antonio's watering holes, the Cowboy's Rest. Bass was reluctant to leave the game—he was winning, for a change. But Underwood insisted, and Bass realized by the tone of his friend's voice that something was very much wrong. So he cashed in and they walked outside. Underwood dragged him into the night shadows of an alley.

"What the hell has gotten into you, Hank?" asked Bass. "You look spooked—and I never took you for a feller who spooked easy."

Underwood gave him the news. "The barkeep said one of 'em is a Pinkerton man."

"Pinkerton!" Bass was surprised.

"You didn't know that you were so important, did you?"

"Well, no, I sure did not. It was just one lousy train, Hank."

Underwood snorted. "You pissed down the wrong legs, Sam—the Union Pacific and Wells Fargo. They aren't going to take it lying down. They'll leave no stone unturned to catch you now."

"Hell. We had better get out of here. Where's Frank?"

"At the hotel, would be my guess."

They went to the livery where their horses were being kept, then went to the hotel. Underwood stayed with the horses in an alley behind the hostelry while Bass went inside to fetch Jackson. His nerves were on edge. He figured the three lawmen would check at every hotel in town; sooner or later they were bound to come here—if they hadn't already. But he wasn't going to run out on Jackson. The only way to find out if the lawmen had been here was to ask, so once he knew the lobby was clear, Bass went straight up to the desk clerk.

"Anybody been here tonight looking for me?"

"No, sir, Mr. Baker, not that I know of."

"Well, they'd give you a fair description of me, I suspect, and tell you that my real name is Sam Bass—which it is."

"Oh, I see. And, um, would these gentlemen be peace officers, by any chance?"

Bass smiled. "You didn't get here with yesterday's rain, I can tell. Fact is, they think I did something that I didn't have no part in."

"You're an innocent man, then," said the clerk dryly.

"In this case, I sure am. I'd swear it was so on a stack of Bibles."

The clerk glanced around. "I don't seem to have a stack of Bibles."

"Do you have any of these?" Bass laid a gold double eagle on the counter.

"Why, no, I don't have any of those, either."

Bass reached into a pocket and took out four more and stacked these neatly atop the first. "If I wanted you to tell those three peace officers that I'd been here but was gone now, and headed south for Mexico from what you'd heard, would this buy me that favor?"

The desk clerk reached out and put his hand over the gold coins. "I take it you and your friends are leaving tonight?"

"You're right on the money. And we are headed for Mexico, by the way."

"Of course you are." The clerk pocketed the twenty-dollar gold pieces.

"So I can trust you?" asked Bass.

"I guess you'll have to," said the clerk with a cold smile and avarice in his eyes.

Bass leaned over the counter, pitching his voice lower. "I know what you're thinking. You're thinking that the reward on my head is bound to be a lot more than a hundred dollars. And you'd be right. Thing you got to remember is that it's awful hard to spend reward money when you're six feet under."

The clerk abruptly stopped smiling. "I see what you mean."

Bass nodded. Now *he* was smiling. "You looked like a smart feller to me."

He went upstairs to find Frank Jackson sprawled on a bed reading a newspaper.

"You'll have to read that later," said Bass. "We've got to make tracks." He told Jackson what Underwood had told him about the trio of lawmen.

"I didn't know it was a crime to strike it rich on a Black Hills claim," commented Jackson.

"I lied to you, Frank. I stole the money. Robbed a train. I didn't tell you on account of I didn't know that you'd come with me if I did."

"Well, I got a confession of my own," said Jackson, pulling one boot on and then the other. "I never really believed that story of yours. I reckon I would have decided to come along anyhow."

"I'm sorry you did now, Frank. You ride with me, the law figures you for an outlaw. I wasn't thinking clear. I just had all this money and I wanted you to help me spend it. Truth is, three of the men who helped me rob that train are dead now, and I guess I figure to end up the same way before long. That being so, there's not much point in saving any of the loot."

"You could go away, Sam. Far away. Start a brand-new life. Settle down, get married."

"Don't reckon I'll ever get married. I was in love once, Frank, and once is enough for me. It broke my heart and damn near killed me into the bargain."

They left the hotel by a back way and found Underwood waiting with the horses. Under cover of darkness they succeeded in slipping out of San Antonio unnoticed—and headed north.

A week later, in a remote camp a dozen miles west of Fort Worth, Sam Bass announced that he thought they ought to rob a stagecoach.

"What for?" asked Underwood. "You've got more money than you know what to do with."

"It ain't about money. It's the excitement I miss. If you want to feel alive, there's nothing like a little risk."

"I've had that feeling," said Underwood, nodding. "During the war. Every day before a battle. You know I'm game for anything, Sam. What about you, Frank?"

Jackson was stretched out on a blanket, head resting on his saddle. He was gazing up at the stars. "You know what I liked most about San Antone?"

"The whiskey," guessed Bass.

"The señoritas," said Underwood confidently.

"Nope. I liked being able to lay in bed and read a newspaper all day long if I was so inclined."

Underwood chuckled. "So a life of leisure suits you, does it?"

"Well, I won't have such a life working in a tin shop, that's for sure. So I'm with you, Sam. I might as well be an outlaw, seeing as how everyone thinks I am one now anyway."

They held up a stage running from Concho to Fort Worth on a rainy, windswept night filled with lightning and thunder. There was only a driver, and he gave them no trouble. There were two passengers, as well, who were asleep when the robbery took place. The bandits shook these men awake and roughly dragged them out into the storm, and then relieved them of their cash.

"Forty-three lousy dollars," Underwood complained to Bass, having counted the take twice, the second time because he couldn't believe he'd had it right the first time.

Bass laughed. "Give them back one dollar each."

"What? Why the hell should we do that?"

"I don't want 'em to miss breakfast."

"Never heard of robbing someone, then giving him his money back."

"I'm making a habit of it."

Underwood shrugged and gave each passenger one dollar.

Bass turned his horse alongside the coach and, standing in his stirrups, peered into the box where the jehu sat, his hands held high.

"You carrying a strongbox by any chance, hoss?" asked Bass.

"No, sir. Just a mailbag."

"Okay, guess I'll have to settle for that, then."

They let the stage go on. The following day, having rifled through the mail pouch only to find a few more dollars, the outlaws rode boldly into Fort Worth. The town was buzzing with talk about the holdup. Unperturbed, Bass and his friends checked into the posh El Paso Hotel. They were gone before first light of the next day. That morning the mailbag was found behind the stage company office.

Returning to Denton, Bass advised his colleagues to stay with him in his Cove Hollow hideout. Frank Jackson took his advice. Unwisely, Hank Underwood did not.

"Hell, Sam," he said, "it's Christmas Eve. I want to spend the next few days with my wife and kids."

"That's risky, Hank, but you do what you feel like you have to."

A few days later they learned that Underwood had been captured. Sheriff Everheart, Deputy Sheriff Tom Gerren, and Pinkerton man Tooney Waits had returned from San Antonio empty-handed, only to lead a posse to Underwood's house when word reached them that Hank had showed up at home. Not wanting to put his family in jeopardy, Underwood gave up without a fight, throwing his artillery out the door before emerging with his hands up.

"I'm arresting you as Tom Nixon," said Everheart, "for your part in the robbery of a Union Pacific train in Nebraska."

"I'm not Tom Nixon. Hell, Deputy Gerren knows that. You know who I am, Tom, so speak up."

Gerren shrugged. "All I know is who you say you are."

"Go to hell," sneered Underwood. "Call me whoever you want, and arrest me, for all I care. I ain't done a damned thing wrong. And I've never set foot in Nebraska, neither."

"Well, that's where you're headed now," said Everheart. "Unless you want to tell me where I can find Sam Bass."

"And what if I did?"

"Well, then maybe I'd have to keep looking for this Tom Nixon feller."

"Oh, so that's it," said Underwood, smiling coldly. "I have no idea where Sam is. Haven't seen him in a coon's age."

"You're a liar, Hank," said Gerren. "You and Frank Jackson were with him in San Antonio about a month ago."

"Prove it," challenged Underwood.

"We don't really have to do that," said Everheart smugly. "We'll just send you to Nebraska and let you try to prove you're *not* Tom Nixon."

Quickly growing bored in the caves and thickets of Cove Hollow, Bass and Jackson robbed another stage west of Fort Worth. This time they got away with four hundred dollars and four gold watches.

"That was better than last time," observed Jackson after they had made a clean getaway. "But it still ain't nothing to write home about."

"No, it isn't," agreed Bass. "This is the most I've gotten from tapping a stage, but if we keep on like this we'll die paupers. Frank, if we want to see real money we're going to have to rob a train. But to rob a train we are going to need at least two or three more men. Men with steady nerves who know how to shoot and can ride like Indians."

"Shouldn't be hard to find such men," said Jackson. "Texas has more outlaws than longhorns, seems to me."

Bass laughed. "Then let's go get some recruits and find us a train."

CHAPTER TEN

———

ON A COLD AND RAINY FEBRUARY NIGHT, SAM BASS AND three men approached Allen Station, a stop on the Houston & Texas Central Railroad that ran north from Dallas to the town of Denison. All four men wore long yellow slickers and red bandannas. Twenty-five miles north of Dallas, Allen Station was an isolated place; better yet, from Sam's point of view, it was not far from Denton County and good hideouts like Cove Hollow and the Elm Creek bottoms.

Bass was confident of success. He had good men riding with him. In addition to Frank Jackson, there was Seaborn Barnes. Though only a kid—Barnes was several years younger than Bass himself—Seab had plenty of grit. He had already spent a year in jail on a charge of murder. Acquitted for lack of evidence, Barnes still had to deal with the fact that few people doubted that he had done the deed, or that he would lead a life of crime. It was the general consensus that "Nubbins Colt"—as many had come to call Barnes—would meet a bad end. The fourth man in the gang was Tom Spotswood, a Missouri hellion who had killed a man for the favors of a calico queen in Sedalia and, breaking out of jail, fled to Texas, where he was suspected of cattle thievery.

The four men waited in the dripping darkness, checking and rechecking their timepieces. Each man had one of the gold watches Bass had confiscated during the last stage holdup he and Frank Jackson had pulled. The Number Four Dallas Express was due in Allen Station at eight that night. The train did not arrive on time, though. By eight-thirty, Jackson and Spotswood were getting a little edgy. Bass noticed that Seab Barnes was as calm as the eye of a hurricane. Nothing seemed to rattle the kid. Jackson had shared with Bass his opinion that Seab was too dumb to be scared. That was okay with Bass, if true. And Jackson thought the kid was dangerous, too. But Bass liked having Nubbins Colt around. Seab idolized Sam, and Bass was young enough himself to let that go to his head.

"You sure you got the train schedules right?" Spotswood asked Bass.

"Don't start sweating. I'm sure. Trains don't run on time in Texas."

"How could they?" joked Jackson. "They're always getting held up."

"You reckon there'll be gold on this train, Sam?" asked Barnes.

"I'm betting on it, Seab." Bass laughed. "Come on, now, boys, lighten up. Number four is my lucky number."

"I hate this goddamn weather," groused Spotswood.

"Being an outlaw is hard work," opined Barnes solemnly.

"Yeah," said Jackson, "and I turned into a desperado to get away from that sort of thing!"

Fifteen minutes later they heard the train whistle.

"Okay, pards," said Bass. "If everybody does their job we'll come through this just fine."

They tugged the red bandannas up over their faces and urged their ponies forward out of the scrub.

Arriving at the station, they found the agent standing on the platform.

"Good evening, mister," said Bass—and pointed his pistol at the man.

Frozen with fear, the agent could only stare at the four

masked men who had so suddenly appeared out of the darkness.

"Seab, take him inside and tie him up," said Bass. "Tom, take the horses around behind the station."

Bass and Jackson stood on the rain-slick platform until Barnes and Spotswood had carried out their duties. All four men went around the corner of the station and waited until the train had come to a halt. Then Jackson and Barnes rushed the locomotive and captured the engineer and fireman. Bass and Spotswood approached the express car just as its heavy door slid open.

"Throw up your hands!" Bass shouted at the messenger, who stood in the doorway holding a package.

The messenger hurled the package at the robbers and ducked back into the car. Cursing, Bass leaped aboard. A pistol boomed in the confines of the express car and Bass thought he could actually feel the bullet passing right by his check. He heard it slap into the door behind him, splintering wood. The messenger had taken cover behind some crates in a corner of the car and was shooting at him. The railroad man fired twice more, and both slugs came too close to suit Bass. He let off one hasty shot in answer and quickly left the car.

"Damn it all to hell," he rasped, infuriated. "Mister, if you don't throw down that smoke-maker and give yourself up, I'm going to set this damn car on fire!"

"I am not coming out!" yelled the messenger—and punctuated his defiant reply with another pistol shot.

Jackson came running from the front of the train. "What's the matter? Who's doing all that shooting?"

"Tell the engineer to back the train up so we can unhook the coupling between this car and the others. Tom, keep an eye on the passenger and sleeper cars. Anybody sticks their head out, fire a shot. But try not to kill anybody."

The engine was put in reverse, the express car was detached from the rest of the train, and then the train pulled forward about a hundred feet from the station.

"What's going on out there?" yelled the messenger from behind his barricade in the express car.

"We pulled the express car away from the station and the rest of the train," replied Bass, "so that when we set it on fire we don't accidentally burn up everything else."

The messenger was quiet for a moment, then said, "Okay. I'm giving up. Only got one shell left anyway."

Bass had the railroad man open the express car safe and inside found several large pouches filled with silver coin.

"Should we visit the passenger car and the sleeper?" asked Jackson. "Engineer says he's got a full load."

"Too many people to handle, then," said Bass. "And in Texas nearly everybody goes heeled. We'd just be asking for trouble. No, looks like we made a good strike here. No need to get greedy." Taking the one remaining cartridge out of the messenger's gun, Bass handed the shooting iron back to its owner. "You should be more careful," he said wryly. "You damn near killed me."

The outlaws left the train, ran to their horses, and rode away into the night carrying the pouches of silver.

THEIR HAUL CAME to a bit more than twelve hundred dollars. Posses from towns all up and down the Houston & Texas Central line scoured the countryside in search of the robbers. Distributing the loot equally, Bass told his cohorts that they should split up for a spell and meet later in Cove Hollow once things had settled down. Seab Barnes went one way and Tom Spotswood went the other. Bass and Frank Jackson headed into the breaks along Hickory Creek—rough country with few farms and plenty of good hiding places for men on the run from the law.

Passing through a cypress bog, Sam's horse came up lame. Bass took a chance and walked his pony right up to a run-down shack located on the edge of the swamp. Jackson hung back under cover, watching his friend's back, while Bass approached a man who sat on the shanty's porch. The man had silver hair and beard and brown weathered skin. He wore old overalls and a straw hat. See-betters were perched on the tip of his nose. He was reading a newspaper laid across bony knees, and he didn't seem to be aware of Sam's existence at all until the outlaw was almost right up on him. Only then did he raise his eyes to peer at Bass over the rim of his spectacles.

"Howdy, stranger," he said in a raspy voice.

"Hello," said Bass with a nod and a pleasant smile. "My horse pulled up lame."

"Yes, I see that." The man stood up stiffly, dropped the newspaper in his chair, stepped down off the porch, and walked past Bass to take a closer look at the leg Sam's horse was favoring.

"Uh-huh. Fistula. Need a poultice of pine tar and axle grease to take down the swelling. Ride this horse anymore, son, and you'll ruin her."

"Got any horses I could buy? I've got money and will pay top dollar."

The man went back to his chair, picked up the newspaper, and sat down with a sigh of relief and a sheepish smile. "Rheumatism," he said with a rueful shake of the head. "It's an awful shame to get old. Can't do half the things I want to do anymore."

"That's what they tell me. Now, about the horse . . ."

"I have an old swayback mule that is blind in one eye. I doubt that's what you had in mind."

Bass grimaced. "You're right. It ain't."

"Isn't."

"Pardon?"

"It isn't. Where are you bound?"

"Denton."

"There are faster and better ways to get to Denton than through that cypress swamp, son. Just about the only people who come down into the brakes on purpose are the ones who live here—or ones who are on the run. Now, I'm pretty sure you don't live here."

Bass smiled. "No, I don't live here. I don't live anywhere, really."

The man nodded. "The name is John Howard. And you are . . . ?"

"Sam Bass."

"Pleasure to meet you, Sam Bass. Are you one of the men who held up that train at Allen Station about a week ago, by any chance?"

"What makes you think so?"

"I'm a good judge of character, if I say so myself. And I keep abreast of the goings-on in these parts. For instance, I know that Governor Hubbard has offered a five-hundred-dollar reward for each of the robbers of that express, and the railroad and the Texas Express Company have matched that reward—which means each of the train robbers has a price of fifteen hundred dollars on his head."

Bass looked around. It was hard to believe that John Howard could be in possession of such timely information, isolated as he was out here, a day's ride from nowhere.

"I also know," continued Howard, "that a certain Sam Bass from over Denton way is wanted for questioning in connection with another train robbery that occurred six months ago near Ogallala, Nebraska."

"Just who are you, anyway, Mr. Howard?"

Howard chuckled, held up a hand. "Don't get your hackles up, Sam Bass. I used to be a judge. But I'm not anymore. Haven't been much of anything, frankly, for the past ten years or so. Every other day I pay a neighbor's boy to ride to the nearest town, Pilot Point, to bring me newspapers and sometimes books. Now, I don't mind that you are a train robber. Like many folks in these parts, I harbor no tender regard for the railroads. As far as I know, you have not killed anyone during the commission of your crimes, and that is an important factor to take into account. Besides, I can see by your face that you are no killer."

"No, sir, I've never killed a man and I hope I never have to."

"I hope you won't have to, either. You are welcome to stay here. I haven't much to offer. But as you can see, this is an out-of-the-way place. You're not likely to see a posse ride through here. If we treat that mare, she will be good as new in a fortnight, perhaps even in less time than that."

"Well, for some reason, I trust you, Judge. But what about that boy you hire to bring you the newspapers?"

Howard shrugged. "I cannot vouch for him. I suppose that is a risk you will have to take, if you stay. But then, my guess is you're quite accustomed to taking risks."

"You live here all by your lonesome, Judge?"

Howard half turned his head toward the shanty door and called out, "Hannah, you can come out here now."

A young woman stepped out onto the porch. She was carrying a double-barreled shotgun and Bass realized then that he had been under that gun since his arrival.

"My daughter, Hannah," said Howard. "Hannah, meet Sam Bass."

Hannah Howard was pretty and slender, with long thick black hair and almond-shaped blue eyes that were startlingly bold and direct.

"Are you an outlaw, then?" she bluntly asked Bass.

"Well, I . . ." Bass quickly sensed the futility of trying to fool her. "Yes, I reckon you could say that," he said sheepishly.

Judge Howard chuckled. "My daughter doesn't beat around the bush, son. She speaks her mind. I have raised her to do just that."

"Well, you've done a good job of it," said Bass.

"I don't think it's a good idea for us to harbor fugitives from the law, Father," she said.

"I don't believe young Mr. Bass here is your run-of-the-mill outlaw, Hannah. He won't abuse our hospitality. Will you, Mr. Bass?"

"No, sir. And I'd be obliged if you'd just call me Sam."

"Besides," said Howard, "I wouldn't mind a little company."

Hannah grimaced and lowered the shotgun. "If you say so, Father." It was obvious that she could muster up no enthusiasm for Sam Bass or his company. That bothered Bass, because he thought Hannah was the prettiest woman he had ever seen. Naturally he wanted her to like him.

"Oh," he said, remembering Frank Jackson. "One thing, Judge. I ain't alone. Got room for one more?"

"Can you vouch for him?" Howard seemed amused.

"That I can do. Blockey is a good man."

"Blockey?"

"That's what I call him, anyway. His real name is Frank Jackson."

"What does he call you, I wonder?" asked Hannah dryly.

"Honest Eph." Bass grinned. "I've got no idea why, though."

"Your friend is welcome," said the judge.

"I suppose two outlaws is no worse than one," said Hannah.

Bass turned, stuck two fingers in his mouth, and cut loose with a shrill whistle that brought Jackson out of the brush.

Hannah watched Jackson approach with a skeptical eye. "Father, I hope you will at least make them wash up before you allow them into our house," she said—and turned to disappear into the shanty.

"Doesn't look like your daughter cares much for our being here, Judge," observed Bass ruefully.

"Oh, on the contrary, Sam. I think she likes you."

"Likes me? She has a funny way of showing it, sir, if you don't mind my saying so."

"You have a lot to learn about women," said Howard, chuckling.

FRANK JACKSON DIDN'T think staying with the Howards was such a good idea. The safest place to hole up, he told Bass, was Cove Hollow, and to his way of thinking they ought to make tracks for that place without delay. Bass pointed out that the lameness of his horse made that impossible. Jackson countered with the argument that they could probably buy a horse, or, failing that, steal one. Bass replied that under no circumstances would he steal a horse. In Texas you could kill a man and sometimes get away with it. But if you turned to horse thieving they would hang you for sure. Jackson wasn't buying into that—he was pretty sure he knew the real reason Bass wanted to tarry in the Hickory Creek breaks. A good clue was the way Bass looked at Hannah Howard.

Bass learned that Hannah's mother had died of the black fever ten years ago. Devastated by the loss of his beloved wife, the judge had sought solace in a whiskey bottle, and his chronic drunkenness soon cost him his judgeship and the respect of his friends and neighbors. So he had moved here, divorcing himself from civilization even though he kept himself well informed of the goings-on in the world beyond the oak thickets and cypress bogs of the breaks. No longer a drinking man, Howard had devoted himself to raising Hannah. She was just as devoted to the task of looking after her father. Bass took the liberty of telling her he thought it a shame she was stuck here. "With your beauty, miss, you would be the toast of the town someplace like Fort Worth or San Antonio." He meant it as a compliment—one that he was rather proud of, too—but all it earned him was a withering look from her.

Judge Howard laughed and took sympathy on the forlorn Sam Bass. "I've told her the same thing, Sam, and received the same response. So don't take it personally. She just won't leave me to my own devices. I've even thought of moving to town and putting out a shingle and taking up the law again—just to get Hannah out of this place. It's suitable for me—all I need, really. But I don't want her to spend the best years of her life here."

Bass and Jackson spent several peaceful days at the Howard place. Then the boy came from Pilot Point with several newspapers for the judge. The boy did not seem unduly curious about the two strangers, but Bass still had to wonder if he would mention the fact that the Howards had company, and if such news would pique anyone's interest. He realized that Jackson was right—lingering too long here was asking for trouble. But he hated to leave. He and the judge got along well, engaging in long and interesting conversations on a host of subjects, from horses to the law, Comanche Indians to the Civil War, hunting and fishing—and the favorite subject of both: Texas. What Bass liked most of all about Howard was that the judge never once talked down to him. Howard was well educated. He was extremely knowledgeable about many things. But he treated Bass like an equal.

But of course the main reason Bass threw caution the wind and stayed longer than he should have was Hannah. He wanted her to like him. Wanted that more than anything. And it didn't look like there was a chance in hell of that happening.

The newspapers brought news of Tom Spotswood's capture, which had taken place in nearby Pilot Point. A posse organized and led by an agent of the Texas Express Company had paid a visit to Spotswood's home in the Cross Timbers. Failing to find their man, the posse moved on to Pilot Point in search of fresh horses, intent on continuing the search. One man's good fortune was sometimes another man's bad luck—Spotswood happened to be in town with his young son, buying supplies. When the posse closed in, Spotswood gave up without a fight. He acknowledged later that but for the presence of his son he would not have gone so quietly. Among the posse members was the express train messenger who had exchanged hot lead with the bandits. The messenger positively identified Spotswood as one of the robbers. The outlaw was hauled off to jail.

When Judge Howard read about the capture, he asked Bass if Spotswood was a friend.

"No, not what you would call a friend," replied Bass. He was disgusted with the news. "But he did ride with me for a spell."

"You are going to try to break him out of jail, then?"

Bass gave the judge a wry look. "Now, if I told you yes, wouldn't you be obliged to warn John Law?"

"You're right. I am better off not knowing."

"Tom was a fool, getting caught like that."

"He might turn you in."

"He might try. But he doesn't know where to find me."

"Well, I think you're safe enough here," said Howard.

Frank Jackson didn't agree. That there was at least one posse so near at hand made him nervous. He had captured a woodpecker and made a cage for the bird out of twigs. "I'm gonna call him Samuel," he told Bass, "after you. Or maybe Honest Eph. Seeing as how you and him both are going to spend the rest of your days in a cage."

"Not me," said Bass. "If they catch me they're gonna have to kill me. I will not go to jail. I don't like feeling trapped."

"Well, now, if the judge's daughter gave you a smile, you'd be trapped, for sure."

Bass grinned. "Yeah—but that's not going to happen."

"If not, then why don't we move on? We'll be a long sight safer in Cove Hollow than we are here."

"I guess you're right," said Bass with a sigh. "We've hung around here too long. Okay. We'll go—on one condition. That you set that woodpecker free."

"It's a deal."

Bass told the judge that he would be leaving in the morning. And at sunrise he and Jackson were saddled up and ready to go. Howard shook their hands.

"You boys are always welcome under my roof—long as you don't start killing people. I won't play host to killers. But you two are good-hearted lads who just took a wrong turn somewhere."

"Yeah," said Jackson, grinning. "My wrong turn was when I started riding with Sam here."

"Don't let him fool you, Judge," said Bass. "He's a natural-born outlaw. Took to it like a fish to water."

Bass was stepping up into his saddle when Hannah came out of the house and shyly presented him with a woolen muffler.

"I . . . I knitted this for you, Samuel," she said.

"Thanks, Hannah." Bass took the muffler and wrapped it his neck, tossing one end over a shoulder. "Nobody ever made me anything before." There was more—much more—

that he wanted to say to her, but he couldn't find the words. So he just stared at her, committing every line of her face to memory, and wondering if he would ever see her again.

"Come on, Sam," said Jackson.

They rode away—and several times Bass turned in his saddle to look back at the Howard place.

"Good thing we left when we did," mused Jackson, "or you might have been trapped after all."

"Yeah," said Bass wistfully.

"So what are we going to do now?"

Bass rode in thoughtful silence for a moment. "Rob another train, Blockey. Let's get us enough money so we can go down to Mexico and live high off the hog for a spell."

"We'll need some help."

"We'll get Seab Barnes. He'll ride with us."

"Can three men pull off a job like that?" asked Jackson dubiously.

"Let's find out."

CHAPTER ELEVEN

"I GUESS YOU COULD SAY THAT I'M A LITTLE SUPERSTI-
tious," Bass told the newspaperman, Jed Banks. "So I
picked the Number Four express that ran between Dallas
and the Gulf Coast on the Houston & Texas Central rails.

"The Union Pacific express up in Nebraska had been
the Number Four, as had been the train me and my boys
had held up at Allen Station just a few weeks earlier. This
time I picked a small station south of Dallas called Hutchins for the place to pull the robbery. The train was due to
arrive in the Hutchins station at ten in the evening, and it
always stopped. With Frank Jackson and Seab Barnes riding with me, I chose a dark overcast night for the job. We
all wore yellow slickers and covered our faces with red
bandannas. Rode right up to the station and got the drop
on the agent there, a man by the name of Gales. The Number Four got there a half hour later. Frank jumped aboard
the locomotive to cover the engineer and the fireman. Me
and Barnes moved on the mail car when the railway mail
clerk rolled the door back to toss out a mail pouch. The
clerk threw the pouch at us, knocking Seab off balance, and
then slammed the door shut.

" 'Robbers on the platform!' he bellowed, loud enough
for the express messenger in the next car to hear him.

Seab was mad as hell. He fired twice into the mail car

*door. I told him to stop that. I could tell that things were
getting out of hand, plenty quick. Frank and I had thought
to bring along a couple of axes—they were leaning against
the wall of the station. I grabbed them and tossed one to
Seab and laid into the door to the express car with the
other. Seab joined in. . . ."*

The ax heads bit deep into the door, sending slivers of
wood flying everywhere. In a matter of minutes Bass was
able to reach in through the jagged hole they had made and
throw the heavy bar lock. Pushing the door open, he ducked
as the express messenger threw hot lead his way.

"Stop shooting, damn it!" he yelled crossly. "Keep that
up and we'll fill the station agent full of holes."

The express messenger cursed them roundly—and then
tossed his pistol out of the car.

"Light a lantern in there," Bass told him.

The messenger did as he was told, illuminating the interior of the express car.

"Now step out here where we can see you," said Bass.

The messenger came to the doorway, holding his hands
high.

"Come on," Bass said to Barnes, and the two of them
climbed up into the car. They found a sack of silver coin,
but that was all they had time to grab before a flurry of
gunshots outside flushed them out of the express car. Hitting the railroad siding in a crouch, Bass heard the crack
and buzz of bullets and looked toward the rear of the train.
He saw the dark shapes of men there, and the muzzle
flashes of the guns they were shooting, and figured they
were some of the passengers—a few brave souls who had
decided to take the law—not to mention their lives—into
their own hands in attempting to foil the robbery.

"Shoot over their heads," Bass told Barnes, and fired a
couple of rounds in the general direction of their adversar-
ies but well to skyward.

"The hell you say," rasped Barnes, and started shooting
on the run, making for the corner of the station.

Bass followed, glancing at the front of the train in time

to see a figure leap from the locomotive. "Blockey! Make for the horses!"

The three outlaws slipped away in the darkness and stayed in their saddles all night. Dawn caught them in the Trinity River bottoms, where they remained, laying low, during the daylight hours.

Their take amounted to less than five hundred dollars in silver. Seab Barnes cussed a blue streak. Frank Jackson took the disappointment in stride. "Well, I think the good citizens of Texas should pay a little more than this for the privilege of taking potshots at me," he said.

"One thing is plain," said Barnes. "We need more men next time we take a train."

Sam Bass walked over to Barnes and gathered up a handful of Seab's shirt and pushed him back against a tree.

"You won't be one of them, Seab, if you don't start doing what I tell you."

Seab Barnes was a prideful and quick-tempered kid—but this time he didn't flare up. Not against Bass. "What did I do?" he mumbled.

"You might have plugged somebody back there."

"Jesus Christ, Sam! They were shooting at us!"

"Sure they were. What did you expect them to do? We were trying to rob them."

"Well, if somebody is trying to kill me, it's only natural that I'm going to try to kill him first."

"I don't want anybody killed, you hear me? And if you want to ride with me, you'd better keep it in mind."

The following morning they arrived at Cove Hollow. A few days later, Jim Murphy rode in and found them. Murphy had started a horse farm located on the outskirts of Cove Hollow. Bass had slipped out to see him from time to time since his return from Nebraska and points north. Sitting on a rock in front of the cave where the outlaws had holed up, Bass and Murphy shared a jug of corn liquor the latter had thought to bring along.

"You boys have stirred up a real hornet's nest, Sam," Murphy said with admiration. "Posses running all over the countryside. The Texas Central wants your hide. Only thing is, they're not sure it's you. Not yet anyway. Sure, plenty of lawmen suspect that you've had a hand in the train robberies that have happened around here. But so far no one's got enough proof to make out a warrant."

"I'd like to keep it that way for as long as I can."

"Well, then you should know what I come all this way to tell you. There's a fella showed up at my place last night. His name is Riley Wetzel. He's Dad Egan's new deputy."

"What does he want?"

"He wants to meet you, Sam. How do you like that?"

"Meet me? Did Dad put him up to this?"

"He says it's all his idea, but Dad gave him the go-ahead."

"What did you tell him?"

"I told him I would ride in here and see if I could find you, and if you were interested in meeting him."

"He's got nerve, I'll give him that."

"I'll just go back and tell him I couldn't find you. But I wanted you to know what is going on."

"Thanks, Jim. But I want you to bring this Riley Wetzel here to see me."

Murphy was shocked. "You can't be serious, Sam."

"Never been more serious in my whole life."

"That's plumb crazy. He's a lawman, and he's out to prove himself at your expense, Sam. That's plain to see."

Bass laughed and draped an arm around Murphy's shoulders. "You worry too much, Jim. You're a born worrier. Just bring him along. Everything will be fine and dandy, you'll see."

"I sure hope you know what you're doing," said Murphy—and it was clear he had serious doubts along those lines.

When they found out about Wetzel, Frank Jackson and Seab Barnes thought Bass had gone loco, too.

"Why the blue blazes are you doing this, Sam?" asked Jackson. "I figure you must have a reason, but damned if I can see what it is."

"The law isn't sure about us. I want them to think we don't have anything to hide."

"If we don't have nothing to hide," said Barnes, "then what the hell are we doing hiding out here?"

"I'll explain all that. Seab, are you going to tell this deputy that we rob trains?"

"Of course not. What do you take me for? I ain't touched in the head."

Bass nodded. "Well, neither will I—and Blockey won't, either. So what's the problem?"

The following day, Jim Murphy brought Riley Wetzel to the Cove Hollow hideout. It didn't bother Bass that the deputy would know how to find the place again—there were a dozen hideouts just as good as this one in the area. Wetzel was a dark-haired, serious-looking young man, an ex-cowboy turned manhunter—lean, sharp-eyed, and smart. His approach was friendly, casual, meant to disarm. Bass took an immediate liking to him. Riley was obviously an ambitious man, and one long on courage. They all sat around a morning campfire and drank coffee and made idle talk for a spell. Finally Wetzel worked his way around to the reason for his being there.

"You know, Sam, some folks think you've been holding up trains and stagecoaches in these parts."

"I know that, Riley, but I'm an innocent man."

"Then why are you living out here? Come to Denton. That's your home and you have a lot of friends there."

"Oh, I kind of like it out here. Nice and quiet. No one to bother me."

"I'm told there are outlaws in these canyons."

"Haven't seen a single one yet," said Bass. "Have you, Frank?"

Jackson sipped his java and shook his head. "No. And I've kept an eye peeled for two-legged varmints, too."

"Riley, I'll tell it to you straight," said Bass. "Just because I pushed a herd of cattle north with Joel Collins, people assume I was with him when he robbed that Union Pacific express up in Nebraska. But when that happened I was still in the Black Hills hunting for gold. And now, every time there's a holdup, like you said, some people jump to the conclusion that I must have had a hand in it. Now, I don't care to end up in the bone orchard on account of some gun-happy bounty hunter. So until you catch the boys who really are pulling these jobs, I'll just lay low right here, if you don't mind."

Riley smiled. "That may take a while. Those robbers are slippery characters. You got enough to live on?"

"Oh, we do fine. Plenty of game in these thickets. White-tailed deer and wild turkeys and rabbits and possums galore. And I struck gold up north—still got enough in my poke for coffee and tobacco and sugar and flour whenever we're in need of it. Don't worry about us. We'll make do."

Riley nodded. "That's good to know, Sam. I'm sure Dad Egan will be happy to hear it. You know he thinks a lot of you."

"Dad's a good man. None finer."

"Yes. Ask me, if anyone has a shot at nabbing these train robbers, it's Dad Egan. He knows his business backwards and forwards."

"If anyone can get the job done, it'll be him," agreed Bass.

By that time Riley Wetzel had figured out he wasn't going to get anywhere with Bass and his friends. A lot of outlaws had loose tongues; reckless pride and often downright stupidity led them to say incriminating things. But Riley realized that Sam Bass was much too smart to talk himself into trouble. The deputy had little doubt that these were the culprits who had hit two Texas Central trains in a month's time. And his visit was not a total loss. At least now he knew better what he was up against. Sam Bass was nobody's fool.

Riley finished his coffee and then stood to go, thanking the outlaws for their hospitality. Bass shook his hand.

"Good luck catching those desperadoes, Riley. Hope you do it soon, so's I can come on home."

Riley smiled thinly. "Oh, don't worry, Sam. I don't reckon you'll be out here much longer."

"One thing I don't do is worry," replied Bass.

A WEEK LATER Jim Murphy was back in Cove Hollow looking for Sam Bass, who had taken the precaution of moving his camp after the visit from the Denton County deputy sheriff. All Murphy could do was ride the canyons and look conspicuous until Bass found him. He told the outlaw leader that he had some good news. Henry Underwood was back, and wanted to find his old friend. Bass told Murphy to let Underwood know where to find him, and the next day Hank appeared at the new camp. He didn't come alone.

"Sam, this here is Arkansas Johnson. A friend of mine. He and I were locked up in that goddamned Nebraska jail together."

Arkansas Johnson was a stocky man with pale blue eyes and a ruddy complexion and a face badly scarred by a long-ago bout with smallpox. He looked like a rough customer. Bass wasn't sure if he could be trusted, but as he was a friend of Underwood's he was made to feel welcome in the camp.

"Didn't think I'd see you again for a good long spell," Bass told Underwood. "What happened, did they finally figure out that you weren't Tom Nixon?"

"Hell, no, and I wasn't going to stew in some iron cage waiting for them to figure it out, either."

Underwood went on to explain how he and Johnson had made their escape. The latter's wife had brought them some steel saws concealed in a bucket of butter. For weeks the two men had worked on the strap iron barring their cell's solitary window, concealing the saws behind loose bricks in the wall when they weren't being used. On the night they made their break, they stole a couple of horses— Arkansas Johnson insisted that the victim of the theft had to be the local judge who had incarcerated Johnson for stealing lumber. Underwood had agreed, thinking that was a nice touch.

"What do you aim to do now, Hank?" asked Bass.

"Why, ride with you, Sam, what else? And Arkansas, here—he don't look like much, but he's a good man."

Bass nodded. Though Arkansas Johnson was an unknown commodity and Hank Underwood found killing a little too easy, Bass decided to wait and see what happened. After the trouble he'd had during the last holdup, he needed more men for the next job. It was just safer that way.

Then Frank Jackson mentioned quitting.

"I'm just plumb tired of riding the outlaw trail," he told Bass. "Sure, I might have more money in my pocket than I would were I in an honest trade, but hell, we didn't get a chance to spend it. We use up all our time trying to dodge posses."

"You can't quit," said Bass.

"Why not?"

"There's no going back to the way things used to be, Blockey. You can't go back to Denton, back to work in that tin shop, like nothing's happened. Folks know you rode with me, and most of them figure me for a lawbreaker, which would make you one, too."

"Far as I can tell, there's no evidence to tie me to any of the holdups."

"Hank didn't rob a train—and he ended up in a Nebraska jail cell. But that wouldn't be your only worry. There's plenty of bounty men out there who'll kill you just on the off chance that they might be able to collect a reward."

Jackson sighed. "I hate to say this, Sam, but I sometimes wish I hadn't let you talk me into going off to San Antonio with you."

Bass put a hand on his friend's shoulder. "I know, Blockey. I wish I hadn't, either. And I'll get you out of this, I swear."

"How you look to do that?"

"All we need is to hit the jackpot one time. Then you and me, we're off to Mexico, and we'll stay clean once we get down there."

"What are we going to do in Mexico for the rest of our lives?"

"Why, I don't rightly know. Raise horses, maybe." Bass grinned. "And go courtin' all those dark-eyed señoritas."

Jackson chuckled. "You can't fool me, Sam. You've got your cap set for a certain judge's daughter."

Bass stopped grinning of a sudden. "She could never be mine, even if she was so inclined. And we all know that she isn't."

They were pensively quiet for a moment. Then Jackson spoke up. "Sam, how did we get into this mess, anyway?"

"Damned if I know, Blockey. But we'll get out of it— all in one piece and with our pockets full of money. So don't quit on me. You're safer sticking with me. Now that Hank and Arkansas are with us, we'll fare better."

"Okay, Sam. I'll stick with you. Guess I knew all along that I didn't really have a choice. And I know something else, too."

"What's that?"

"That you and I will never have to worry about growing old."

"Yeah," said Bass. "But that's okay. I never really wanted to."

CHAPTER TWELVE

WHEN GRAYSON COUNTY'S SHERIFF EVERHEART CAME TO Denton to talk to Dad Egan about the rash of recent train robberies, he found his Denton County counterpart at home. It was a cool and starlit April evening and Egan was sitting on his front porch with Riley Wetzel; he had invited his deputy over for supper. Being a bachelor, Riley had jumped at the chance to fill his belly at a table set by the sheriff's wife, Dillie. Egan was taking his ease in a sturdy rocking chair, smoking his evening pipe and talking politics with Wetzel, when Everheart rode up.

"Howdy, Bill," said Egan, recognizing the lean, craggy, gray-haired lawman as Everheart steered his trail-weary cayuse closer to the house. "Climb on down and stay awhile. We just finished eating, but I reckon there's plenty of grub left, and hot coffee."

Everheart dismounted stiffly. "You know," he said, wincing as he pressed a fist against the small of his back, "I'm getting too old for this kind of thing. I need to spend more of my time in a rocking chair, like you, Dad." He grinned at Egan.

Egan grinned back, and stood up to gesture at the rocker. "Try her on for size and I'll go tell the missus to make you a plate of vittles."

"Just some coffee suits me."

When Egan returned with a mug of steaming black java, he found Everheart in the rocking chair. The Grayson County sheriff nodded enthusiastically. "This is a sight more comfortable than that old hull I've lived in for the past twenty-five years," he said, pointing with his chin at the saddle strapped to the back of his pony.

Egan chuckled. "You can't retire, Bill, any more than I could. We would both die of boredom."

"You've been lawdogging in these parts for a good while, haven't you?"

"Long enough."

"Long enough, then, to know that we've got a problem with that gang of train robbers."

"Yeah, I know that."

"Governor, he knows it, too. That's why he's bringing in the Texas Rangers, I reckon."

Egan glanced at Wetzel in surprise. "That's the first I've heard of it."

"Friend of mine down Austin way sent me a telegram telling me." Everheart sipped his java gratefully. "Mighty good coffee."

"Mrs. Egan made it, that's why," said Wetzel. "If Dad had made it, you'd need a spoon to eat it with."

Everheart chuckled. "You can use my coffee in place of axle grease if you've a need to."

"So first it was railroad detectives," said Egan. "Then the Pinkertons. And now the Rangers."

Everheart nodded. "The railroads went to the governor and talked him into it. I guess these owlhoots are just too crafty for us local tin stars, Dad. The Rangers, now, they always get their man, you know."

"So you came all this way to tell me that?"

"Nope. There's been another train robbed."

"Where?"

"Mesquite."

"Damn," muttered Egan. "They just struck at Eagle Ford. Think it's the same bunch? That's pretty quick work, if so."

"Everyone seems to think so."

Egan tried to recall everything he had heard about the Eagle Ford robbery. The Texas & Pacific train out of Dallas had paused at that remote station on the evening of April fourth—and was promptly boarded by four masked men. One outlaw leaped aboard the engine to put the engineer and fireman under the gun. A second man moved down to the passenger car, entered it, and told all those within to keep their seats if they didn't want their heads blown off. When the messenger refused to open the express car, the other two bandits had attacked the door with axes. Accompanying the messenger was a gun guard—the railroads in these parts had taken to hiring extra security because of the rash of robberies. But both the gun guard and the express messenger were buffaloed—they gave up without a fight. The messenger compliantly opened the safe, but the robbers found only fifty dollars inside.

Moving to the mail car, the bandits confiscated some registered packages. Meanwhile, the baggage handler, conductor, and brakeman were herded onto the station platform to join the Eagle Ford agent, engineer, and fireman. A cattleman named Wilson tried to slip away but was apprehended. One of the bandits knew him by name. Unfortunately, Wilson could not identify the outlaw, though he said the masked man's voice was familiar to him.

The desperadoes made a slender haul at Eagle Ford—a few hundred dollars at most—because they were unaware that the Texas & Pacific had started entrusting most of the money it carried to a special messenger who posed as an ordinary passenger. The bandits had not taken the time to search every single passenger for valuables—only a handful, those who appeared to be well off, were relieved of their wallets and gold watches. "We don't aim to rob ordinary folks," said one of the outlaws, "just the big augurs who can afford it." All four men wore dusters and used red bandannas to hide their features. Not a shot was fired, and the quartet of highwaymen made a quick getaway. A posse out of Dallas found their trail the next morning and followed it as far as the Hickory Creek breaks, but there the sign disappeared.

"It seems clear that the same men who robbed the Texas & Pacific at Eagle Ford were the ones who boarded the Texas Central expresses," said Everheart. "The red bandannas, for one thing—and they used axes on the express car door. The editor of the Dallas newspaper said he was convinced the gang was led by Sam Bass and included Frank Jackson and Hank Underwood. I guess you know Underwood broke out of jail up Nebraska way, with a hardcase who goes by the name of Arkansas Johnson."

"So I've heard," said Egan. "But Frank Jackson was seen around here the day of the Eagle Ford robbery."

"Are you sure about that?"

"The witnesses are reliable. Jackson and Bass are good friends. If Bass had been at Eagle Ford that night, Jackson would have been with him. As for Underwood, he was arrested and taken to Nebraska because you and that Pinkerton man identified him as Tom Nixon, one of the men who robbed the Union Pacific express."

"I never did think he was Tom Nixon," admitted Everheart. "But I did think he might spill the beans about Sam Bass to save his own hide. I was wrong about that."

"Could have told you you would be," said Egan dryly. "Hank Underwood is a hellion. Crossed over the line more than once, I'm sure. But so far I have no evidence—and I won't lock up a man on a whim."

"If I didn't know better, Dad, I'd say you were giving Bass and those other boys too much benefit of the doubt."

Egan's eyes flashed with quick anger, but he managed to keep it in check. Everheart was a fellow lawman. Furthermore, he was a guest. He was a candid man, too, and Egan could not fault anyone for being forthright.

"I'll give you the benefit of the doubt this time, Bill," he said, "and assume you don't hold to that misbegotten opinion yourself."

Everheart smiled. "No. But there are others up my way and over in Dallas who wonder why you haven't done anything about a nest of thieving varmints who live right out your back door, almost."

"I just told you why. No proof. I don't know if Sam Bass was at Hutchins, or Allen Station, or Eagle Ford—or at Mesquite, either. When and if I find out that he was, I'll bring him in."

"I rode into his camp," said Riley Wetzel, "hoping I could find such proof. I came away empty. If Sam Bass is the leader of this gang, he's a clever one. He won't be easy to catch."

"My old deputy, Tom Gerren, did the same thing a couple weeks back," Egan told the Grayson County sheriff. "I told him not to go, that it was a waste of time, not to mention dangerous, but he went anyway. He found Bass and Jackson and talked to them for a spell. They didn't seem to him to be the least bit worried. Then he saw why that was so. A rough-looking character with a scarred face was sitting at the base of a tree off to one side, a cocked rifle in his hands. Tom knew that if he made one wrong move that fellow would put a hole in him."

"That sounds like Arkansas Johnson," muttered Everheart.

"If they'd spent any of the gold or silver they were supposed to have stolen, then I would jail 'em," said Egan. "But they haven't. So all I can do is wait."

"For what?"

"For them to make a mistake."

"I don't know," said Everheart skeptically. "You might be waiting a long time. These boys don't make many of those."

"Everybody makes one, sooner or later. Just a matter of time."

Everheart grunted. "Meanwhile, they've robbed another train. Another Texas & Pacific express out of Dallas. Happened last Wednesday night. There were seven robbers this time."

"Dusters and red bandannas again?"

Everheart nodded. "Every last one of them. Makes them

all look alike, so it's hard to pick up any distinguishing marks or habits."

"And in a gunfight they'll have no trouble picking out their own from the enemy. So what happened at Mesquite?"

"The westbound out of Dallas stopped to pick up the mail. When it did, one of the bandits jumped aboard the locomotive and took off the engineer and the fireman. But then the conductor stepped off the passenger car platform and pulled a gun and started shooting when he realized what was going on. A couple of the robbers shot back at him, but the conductor ducked back inside. Then the station agent's wife came out to see what the ruckus was all about. A bandit ordered her to put her hands up. She told him to go to hell and rushed back inside, locking the station door. The robber put a bullet through the door. The woman wasn't hit."

Egan frowned. "Damn it. What kind of bastard would try to shoot a woman?"

"In all the confusion the engineer made a break for the locomotive, but he was pistol-whipped for his trouble. He'll live, though. And the fireman escaped, hiding under a trestle until it was all over. The conductor came back out of the passenger train right about then and commenced to shooting again. Several of the robbers fired back at him and this time he caught a bullet in the arm. He managed to climb back into the passenger car and bind up his wound. By that time several other men were making things hot for the robbers. The express manager emptied his pistol at them before shutting and bolting his door. The baggage master cut loose with a shotgun. And the Texas & Pacific had a couple of train guards on board. They started shooting from the windows of the passenger car."

"Sounds like it was a hot night in Mesquite," remarked Riley Wetzel. "Did any of these men hit what they were aiming at?"

Everheart smiled ruefully. "Well, no one knows for sure. But the gang didn't leave any bodies or blood behind. By this time the leader of the robbers had told his boys to bring some oil from the locomotive, which he used to douse the express car door. He told the messenger that if the door wasn't opened by the time he had counted to fifty, he would set the car on fire and kill anyone who came out of it. According to witnesses, the gang leader was striking a match when the messenger gave up and threw open the door."

"How much did they get away with?" asked Wetzel.

"Not much. About one hundred and fifty dollars. See, the express messenger had his wits about him. He hid fifteen hundred dollars in gold coin in the ashes of the express car stove."

Wetzel laughed. "The railroad ought to give that man a bonus."

"Yeah, well, listen to this. The messenger asked the gang leader for a receipt for the money he was stealing. The robber laughed and called the messenger a game rooster. Said he was sorry but there would be no receipt because he couldn't write. Can Sam Bass write, do you know?"

"No," said Egan. "But then a lot of folks around here can't."

"Well, anyway, the leader left the express car, called his accomplices together, and they all pulled back, making for their horses, and still shooting it up with the train guards. They got clean away."

"A posse go looking for them?" asked Egan.

"What do you think? It was big one, too, out of Dallas. Within hours of the holdup."

"And did they do any good?"

Everheart snorted. "You really need to ask me that question?"

"This bunch isn't having much luck, when you think about it," observed Wetzel. "If it's the same men who pulled all four train robberies, they pretty much came away empty-handed from three of the four jobs."

"What's your point?" asked Everheart.

"They might decide to move on to greener pastures. It's

getting a little hot for them in these parts. And every train will be heavily guarded from here on out."

"Or they could try their hand at robbing a bank," said Egan.

Everheart gave Egan a long and somber look. "Just a matter of time, you know, before somebody gets killed in one of these holdups. That's why I'm not sorry that the Texas Rangers are coming in. I don't care who catches these boys, as long as they get caught. And you know the Rangers always get the job done. They've cleaned up the Mexican border and made the Comanches think twice about raiding our frontier towns. I reckon in a fortnight our problem will be solved once and for all." Everheart glanced into his empty cup. "Got any more java, Dad?"

"I'll get it for you," said Egan.

Everheart surrendered the cup and looked around, rocking away in Egan's chair. "Yes, sir," he said. "This is surely the life."

Riley Wetzel followed Egan inside. "Dad, that son of a bitch talks like he thinks you're protecting Sam Bass."

"I've learned not to care too much what others think."

"And he's lying about one thing. He cares who catches these robbers. He wants to be the one so bad he can taste it."

Egan nodded. "Whoever does it will be a big man."

"You reckon Bass is leading this wild bunch?"

"I don't know. Could be."

"Well, whoever it is, he's as good as dead, what with the Rangers involved."

"I reckon you're right," said Egan. "We're about to have a war, Riley, and you and me, we're going to be right smack-dab in the middle of it."

IN A WEEK'S time Denton resembled an armed camp. Major John B. Jones of the Texas Rangers arrived to take a look around. Jones was a man of few words. He said very little—and missed even less. Then along came a United States marshal named Lane with a warrant signed by a U.S. commissioner for the arrest of Sam Bass, Frank Jackson, and Henry Underwood for the Mesquite train robbery. Over in Dallas, a United States district attorney opened up shop, while William Pinkerton brought a dozen of his best detectives down from Chicago at the behest of the Texas Express Company. Pinkerton made the Grand Hotel his headquarters and dispatched his men in all directions with orders to learn the identities and locations of the train robbers. "I don't care how you do it," Pinkerton told his men, "but get me those names before anyone else gets them. This company's reputation is on the line. Make a deal with devil himself if you have to. Sell your firstborn into slavery. Spend as much as you have to in bribes. Just find me those goddamned train robbers!"

Pinkerton, however, lost the race. Major Jones knew that Bass had ridden with Joel Collins; he also knew that Joel's brothers Billy and Henry lived near Denton, and rumor had it that Billy Collins was a friend of Sam's. Billy Collins, in turn, was friends with Billy Scott, who liked to boast that he knew a lot of notorious outlaws, all of whom took him into their confidence. Most folks wrote Scott off as a big talker and a bit of a buffoon who thought the outlaw life was a glamorous one but lacked the guts to pursue it and so just talked a good game. The Texas Ranger wanted to find out for sure. He located Billy Scott and pulled a bluff. The first words out of his mouth were, "You're under arrest."

All the color drained out of Scott's face. He stammered that he was innocent of any wrongdoing.

"That's what they all say," sneered Jones. "I have it on good authority that you were one of the seven men who robbed the Texas & Pacific train at Mesquite last month."

"I wasn't anywhere near Mesquite. I've got people who can tell you where I was when that holdup took place."

"I'm glad you have friends who will lie for you. I've got reliable witnesses that say otherwise. So you're coming with me." Jones held up some iron shackles. "You're going to be wearing these for a long time, so get used to them."

"No!" gasped Scott. "I didn't rob no train! Please, you got to believe me!"

"Why do I have to do that? It was you, Sam Bass, Frank Jackson, Henry Underwood, Arkansas Johnson, Billy Collins, and one other I haven't been able to identify yet."

"No, no, no!" Scott seemed to be having trouble breathing. "I wasn't there and neither was Billy Collins, I swear."

"Billy Collins was seen in Mesquite the day before the robbery. He was asking about train schedules."

"Yeah, he rode into Mesquite to take a look around for Sam."

"Sam Bass, you mean."

"That's right, Bass. But Billy didn't take part in the holdup. He just did a little scouting."

"Then who were the seven men who robbed that train?"

"Bass and Jackson, Underwood, Arkansas Johnson, Seaborn Barnes, Sam Pipes, and Al Herndon. Billy Collins wanted to go along, but Bass told him no, seven men was enough. Barnes got hit in both legs, too, during the holdup."

"Is he alive?"

"Far as I know. He's with Bass and Jackson and Underwood and Johnson at one of their hideouts."

"Do you know which one?"

"No, I don't. Honest."

"You're lying to me."

"No, I swear, I'm telling you the truth!"

"What about Pipes and Herndon?"

"I don't know where Al Herndon is, but Sam Pipes is staying with Henry Collins. That's Billy's brother."

Jones nodded and turned to leave.

"You—you're not going to arrest me?" asked Scott.

"Not right now. But I'm going to give you some advice, and if you want to stay alive you'll take it."

"What's that?"

"Get some new friends," rasped the Texas Ranger.

Major Jones had the authority, given to him in writing by the governor, to organize a special company of Rangers.

To lead them he chose a Dallas man named June Peak. Born in Kentucky, Peak had ridden with Nathan Bedford Forrest during the war and was wounded at the Battle of Chickamauga. After the war he had served in Dallas as a deputy sheriff and then the city marshal. He had been hired by New Mexico cattle barons to get rid of a plague of rustlers, and had done so with dispatch. He was skilled with rifle and pistol and could read sign like an Indian. And he was well liked, a born leader of men, from what Jones could see. At first Peak didn't want the job. He knew some of the suspects, and liked them personally.

"That's okay with me," said Jones. "You can try to talk them into giving themselves up, if you want to. That's the only way they're going to stay alive. You would be doing them a favor."

Peak agreed. Jones gave him a commission as a lieutenant in the Texas Frontier Battalion—the official name for the Rangers—and together they selected eighteen men to serve for a period of one month in a special company charged with a single task—to stop Sam Bass and his gang of train robbers.

Three weeks after the Mesquite holdup, Jones and Peak and their men showed up at the home of Henry Collins and arrested Sam Pipes. Pipes told them that Al Herndon was hiding out at a nearby farm, and a couple of hours later Herndon was in custody, too. The prisoners were taken to Dallas and thrown in jail. Friends, including Collins, made bail for both men as soon as they had been charged with assault by a local justice of the peace. But Major Jones went to the United States commissioner and obtained a warrant that charged Pipes and Herndon with mail robbery, a federal offense. The bail for that charge was set at fifteen thousand dollars apiece. Jones was confident that this would keep the two outlaws in their cells. But Collins and others managed to make that bail, too, and hired a top attorney, Henderson Barksdale, to represent the pair of lawbreakers.

Incensed, Jones rearrested Pipes and Herndon on a state

charge of robbery before they could slip out of town. Barksdale complained that no man could be tried twice for the same offense. Peak warned Jones that some of the local citizens were beginning to mutter about how the two men were being railroaded. Guarded by Peak's Rangers, Pipes and Herndon were smuggled out of the Dallas jail under cover of night and transferred to the jailhouse in Tyler, two days' ride away.

"That takes care of them," Jones told Peak. "Now it's time to get Sam Bass and the others. I'm sending you to Denton. I'll stay here and deal with the likes of Collins and Barksdale."

"Those boys have a lot of friends," observed Peak. "Nobody much cares for the railroads, you know, and so far the gang hasn't killed anybody, so public sentiment is on their side."

Jones gave June Peak a hard stare. "I wouldn't care if they were the Twelve Apostles. You're a Texas Ranger now, Peak. Those boys broke the law. We represent the law. So do your job. Bring them back, dead or alive."

Peak took his special company to Denton. He carried state and federal warrants for the arrest of Sam Bass, Frank Jackson, Henry Underwood, Arkansas Johnson, and Seaborn Barnes. He also carried a letter addressed to Sheriff Egan and penned by John Jones, who made it plain that the state of Texas expected Denton County's chief lawman to cooperate fully.

When Egan read the letter, he turned to his deputy, Riley Wetzel.

"I want every man in Denton who can ride a horse and knows one end of a gun from the other to sign up for this job. We're going into Cove Hollow and bring those boys out. A long time ago I warned Sam Bass that he would one day have a reckoning with the law. I believe that day has finally come."

CHAPTER THIRTEEN

I WAS WHILING AWAY A HOT MAY AFTERNOON IN A CAMP IN Cove Hollow, listening to the sawing of locusts in the mesquite and cottonwood trees, when the posse showed up. Frank Jackson, Henry Underwood, and Arkansas Johnson were with me at the time. Seab Barnes, who had been hit in both legs during the Mesquite robbery, was safely tucked away at the nearby farm of a friend.

There wasn't much to do at the hideout. Word had come to me from several sources that the countryside was fairly crawling with lawmen dead-set on bringing us in. We had heard about a special company of Texas Rangers created in Dallas. We also knew that Tom Pipes and Al Herndon had been arrested. Now everyone knew for sure that the rest of us were part of the train-robbing gang. That didn't bother me much. It was bound to happen sooner or later. What bothered me more was the fact that I had profited little from all the effort I'd put into becoming the most wanted outlaw in Texas. There were thousands of law-breakers in the state, but me and my friends were the ones everyone was talking about. We were also probably the poorest. The last three train robberies had been failures in terms of the loot we had gotten away with. I was still a long way from having enough of a grubstake to start a new life in Mexico.

All we could do was lay low in the ravines and caves and thickets of Cove Hollow. But even that wasn't as safe a prospect as it had once been. The law knew we were likely to be in that vicinity—so it came as no real big surprise to any of us when the posse appeared. . . .

Arkansas Johnson was the first to see the band of horsemen on the other side of a steep, brush-choked ravine from their camp.

"Who the hell is that?" he asked no one in particular, reaching for the rifle that was always near at hand.

Sam Bass was lying in the shade on a blanket, looking up at the sky through the dusty branches that sheltered him from the blazing sun. At Johnson's words he sat up and took a look at the six, seven . . . no, make that eight riders across the ravine.

"Aren't we in Denton County?" asked Underwood.

"Last time I looked," said Frank Jackson.

"Well, that's Bill Everheart, sheriff of Grayson County," said Underwood. "That's the son of a bitch who arrested me and had me hauled off to Nebraska when he knew damned good and well I was not Tom Nixon."

At that moment the posse spotted the outlaw camp. Men drew long guns from saddle scabbards and leaped from their horses to seek cover.

"What do we do, Sam?" asked Johnson. "Looks like they got some fight in them."

Before Bass could answer, the men across the way started shooting. The outlaws scurried for cover. Bass got up and started to run for the horses, fearing that the gunfire would spook them. Then something hit him in the midsection so hard that it knocked him off his feet. Frank Jackson scrambled to his side.

"My God, Sam, are you hit?"

Bass felt for a wound, for telltale blood. Nothing. A closer inspection revealed that a bullet had struck his gunbelt, crushing a cartridge in one of the belt's loops before careening harmlessly away. More hot lead was filling the air around them. Bass reached up and pulled Jackson down flat on the ground beside him. "We need covering fire!" he yelled—and Arkansas Johnson and Hank Underwood obliged, firing their repeating rifles as fast as they were able, and causing the posse members to pay more attention to saving their own skins than shooting off their guns—at least long enough for Bass and Jackson to find some shelter.

At this spot the ravine resembled a canyon in depth and width, and the sides were too steep to permit a crossing by horseback, but Bass feared that sooner or later Sheriff Everheart would send some men either up the ravine or down it with orders to find a way across. After a few minutes of fierce gunplay with the posse, the outlaws broke for their horses.

Everheart tried to give chase, but the ravine slowed him down too much and the posse lost track of their prey. They could not know that Bass and his men had doubled back and were keeping an eye on Everheart's progress from a distance, using Frank Jackson's field glasses. Finally Bass relaxed, convinced that they had thrown their pursuers off completely.

"Where do we go now?" asked Underwood.

"Cove Hollow's no good anymore," said Bass. "It will be crawling with posses from now on." He glanced at Jackson. "I think the safest place for us right now are the Hickory Creek breaks."

They had just turned in that direction when a smaller posse spotted them and gave chase. Bass and the others ran their horses full tilt for several miles. They were all heartily glad that Bass had shown foresight in buying the fastest ponies he could find through his friend Jim Murphy. He had paid top dollar, and in every case spent his money on horses that had that wildfire in their eyes—the same kind of fire he had seen in the eyes of the famous Denton Mare that he had once owned.

Using his field glasses, Jackson identified the leader of the posse as Dad Egan's deputy, Riley Wetzel. "That's one man I don't ever want to tangle with," said Bass, recalling the pluck Riley had displayed in visiting the outlaw hideout all alone a couple of months earlier. Bass didn't have to tangle with Wetzel this time—they soon outpaced the posse and then shook the pursuit off completely by swimming their horses more than a half mile downstream in a creek still swollen from the spring rains. Darkness fell before Wetzel and his men could find the trail of the outlaws again.

But Riley Wetzel wasn't one to give up easily. "If they keep going, east they'll end up nighting in the Clear Creek breaks," he told his men. He sent a rider back to Denton with orders to tell Sheriff Egan to bring reinforcements and meet him at Hard Carter's farm, located on the edge of the breaks.

Joined by Egan and six more men a mile from the Carter farmhouse, Riley pushed on at dawn. As they approached the isolated farm, they saw four men encamped at the edge of some trees within sight of the Carter place. Assuming correctly that this was Sam Bass and his gang, the posse charged forward.

Bass and his men were just sitting down to a breakfast of biscuits and coffee. They had been in their saddles until late, and had only had a few hours' sleep, and they were tired and sore and hungry. When the bullets from the posse's guns started ripping through the camp, Hank Underwood threw down a cup of coffee in complete disgust. "Goddamn it!" he roared. "A man can't even eat in peace around here."

"Head for the creek, boys!" shouted Bass, and all four jumped onto their saddles and kicked their ponies into a gallop, heading deeper into the trees. It was a brief but harrowing chase, pursued and pursuers weaving their horses through the thick growth, ducking low-lying limbs and praying their mounts did not step into a hole. There was much lead-slinging back and forth, but it was nearly impossible to hit a moving target from the back of a galloping horse. Once again the outlaws outdistanced the posse, and eventually a keenly disappointed Dad Egan called off the chase, gathered up his scattered men, and returned to the Carter farm, where the outlaw camp was inspected. All they found were some blankets and pots and pans.

"I was hoping we would at least recover some of the stolen loot," Egan told his deputy.

Riley smiled ruefully. "That Sam Bass is about as hard to catch as the wind."

"There's one difference," replied Egan grimly. "The wind can't stop a bullet."

Leaving Riley in charge of the posse with orders to scour the countryside thoroughly, Egan returned to Denton to meet June Peak and his special company of Texas Rangers. He found thirty of Denton's male citizens armed and mounted and on their way out to help catch Sam Bass. Egan directed these men to the Carter farm to join Wetzel. The posse searched the Clear Creek breaks all that day. Only one man came back to Riley with anything worthwhile to report.

"I seen him!" gasped the man. "I seen Sam Bass!"

"Where?" asked Wetzel.

"Well . . . I ain't quite sure where I was," admitted the man, shamefaced. "See, I was a little lost. Somehow I got separated from the others. And hell, you know how it is down in there, Riley. It's easy to get turned around, and easier still to stay that way. I was just about to the point where I thought I was going to spend the rest of the year in that jungle when I looked up and seen Sam Bass."

"You sure you weren't seeing things?"

"I'm sure. I know Sam by sight. He wasn't thirty feet away from me, either. Just sitting on his horse on the edge of a cutbank, smiling at me."

"Smiling at you?"

The man nodded. "Smiling—like an old fox. He said, 'Hello, Ben. I reckon you are going the wrong way if you're looking for your friends. They are all over in that direction.' And he pointed me down the right trail, then turned his horse and disappeared into the brush."

"You didn't think to place him under arrest, I guess."

The man chuckled. "Yeah right, Riley. Sure thing. I figured I had at least one rifle trained on me all the time—

don't you? But I went the way Sam pointed, and here I am."

"I hope you get the chance to thank him personally, Ben."

"Oh, I already did that. And I told him I hoped he knew that my hunting for him was nothing personal. He said he understood that. Sam Bass is a nice fella, Riley, when it comes right down to it."

"He's an outlaw, Ben. Never forget that. Under different circumstances he would shoot you full of lead."

Riley and his men searched all that day and most of the next for the robbers. But it was all in vain. Bass and his men had somehow slipped through their fingers.

WHEN SAM BASS saw Judge Howard for the second time, the latter was as he had been before, sitting on the porch of his rickety house on the edge of the cypress swamp in the Hickory Creek breaks. Once again Howard was perusing a newspaper. Bass didn't bother going in alone, with the others hanging back to keep him covered; all four of the outlaws rode right up to the house. The judge looked up at them and turned his head slightly to call inside.

"Hannah, Sam is back."

She came running out, wiping her sourdough-encrusted hands on an apron—and the smile of delight froze on her lips as she saw the condition Bass and his followers were in. The desperadoes had obviously been on the dodge for days. They were dusty and dirty, their gaunt cheeks unshaven. Their horses looked about ready to drop, and the men looked like they were in the same condition.

"Sam," she said softly. "Are you . . . okay?"

"Hello, Hannah." Bass managed a smile. It was almost too much of an effort for him. "I've had better days, but things are sure looking up now."

"You just missed the Texas Rangers, son," said Howard.

"Rangers?" rasped Underwood. His hand automatically moved to the butt of the Remington Army in his holster. "How many of them?"

"Enough. Led by June Peak. Know him, Sam?"

"No, sir, I don't. But I have heard of him."

"Then you know you don't *want* to know him," said Howard. "They passed through here this morning, headed north."

"I guess we got lucky, boys," said Bass.

"Makes you wonder how long we'll stay that way," remarked Frank Jackson.

"What's going on, Sam?" asked Howard.

"They've made up their minds to be rid of us, Judge."

"Reckon those Rangers will swing back through here anytime soon?" asked Underwood.

Bass suddenly realized that Underwood was afraid—afraid of the Texas Rangers. That caught him by surprise. He had never seen fear in Underwood before, and it was unsettling.

"You never know about them," said Howard. "They could turn up anywhere."

"I think we ought to move on," Underwood told Bass.

"You could be right, Hank."

"No," said Hannah, with a vehemence that startled everyone—including herself. "No, don't go just yet. You need some food, and some rest."

"She's right about that," agreed the judge. "And your horses are bottomed out."

Bass hesitated, torn between a desire to spend some time with Hannah and concern about putting her—and her father—in harm's way. "I don't know," he said. "Would purely hate to get you into trouble, Judge."

"Why don't you let me worry about that? Besides, I want to have a talk with you, Sam."

Bass dismounted, wincing at the stiffness in his joints that came from too many hours in the saddle. Jackson and Arkansas Johnson followed suit. But Underwood lingered in his saddle, scowling.

"Hank, we're as safe here as we are anywhere else," said Bass wearily. "But if you want to move on, go right ahead."

Underwood grimaced. "Reckon I'll stick with you for a

while longer, Sam," he said, climbing down off his horse. "Maybe your luck will hold out for us a little longer."

They unsaddled their ponies and put them on long tethers in the trees behind the house, then tried to clean up as best they could before sitting down at the table. Hannah had made biscuits and stew, and the outlaws ate like they had been without sustenance for a month. Afterward, Howard and Bass went for a walk. The sun was setting, and the woods were coming alive with sounds—frogs, crickets, and night birds, even an owl hooting from way back in the swamp.

"Sam," said Howard, gnawing on the tip of a cold briar pipe. "They aren't going to stop until they have run you into the ground."

"I reckon that's true, Judge."

"Tell me straight—how many crimes have you committed?"

"Well, I've robbed four trains here in Texas. And the Union Pacific up in Nebraska. Also, nine stagecoaches in the Black Hills and several more west of Fort Worth."

"Did anybody get killed?"

"Yes, sir. A stage driver, up in the Dakotas. But we run the man who did the killing out of the gang."

"So you have never killed a man, Sam?"

Bass thought about the gambler Penrose. He had an urge to tell Howard about that, too—but decided against it. Technically he hadn't killed Penrose. Underwood had done that deed, so it wasn't like he was lying to the judge.

"No, sir, I have never killed anyone."

Howard nodded. "Good, good. Sam, I think you should turn yourself in. Do it before someone does get killed. Do it now, before it's too late. I will defend you at your trial."

"You?"

"That's right. I used to be a pretty damned good lawyer, if I do say so myself."

Bass smiled. "I'm sure you were. Thanks, Judge, but you know it wouldn't do any good. They've built me up way too high. They will nail my hide to the barn door, and nothing you could do or say will change that. You know what I'm trying to say?"

Howard nodded again. "Yes, I think so. They are going to make an example out of you. The railroads want your blood, and the Rangers have staked their reputation on getting you."

"I reckon if they didn't hang me, I would spend the rest of my life behind bars."

"That's where I might be able to assist you. Perhaps I could get your sentence down to something reasonable."

"How long would a reasonable sentence be?"

"Well, now, that's difficult to say. Ten or fifteen years, perhaps."

Bass stopped dead in his tracks. Thumbs hooked under his belt, he stood there a long minute, hipshot, gazing at the toes of his boots. Finally he shook his head.

"No, I guess not, Judge. I don't want to spend even ten years in an iron cage. I couldn't."

"You would still be a fairly young man when you got out, Sam. You could start all over, with a clean slate."

"There's no such thing. First train that got held up, they would be breaking down my door, and you know it."

"You could go away, Sam. Leave Texas. Start fresh somewhere else."

Bass shook his head, smiled ruefully. "I like it here."

Howard looked at him pensively. "You're not going to let them take you in, are you?"

"Well, Judge, they seem to be inclined to shoot first and ask questions later."

"I wish you would reconsider, son. You know there is a certain satisfaction to be derived from getting old. You beat the odds a little more with every winter you manage to tack on."

"I don't feel right being here," said Bass. "I am putting you and your daughter in danger and that doesn't sit right with me."

"Hmm." Howard chewed some more on the pipe's stem.

"Hannah is kind of partial to you, Sam. Who knows, maybe she could change your mind."

"I wish she could."

Later that evening, Hannah found Bass sitting alone on the porch. She asked him if he would like to walk with her.

"It would be an honor," he said. "But you ought to know, I talked to your pa earlier and he tried to talk me into turning myself in. I won't do that, Hannah. I just can't. I'd rather be dead than locked up in an iron cage."

"Just walk with me," she said quietly, and he fell in alongside, accompanying her to the edge of the cypress bog. She carried a lantern to light the way. Off in the darkness an alligator grunted. Bass wondered what other dangers lurked out there. Wondered if there was a Texas Ranger watching them, lining him up in his rifle sights. It wasn't his health as much as Hannah's safety that concerned him. She gazed at him by the lantern light, gazed so intently that it made him more than a little uncomfortable.

"You have haunted eyes," she said, and she sounded profoundly saddened. "They are very old eyes for someone so young."

"I don't feel young. Guess I stopped feeling young a long time ago."

"Why, Sam? Why does it have to be this way?"

He shook his head, too ashamed to look at her. "I just wanted my share."

"By stealing from others?"

"That never bothered me, taking money that belonged to the railroads, or to Wells Fargo, or to the mining companies. But I never was much for robbing the ordinary folk who rode the trains or the stages, if that counts for anything."

"You should go away. Far away from Texas."

Bass swallowed the lump in his throat. "I might consider doing that, Hannah—if you would go with me."

She shook her head. "I can't, Sam. I'm so sorry."

"Because I'm an outlaw?"

"Well, that's part of it, yes. But mostly it's my father. He needs me. He would be lost without me. I am all he has."

"I understand."

Hannah tentatively reached out and took his hand. "Please leave Texas, Sam. I—I don't think I could bear to hear that you had been gunned down. And we both know that's what will happen if you stay."

"Wouldn't do any good to run. They would find me no matter where I went, or how deep the hole I crawled into."

"Who would find you?"

"The Rangers. The Pinkertons. Or the railroad agents. Take your pick." He looked at her then, marveling at her beauty, and smiled. "You sure are pretty, Hannah. I know I shouldn't have come back, but, well, I just wanted to see you one more time."

She stepped in very close and laid her head on his shoulder with a sigh, and Sam Bass put his arms around her and held her close, savoring the moment, treasuring it as he knew he always would, and for a little while forgetting about what was and losing himself in dreams of what might have been.

CHAPTER FOURTEEN

FOR THE BETTER PART OF A WEEK SEVERAL POSSES AS WELL AS June Peak's special company of Texas Rangers thoroughly combed the thickets and swamps along Hickory Creek. At one point a Denton posse mistook a squad of Peak's men for the Bass gang and started shooting. The mistake was quickly realized, and fortunately no one was hit. There was, in fact, only one casualty of the manhunt—a posse member who managed to shoot himself in the foot.

Though Bass and his followers weren't apprehended, several others were arrested and thrown in jail on charges of aiding and abetting the outlaws. These included Billy Collins and Jim Murphy. Bass hated that others were being made to suffer on his account. But he understood what the lawmen were trying to do. Judge Howard and his daughter weren't the only ones who had proffered help to him; particularly in Denton County there were quite a few citizens willing to provide food and a hiding place to the desperadoes. Anyone the railroads hated as much as Sam Bass couldn't be all bad, they said.

Bass dared not linger too long at the Howard place, as much as he wanted to be near Hannah. He stayed one night and then was gone the following morning, vanishing back into the swamps. After several days of playing cat and mouse with the groups of armed men on the prowl for him,

Bass told the others it was time to get the hell out of the county. They had two choices—they could head north into the Nations or west to the sparsely populated and virtually lawless Texas frontier.

"I don't think we should take a chance on the Indian Territory," said Hank Underwood. "The tribal police and the United States marshals out of Fort Smith would give us hell. Besides, you and I are well-known up that way, Sam, and we're not exactly thought highly of."

"How come?" asked Arkansas Johnson.

Underwood explained to his friend how he and Bass had made plenty of enemies among the Indians when they had taken the Denton Mare into the Nations a couple of years ago. "And you know how those damned Indians are," concluded Underwood sourly. "They never forgive a slight."

"Neither do you, as I recall," said Arkansas Johnson, and they all laughed.

"Then it's agreed—we'll head west," said Bass.

"And what do we do when we get out there?" asked Frank Jackson. "Rob another train?"

"Reckon I'm finished with trains," said Bass. "They're on to us now. Every train carrying anything of value will be loaded down with guards."

"Not stagecoaches again, I hope," said Jackson wryly. "I already got three gold watches, Sam. I don't need any more timepieces, thank you all the same."

"Oh, we sometimes got more than watches when we held up a stage."

"Not often enough to suit me."

Bass smiled. "No, I was thinking we might try a bank on for size. You game for that, Blockey?"

"Well, now, I don't know. Do I have a choice? I sure can't go back to work at the tin shop, now, can I?"

So they rode west, and a few days later decided to hole up in a likely looking spot on Big Caddo Creek. They were about a hundred miles away from Denton. This was rough country, and the towns were few and far between. The only drawback to the move was that they did not have any sympathizers to count on in these parts. Still, they felt a little better off. And they were pleased to find a deserted cabin by the creek. It was well off the beaten path. Using stolen gold, they bought provisions from a couple of nearby farms. Bass knew that was risky, but he hoped their generosity with the gold would persuade the locals to keep their mouths shut.

The outlaws discussed robbing a bank at nearby Weatherford, but changed their minds when they heard that another gang of desperadoes had tried to pull that off only a month earlier. The banker and some of the townsfolk had put up one hell of a fight, and two of the would-be bandits had been dispatched to boot hill.

"Never underestimate dirt farmers," said Underwood. "They'll fight like wildcats to keep what's theirs."

"Doesn't sound like bank robbing is all it's cracked up to be," remarked Frank Jackson. "Seems to be a pretty risky proposition."

"Well, what do you expect?" asked Arkansas Johnson. "We're in a risky line of work."

"Besides, Blockey," said Bass, "I know for a fact that you don't want to grow old."

They had been at the cabin for several days when Sam Bass suddenly got edgy and told the others it was time they moved on again. "I can't explain it, but I've got a hunch we've overstayed our welcome."

"It's a good thing I'm fond of travel," said Jackson.

They left the hideout the next morning—and an hour later, on the Palo Pinto road, ran right into a posse out of Breckenridge, led by the Stephens County sheriff, Berry Meadors.

It occurred to Bass when he saw the posse that someone had informed John Law of their presence. Apparently he hadn't spread enough of those double eagles around to keep lips from flapping. But he had no time to dwell on his mistake; the immediate problem was that neither party of men was aware of the other's presence until they were within spitting distance. Meador's posse came around a sharp bend in the road that at this point cut through a bosk of live oak, and found themselves nose to nose with the four hardcases they had come out to find.

On both sides the men abruptly checked their ponies, and for a moment no one moved. The outlaws realized that if they turned to make a run for it, they would fall under a hail of bullets. Even a store clerk couldn't miss at this range. So there was only one thing left to do.

For his part, Meadors hesitated. He had the desperadoes outnumbered, but he also knew that in a shootout at such close range the outlaw gang was bound to empty some of the posse's saddles. The men who rode with him had volunteered, but Meadors didn't figure that would make telling their widows and children any easier when he took them home draped over their horses in the dead man's ride.

So the deputy sheriff tried to bluff his way through. "You boys take it nice and easy, now," he told the outlaws. "Just throw down your guns and put up your hands. You've been caught and you might as well face facts."

Underwood looked at Bass, then back at Meadors—and grinned. "I think you're the ones who've been caught."

"There's no need for—" Meadors didn't get a chance to finish. One of his men lost his nerve and went for his pistol. Bass and his companions didn't hesitate. They, too, reached for their guns. Everybody started shooting. In no time at all Meadors was shrouded in acrid gunsmoke that stung his eyes. He was slinging lead right along with the rest, even though he didn't have a definite target. Men were shouting and cursing above the din of gunfire. It sounded like the crackle of lightning that strikes too close—only it went on and on and on.

And then, as suddenly as it had started, the shooting spree came to an end, and Meadors found himself out of the haze of powder smoke—and surprised to see that the outlaws had disappeared. Most of his men were either reloading or trying to get their horses under control. Two had been wounded, though not mortally. Meadors couldn't believe that with all the bullets that had been flying no one was dead or dying. And he was keenly disappointed that after firing at least forty rounds he and his men had not managed to drop a single bandit.

Instructing the two wounded men to return to Breckenridge and send up reinforcements, Meadors found the trail of the outlaws and followed it. Though he tried all day, he could not catch up to them. After their brush with death on the Palo Pinto road, some of his men seemed to have lost a lot of their enthusiasm for posse work. That night Meadors made camp at King Taylor's trading post.

He had no way of knowing that Bass and his gang were in a cold camp only a quarter of a mile away. Bass knew about the posse, though—he had ridden toward the trading post hoping to buy some supplies and seen Meadors and his men at a distance. Turning right around, he told his saddle partners, and Arkansas Johnson suggested they slip in at night and run off the posse's mounts. Bass didn't think that was a good idea. He couldn't believe their luck—all four of them had come away from the earlier shooting scrape without even a scratch. He didn't care to test that luck any further than he had to. Johnson scoffed at his caution. "Those boys can't shoot worth a damn. We wouldn't have nothing to worry about."

"I'm with Sam," said Frank Jackson. "I would hate for one of them to kill me by accident."

At daybreak Bass and Jackson were at a vantage point from which they could watch the posse's camp with the latter's field glasses. Meadors was joined by two groups of men. The first bunch looked like townsfolk. The second looked to be much tougher hombres.

"Who do you reckon they are?" asked Jackson.

"I don't rightly know. But if you wanted me to guess, I'd say they were Texas Rangers."

"Oh, that's just dandy. Must be twenty-five men down there now. What do we do?"

Bass grinned. "Now, what do you think, Blockey?"

"We run like hell?"

"Let's get started."

They dodged into the cedar breaks of the Palo Pinto, and soon shook off their pursuit. It was agreed that they would split up and meet a few days later at Black Springs. Bass and Jackson rode due east and late that night arrived at an isolated ranch house. A woman of about forty hard years opened the door. Hat in hand, Bass asked for food and shelter and assured her that he was willing to pay handsomely for whatever she could provide.

"I am Mahala Roe," she said. "These are my daughters, Sarah and Lucy. Their husbands are away to help build a church. Since the menfolk are gone we will have to trust that you two are gentlemen."

"We're willing to sleep in the barn, ma'am," said Bass.

"Nonsense. I have a spare room and you are welcome to it. Put your horses in the barn and then come back here. I will warm up some dinner for you."

"We're obliged, ma'am," said Bass.

On the way to the barn Jackson commented on the fact that Mrs. Roe had not asked them for their names.

"Maybe she already knows who we are," said Bass. "There is a lot of paper out on us, Blockey."

"I saw a wanted poster with your name on it, but the picture didn't look at all like you, Sam. The feller in the picture was twice as handsome as you are."

After they ate, Mrs. Roe showed them to the spare room. By then it was very late, and she told her daughters it didn't look as though their husbands would be getting home that night. Both Sarah and Lucy were concerned about the two strangers in their house. "Ma, what if they are outlaws?" asked Lucy.

"They are," said Mahala Roe. "The dark-haired one is Sam Bass."

Lucy gasped. "Oh, my God—what are we to do?"

"Mother, why did you let them in if you knew they were outlaws?" asked Sarah.

"They are train robbers, not murderers."

"But how can you be sure that they will not harm us?"

"My dear," said Mrs. Roe patiently, "I have lived

twenty-five years on the Texas frontier. I have seen ruffians and cutthroats of every stripe. I can look into a man's face and tell if he intends to do me or mine mischief. And those two have no such intentions, on that you may rely. Now go to bed, and sleep well."

After Sarah and Lucy had turned in, Mrs. Roe tapped on the door to the spare room. She was told to come in and entered to find Bass and Jackson on their feet—and a small arsenal of rifles, pistols, and knives laid out on the bed. The outlaws had been cleaning their weapons and discussing plans for the future.

"Mr. Bass," she said, with barely a glance at the guns and knives, "I have told my daughters who you are and they are frightened. I also assured them that you would do us no harm. Now, do not make a liar out of me."

"No, ma'am," said Bass, astonished. "I wouldn't dream of doing any such thing."

"Very well, then. Good night."

THE FOLLOWING MORNING the Meadors posse arrived at the Roe house, only to learn that Bass and Jackson were long gone. One of the Texas Rangers sternly admonished the widow woman for not being more particular about her houseguests.

"Do not presume to tell me who I can invite into my own home," Mrs. Roe snapped back. "Sam Bass may be a train robber, but he is also a perfect gentleman. Which is more than I can say for you!"

Chastened, the posse watered their horses and pressed on. But they soon lost the trail again. Sensing that his men were discouraged to the point of quitting, Meadors abandoned the chase. He justified the decision to the Texas Rangers by pointing out that the outlaws were no longer in his jurisdiction. Returning to Breckenridge, Meadors telegraphed Dad Egan, informing the Denton County sheriff that it appeared to him as though Sam Bass was on his way home. Egan discounted this—he didn't think it likely that Bass would dare come anywhere near Denton, which was still chock-full of Rangers, Pinkertons, railroad men, and bounty hunters. Denton was probably the most dangerous place in Texas for Bass and his gang right now. Egan conceded that Bass was bold. But he was not a fool.

Dad Egan would soon find out just how bold Sam Bass could be.

Less than a week later, Bass and his companions rode right into Denton at daybreak, arriving at Work's Livery Stable just as the hostler was opening the barn doors. The hostler looked up at the four horsemen—and down the barrels of their six-guns—and could not believe his eyes.

"Good morning," said Bass pleasantly. "I'm told you have a couple of horses that belong to me."

"I—I don't know what you're talking about," gasped the hostler.

"The hell you don't," snapped Underwood. "Your boss has been charging two bits to anyone who wants to see the getaway horses of the Bass Gang."

"Those ponies were taken from Jim Murphy's ranch," explained Bass. "Back when they arrested Jim. They belong to me. I paid good money for them. They were at Murphy's to be reshod, that's all. Now I want them back, pronto."

Underwood dismounted, handed his reins to Arkansas Johnson, and walked into the barn. A moment later he emerged and nodded to Bass. Then he grabbed the hostler roughly by the collar and rammed the barrel of a pistol hard against the man's jaw.

"Don't play stupid," warned Underwood. "Put some saddles on those two horses back there—you know which ones—and be quick about it, or I'll put a hole in your head."

"Easy, Hank," said Bass.

Underwood scowled. "We need to show these people that they can't just go around stealin' what belongs to us. It ain't right."

Frank Jackson found that amusing. "Thou shalt not steal. By God, that's one of the Commandments, isn't it? I'd almost forgotten."

"It just rubs me the wrong way when so-called honest folk get light-fingered," said Underwood. "That's all I'm saying."

Arkansas Johnson was keeping a wary eye on the street, and had noticed that several of Denton's early risers were paying particular interest in what was going on in front of the livery. "Boys," he said, "can we talk about who should and should not steal some other time?"

Underwood marched the hostler into the barn at gunpoint. A few minutes later he came out with two saddled horses, but no hostler. He glanced at Bass and anticipated the question.

"No, I didn't hurt him, damn it. I wonder how much John Work will charge folks to see a hostler tied up by the Bass Gang."

Bass laughed. Leading the two extra horses, the outlaws raised dust dashing north out of Denton. The road they took led them past the Egan place. As they galloped by, Bass spotted Dad's boy, Johnny, on his way to the barn carrying a milk pail. Johnny Egan stopped in his tracks and gaped at the bandits, slack-jawed with astonishment. "Hello, there, little pard!" called Bass with a wave of the hand. Then he noticed Dillie Egan standing in the doorway of the house—and tipped is hat. Dillie nodded back. An instant later the outlaws were gone. As the dust settled, Johnny ran back to the house, shouting excitedly.

"Ma! Ma, that was Sam Bass himself!"

"Yes, I know, son. Keep your voice down. Your father is still sleeping."

"Oughtn't we to wake him up, Ma?"

Dillie ran her fingers through her boy's unruly mop of hair. "Go about your chores, Johnny."

A quarter of an hour later a dozen Denton men thundered up to the Egan house on hard-run horses. By now a steady drizzle had begun to fall from the low, powder-gray sheet of clouds that covered the sky. Dad Egan was roused by all the commotion the excited posse made. Bleary-eyed and half clad, he came out onto the porch to learn what the ruckus was all about, and was informed of the latest exploit of the Bass Gang.

"They must have rode right by here not more than twenty minutes ago," said one of the posse members. "Hurry up, Dad. This time we'll catch 'em."

Egan glanced at his wife. Dillie nodded. Ordering his son to saddle a horse, the Denton County sheriff went back inside to grab the rest of his clothes and his guns.

"Why didn't you wake me up?" he asked Dillie as he pulled on his boots. He wasn't angry, just curious.

"Because you would have gone charging after them."

"Well, you know, that is my job."

"I know that. But I don't want you to be killed. I doubt that Sam would ever take a shot at you. But I'm not so sure about some of the men who ride with him."

"Damn it, Dillie, Bass is making a fool of me. Of all of us."

"Oh, now," she said gently, handing him a cup of coffee, "he won't be doing that much longer, and we both know that's true."

Egan said no more. He knew his wife still had a soft spot for Sam Bass. Though he would never admit it to anyone, he did, too. He gulped the coffee, grabbed his coat and slicker, and gave Dillie a peck on the cheek before going back out into the morning rain.

CHAPTER FIFTEEN

IT RAINED ALL THAT DAY. THE WEATHER SUITED DAD EGAN'S mood perfectly. He had hoped that the conditions would make tracking the outlaws a bit easier. But the rain didn't seem to slow Sam Bass down in the least. The same could not be said for the posse that followed Egan. They trailed the gang of train robbers into the Clear Creek bottoms—and there lost the sign. Some of Egan's volunteers gave up and went home. But more arrived to take their places. By the end of the day Egan had fifty men riding with him. That was too many. In fact, Egan would have preferred going after the longriders with just a few handpicked men. He figured he would have a better chance of catching his prey that way. But he didn't try to send his posse home. He knew they wouldn't go until they were good and ready. These men all had one thing in common—they had a hankering to be present and accounted for when history was being made. They wanted to take part in the capture or the killing of Sam Bass—or at least to be on hand when that momentous event transpired. The rigors of pursuit were weeding out a few of the faint-hearted, but most of the men who rode with the sheriff were willing to endure reasonable hardships in return for bragging rights when it came time to tell their children or grandchildren about the role they had played in tracking down the legendary Sam Bass and his gang of hellions.

After a wet and miserable night camp, Egan split his posse up and sent the groups off in various directions, hoping that one of them might get lucky and flush the fugitives out of hiding. Egan himself decided to ride back to Denton and wait for word. With him rode two men. A few miles out of town they were startled to see the outlaws crossing the road right up ahead of them. Egan shouted at the lawbreakers to stop and surrender, but one of his companions got nervous and started shooting. A couple of the bandits fired back. The rain was coming down hard now, and Egan could not see much in the gray gloom—nothing except the bright yellow blossoms of muzzle flash. Then the outlaws vanished into the brush. The sheriff gave chase, but again he lost them, in the thickets along Elm Fork. The rain-swollen stream stopped him altogether. Thoroughly disgusted with the way things had gone, Egan resolved to go home.

The following day brought news that Bass and his boys had been spotted in the vicinity of Pilot Knob, a cap rock six miles from town. Egan sent a deputy named Clay Withers and two brothers, Tom and Jack Yates, who were experienced trackers and very good shots with both rifle and pistol. Noted Indian fighters, the Yates boys were men Egan knew he could count on. As they neared the prominent landmark, a dome of limestone rock rising above the prairie, Withers and his party were joined by George Smith, the city marshal of Denton, and three other men. As Bass had "stolen" two horses inside the town limits, said Smith, that made the outlaws his problem. A short while later the posse neared a farm and spotted four horsemen sitting their saddles and talking to an old woman who stood on the farmhouse's rickety porch.

"There they are!" yelled Smith. "Let's go get 'em!"

"Hold up there!" called Clay Withers, but to no avail. Smith and his boys were galloping hell for leather toward the farmhouse, guns brandished. Withers and the Yates brothers had no choice but to follow.

Sam Bass was paying for a sack of eggs with a twenty-dollar gold piece when Arkansas Johnson, who had a deeply ingrained habit of checking his back trail at least every other minute, shouted that they had company coming. Hank Underwood dragged a rifle out of his saddle boot, but Bass grabbed the long gun's barrel and pulled it down.

"This isn't a good place for a shooting scrape," he said.

Underwood glanced at the old woman, understanding that Bass didn't want any innocent bystanders to get hurt. "Okay, Sam," he said. "Have it your way."

Bass handed the eggs back to the old woman. "Hold on to these for me, will you, ma'am? I'll be back pretty soon."

She offered him the double eagle that he had given her in payment, but Bass told her to keep it—and raked his spurs across his pony's flanks before she could voice a protest. The horse leaped into a stretched-out gallop and Bass led his companions away from the farm, the posse in hot pursuit about a hundred and fifty yards behind. The outlaws bent low in their saddles as some of the posse members began shooting. When Bass reached a line of trees, he checked his horse sharply and jumped out of the saddle. Holding rein leather in one hand, he pulled out his pistol and drew a bead on the pursuers.

"What are you doing, Sam?" asked Frank Jackson.

"Got to slow them down, Blockey," said Bass—and pulled the trigger.

Marshal Smith's horse went down, hurling its rider a good twenty feet.

Hank Underwood let out a whoop of pure joy. "I'm sick and tired of running! Time to stand and fight." Dismounting, he handed his horse over to Arkansas Johnson and brought his repeating rifle up to his shoulder, aimed, and fired.

Marshal Smith, who had just regained his footing, and who was still stunned by the fall, went down again. Levering another round into the rifle's breech, Underwood glanced at Bass.

"Hell," he said defensively, "they're going to kill us anyway. Don't you know that by now?"

Bass didn't say anything. He and Underwood fired several more times. The posse gathered up its wounded leader and withdrew to the distant farmhouse, out of rifle range. Using Frank Jackson's field glasses, Bass watched as Smith was carried into the house. A few minutes later he saw one of the posse members riding all-out in a westerly direction.

"Come on," said Bass grimly, and got back into the saddle.

They caught the posse member on the Denton road ten minutes later.

"I know you," said Bass. "Matt Martin, isn't that right?"

Martin nodded, trying very hard to keep the hands he held over his head from shaking. "You—you going to kill me, Sam?"

"Were you trying to kill us back there?" snapped Underwood. Leaning out of his saddle, he angrily backhanded Martin. "Damn your hide."

Martin's eyes flashed anger as he spit blood. "Damn yours, Underwood."

Underwood reached for his pistol, muttering an epithet, but Bass swung his pony between Hank's and that of the Denton man.

"You aiming to cut him down in cold blood, is that it?" asked Bass.

"I've done such a thing before," replied Underwood coldly.

"Yes, I know," said Bass, vividly remembering the business with the gambler Penrose. "I guess you've been sent to fetch Dad Egan," he said to Martin.

"What if I am?"

"You're going to have a long walk ahead of you. Climb down off that horse."

Martin did as he was told, and watched as Arkansas Johnson stripped bridle and saddle from his pony before hazing the animal off down the road. That done, Johnson climbed down himself and drew a Bowie knife from the top of his right boot. He cut Martin's bridle into pieces, then did the same to the saddle's cinch strap. Next he turned on Martin, still brandishing the big knife.

"You got any money on you?" he asked.

"You're gonna rob me, too?" asked Martin, outraged.

"Call it a fine," said Johnson. "That's what you get for shooting at us."

"Besides, we're outlaws," said Frank Jackson. "Robbing people is what we do."

"How bad off is George Smith?" Bass asked Martin.

"Took a bullet in the hip. He'll live, no thanks to you. Which one of you bastards shot him, anyway?"

"I'm proud to say that would be me," said Underwood defiantly, "and I'd be happy to do the same for you."

"Come on, let's get out of here," said Bass.

"You'll all be dead before winter," predicted Martin. "And Texas will be a lot better off when that happens!" he added, shouting after them as they rode away.

Later that day Bass and his friends had yet another shooting scrape. They paused in a thicket to dismount, loosen saddle cinches, and let their hard-run horses breathe. A few minutes later they heard a man shout: "Over here! We've got them now!" The outlaws spotted two men about fifty yards away. Slinging some lead in that direction, they hurriedly got back in their saddles and rode eastward. A couple of miles from the thicket, Arkansas Johnson announced that a posse was coming up fast. Bass looked back to see twenty riders, pushing their horses hard. He didn't know it, but both of Dad Egan's deputies, Riley Wetzel and Clay Withers, were with the pursuers now. Both were excellent horsemen, good shots, and brave men. Pulling ahead of the others, they didn't worry about getting separated from the rest of the posse. They only cared about one thing: catching the bandits.

When they had closed to within one hundred yards of the Bass Gang, the pair of Denton County deputy sheriffs started shooting. Bending low in their saddles, the outlaws fired back. This continued for another mile or so before the greater stamina possessed by the bandits' horses began to show itself. Gradually the lawmen's spent mounts gave ground. Reaching the rain-swollen Denton Creek, Bass and his companions urged their horses into the fast-moving stream without hesitation, and got across without a mishap. Wetzel and Withers realized that their own ponies were too exhausted to make the crossing safely, and they wisely—though reluctantly—waited there to let the rest of the posse catch up.

On the other side of the creek, Bass and his boys struck a road and turned south, soon to arrive at a store run by a man named Hardy Troope. Through the trees Bass could see a sawmill off in the distance. He told the others to wait and entered the store alone. Hardy Troope was waiting on a man Bass instantly pegged as a lumberjack. He knew such men from his days working in the mill at Rosedale, Mississippi, and his Uncle Dave's mill up in Indiana, too. Seeing the man made Bass wax nostalgic. It hadn't been that long ago since he had worked alongside such men in an honest trade—though it seemed like ages. Those had been simpler times, and happier ones, too, and Bass wondered why he hadn't been able to recognize them as such back then.

"I need coffee and ammunition," he told Troope.

"I'll be right with you, as soon as I am finished with this customer," said the storekeeper.

"You'll have to finish with him later. I'm in kind of a hurry."

The lumberjack gave him a long look. "You shouldn't be in such a big rush, young fella."

"I can't help it. My name is Sam Bass and there's a posse hot on my trail."

"Go ahead, Hardy, help him out," said the lumberjack. "I've got all day."

Bass paid for the coffee and cartridges and left an extra twenty-dollar gold piece on the counter. "This will pay for whatever the gentleman wants," he said, nodding at the lumberjack, who had wandered to the door to look out at the other three outlaws sitting their horses in front of the store. "Don't say anything about this to him until I'm gone," continued Bass. "If he won't take it, you keep it for yourself."

Hardy Troope turned the double eagle over and over in the palm of his hand. "Well, Joe may be too proud to take it, but I'm not. Think maybe I ought to put it aside as a keepsake. Folks will want to see it when they hear who gave it to me."

"If it brings you luck or profit, I'll be glad for that. As for me, they haven't given me much of a chance to spend it." Bass smiled ruefully. "I got into the train-robbing business because I thought there would be easy money in it. But it's been hard to steal, and even harder to spend."

"Hope you don't kill any decent folk with those bullets I just sold you," said the storekeeper.

"My luck has been holding out in that department," said Bass as he headed for the door.

Getting across Denton Creek at a better crossing a half mile upstream, Wetzel and Withers and their men took up the chase again. Once more that day the deputies got close enough to throw some hot lead at the outlaws, this time using their long guns. But the bandits dodged into some thick timber and disappeared unscathed.

"This has not been what I'd call a good day," was all Withers could say. He was keenly disappointed. They had come awfully close to stopping Sam Bass, but catching train robbers was not the same as pitching horseshoes. Close didn't count for much, and Clay Withers knew it.

"Oh, it's not been so bad," said Wetzel, for he had a habit of looking for the bright side to things. "We've pressed them hard. Sooner or later they'll get tired of running, and then they will turn and fight. That's when we'll finally get them."

Dusky evening shadows were stretching across the land, so the posse made camp. Somewhere along the way they had misplaced two of their number. Several hours later the stragglers showed up. Tired and overwrought, the pair mistook the posse for outlaws and started shooting. Before they realized their mistake, Riley Wetzel had been shot in the leg.

Dad Egan arrived a short while later. He ordered the two stragglers home, cursing them roundly for fools, and told Riley he needed to go back, too, so that a doctor could examine his leg. Wetzel steadfastly refused. "Tomorrow we're going to get Sam Bass and his boys and I intend to be there when we do."

"Riley, I hate to mention this, but you've got a slug in you."

Wetzel handed Egan a knife. "Only until you cut it out of me," he replied.

Egan performed camp surgery on Wetzel. A posse member supplied a bottle of whiskey. Egan took a swig to steady his hand and Wetzel drank some as a painkiller. After removing the bullet, Egan used some more of the whiskey to cauterize the wound. Then he turned to the man who had brought the who-hit-john along—and turned the bottle upside down, pouring the remainder of its contents out onto the ground.

"I've told you before, damn it," said Egan sternly. "No liquor when you're riding in one of my posses."

Early the next morning the posse was in the saddle again. Thanks to the expertise of the Yates brothers, they soon located the trail of the men they were after and followed these tracks to the place where Bass and his friends had camped the night before, which happened to be only a couple of miles from where the posse had spent the night. Jack Yates informed Egan that the bandits had ridden out no more than an hour earlier.

"Then we have a pretty good chance of ending this today," said Egan. "Let's ride."

The rain had stopped but the sky was still overcast. The wet ground made tracking the train robbers fairly easy, and in an hour's time Egan and his posse were entering a soggy pasture to spot four men gathered around a cookfire at the other side of the clearing, on the edge of a bosk of live oaks.

"There they are, boys!" cried Egan. "Let's go 'get 'em!"

Clay Withers had already unlimbered his rifle. The deputy drew a bead and fired.

The bullet caught Hank Underwood in the arm. He was sitting on a log right beside Sam Bass, drinking coffee, when the impact bowled him over backward.

"Blockey, Arkansas—hold 'em off while I see to Hank!" said Bass.

The other two longriders scrambled for their guns and began shooting at the riders who now thundered right at them across the·muddy pasture. Frank Jackson was standing alongside Arkansas Johnson when he felt a spray of hot blood on his cheek. Wiping at it, he looked at his fingers, then at Johnson—and saw that a bullet had gouged Johnson's neck, just missing the artery.

"Arkansas, you've been nicked," he announced.

"Tell me about it later, I'm busy," replied Johnson, firing at the posse as fast as he was able.

The outlaws were hitting their marks sometimes, too. The horse of the Denton stable owner, John Work, was shot out from under him, and even as horse and rider were going down, Work received a bullet in the shoulder. In short order another horse was killed and two more posse members received minor wounds. Dad Egan called off the headlong charge and led his men into the trees. He and his deputies laid down a covering fire to give the others time to carry the injured to safety.

"Why did you call us off?" Withers asked Egan. He was breathing hard, his eyes bright with excitement as he reloaded his rifle. "Damn it, Dad, we almost had them!"

Egan was serene in the face of this criticism. Ordinarily he did not tolerate subordinates questioning his orders. But he could tell that his deputy's blood was up. Withers wasn't thinking clearly. That happened all too often to men when they got into action. Egan could recall the same thing happening to him back when he had been a young turk. His luck had held out—he had survived his youthful recklessness—and he hoped Withers would live long enough to grow out of his impetuous stage, too. So he cut his deputy some slack this time and explained his actions.

"Sure, we could have gotten to them," he told Withers. "But several of our men would be lying dead out there in that pasture."

"They signed on for this job. They knew the risks."

"Maybe. But I'm responsible for their lives. Yours, too, even though you knew the risks when you pinned on that tin star."

"I'll die if I have to, to stop men like Sam Bass."

"That's mighty noble. But you don't have to die, not today, not here. We will get them, don't worry about that."

Clay Withers wasn't convinced, but he didn't say anything more.

Egan left Riley Wetzel to look after the wounded— Wetzel himself was bleeding again from the wound he had received the day before. Then the Denton County sheriff took Withers and the Yates brothers and two others through the timber, cautiously closing in on the outlaw camp.

When they got there the gang was gone. Jack Yates studied the blood on the ground and announced that two of the outlaws had been hit, one more seriously than the other. Leaving his wounded behind, Egan and the rest of the posse went after them. There had been one dead horse in the outlaw camp, too; that meant two of the bandits had to be riding double. Egan hoped this might slow the fugitives down a bit.

A few miles farther on, they reached another farmhouse and learned from a youth who was visiting there that four men on three horses had passed that way less than half an hour earlier.

"They took my horse," said the youth.

"Then why the hell are you standing there grinning like a jackanape, boy?" asked Egan, perplexed.

"Well, one of them said he was just going to borrow my

horse and he'd see to it that I'd get it back. But then another one of them laughed and said, 'You ought not make promises you might not live long enough to keep, Hank.' And then that one, he paid me for my horse."

"How much did he pay you?"

"Oh, about twice what it was worth." And the young man's grin broadened.

Egan noticed the lad's pockets were bulging. "What did he pay you with?"

"Gold double eagles, that's what. And I don't care if they are stolen or not, Sheriff."

"Don't worry, I don't aim to take them from you. Was one of those men shot up?"

"Two of 'em were. But don't let that fool you. They've got plenty of fight left in them. One of the wounded ones was the man who took my horse, the one called Hank. The other one had a scarred face."

Egan and his posse pressed on. "So Henry Underwood and Arkansas Johnson are hit," he told Withers.

"Yeah, and Bass is still spending that Wells Fargo gold like there's no tomorrow." Realizing the irony of what he had said, Withers added, "And I hope in his case there won't be."

Egan tracked the outlaws along the McKinney Road until, about six miles from Denton, the gang's trail veered off into the thickets of the Elm Fork. A little while later the trail was lost. Try as they might, the Yates brothers could not rediscover it. They could not explain their failure, either. It was, they told Egan, as though Bass and his boys had just vanished into the mist rising up out of the soggy bottoms as the cool shadows of night stretched across the sun-hammered north Texas prairie.

CHAPTER SIXTEEN

❧

"I'M CURIOUS," SAID JED BANKS, LOOKING OVER THE NOTES he had taken, "just how you felt about Sheriff Egan."

"I don't know what you mean," said Bass.

The Galveston newspaperman could tell that the wounded outlaw was being evasive, that Bass didn't want to discuss his personal feelings. But Banks persisted. The relationship between the older lawman and the younger lawbreaker fascinated him.

"I just mean that you lost your father when you were pretty young," said Banks, "and I'm just wondering if maybe Dad Egan wasn't a father figure for you."

"I don't know anything about that kind of stuff," insisted Bass.

"Well, let me ask you this, then. If it had come down to it, would you have shot Egan? Let's say in self-defense—would you have thrown down on him?"

Bass thought it over. "I don't know. I'm just glad it never came to that. Though we threw some lead at him, same as the rest of that posse. Could have been him that got hit instead of some of the others."

"Yes, but you never shot at a posse led by Dad Egan, did you?"

Bass managed a smile. "There were so many posses after us I couldn't keep track of them all."

"And I wonder, too, if it was true what some people said about Egan—that he was less than enthusiastic about catching you because he thought highly of you."

Bass shook his head. "He tried his best to catch us. And his deputies, Clay Withers and Riley Wetzel, they were hell on wheels. Dad Egan did his job, and anybody who says otherwise doesn't know beans."

Jed Banks set the issue aside, though he wasn't fully convinced. The relationship between Egan and Bass might be, he thought, one of those mysteries that never got solved. He had some tantalizing clues, but no answer....

Sam Bass and his three companions emerged from the thickets along the Elm Fork two days later near the town of Bolivar, appearing at a general store on the Denton Road early one morning just as the proprietor was opening up for business. Bass told the man he wanted to buy some supplies, but the store owner recognized him and refused. "I don't trade with outlaws," he declared.

Bass sighed. "Mister, I'm damn tired and on a short fuse." He laid a hand on the pistol at his side. "I'm going to ride away from here with what I want. Now, I can either pay for the supplies or take them. It's up to you. You name the tune and we'll dance."

The storekeeper's ill-advised defiance wilted. "Okay. What is it that you want?"

"A sack of coffee, another of flour, and as much ammunition as you've got handy."

"I've got about a thousand rounds, would be my guess."

"We'll take all of it."

"All? Are you going to start a war or something?" asked the storekeeper, nervously trying to make a joke.

"We're already in the middle of one," said Underwood. "I seen some horses in a pasture out yonder. Who do they belong to?"

"Those are my horses."

"We need fresh mounts, Sam," Underwood told Bass.

Bass nodded. "And we'll be trading horses with you, too," he informed the storekeeper.

"Your horses are used up," protested the man. "That isn't a fair trade. You might as well be robbing me."

"We could do that, too," said Underwood, with a cold smile that made the storekeeper extremely uncomfortable.

"No, you're the one trying to rob us now," said Bass. "You will make a lot of money off our horses because we rode them."

"You know," remarked Frank Jackson, "it seems like everybody stands to make a nice profit off our careers as outlaws—everybody but us!"

"So what's it going to be?" Bass asked the storekeeper.

"Take the horses. I can't stop you."

"Thanks. Oh, and one more thing. When the posse shows up, ask them for me to ease off. We haven't had much rest for three days and nights."

The storekeeper stared at Bass in disbelief. "Wait just a minute. Let me get this straight. You want me to ask the posse to stop chasing you so that you can get some sleep?"

"He's just pulling your leg," said Frank Jackson. "We don't really need sleep."

"Besides, we'll be sleeping for all eternity before too much longer," said the dour Arkansas Johnson.

Bass grinned at the scar-faced hardcase—who now had a blood-soaked dressing around his neck. "You sure are a cheerful cuss, Arkansas. Did you know that?"

"Imagine being locked up in a cell with him for months," said Underwood. "I'm telling you, I thought about hanging myself on more than one occasion!"

Bass and Jackson laughed, and even Johnson smiled, albeit grudgingly. The storekeeper just shook his head in wonder. "I don't get it," he said. "You boys are likely going to die any day now. How can you be joking around like this, knowing that?"

"Why worry about it?" asked Bass.

Leaving the Bolivar store on fresh horses, the gang stuck to the road for a spell. An hour later they saw a solitary rider approaching them. When he saw them, the man waved and urged his horse forward.

"Howdy," he said affably. "I'm Zeke Dawson. Are you boys part of the posse?"

Underwood glanced at Bass, then asked, "Which posse do you mean?"

"Why, Sheriff Egan's posse, out of Denton. The one chasing Sam Bass and his gang of cutthroats."

"Cutthroats? Why, I have never cut a throat in my whole life. Have you, Sam?"

"Nope. Can't say that I have."

Underwood leaned forward in the saddle to look past Bass and Jackson at Arkansas Johnson. "What about you, Arkansas? Ever cut any throats?"

"Haven't had the pleasure—yet," said Johnson, and grinned at Dawson. Bass figured it was probably due to lack of practice, but Johnson's grin wasn't a very good one. It looked more like a wolf's snarl.

Dawson was perplexed. "No, you boys misunderstood me. I said the Bass Gang were cutthroats."

"I know what you said," replied Underwood. "You must be new to Denton County. I don't think I know you."

"Just been here a couple of weeks. Brought my family down from Tennessee to make a fresh start."

"Gallivanting around the countryside looking for cutthroats is not a good way to make a fresh start," opined Underwood. "Especially when you're twice as dumb as a fence post."

"I beg your pardon?" Dawson scowled, offended.

"Well," drawled Bass, "it's like this. I'm Sam Bass. And these boys are ... well, they're the cutthroats you mentioned."

All the color drained out of Dawson's face. "Oh, my God," he croaked.

"Get down off that horse," snapped Arkansas Johnson.

Dawson realized that Johnson was pointing a gun at him. He hadn't even seen the outlaw draw his shooting iron. The gun barrel aimed his way looked bigger than a twelve-pounder cannon.

"I—I don't have any money on me, boys. But you—

you can take my horse. Just please, for God's sakes, don't kill me!"

"You know," said Underwood, "it riles me something fierce that you would be out here hunting us. I mean, we haven't done a damned thing to you, have we? So what business is this of yours, anyway?"

"It's—it's none of my business, you're absolutely right. Tell you what, I—I'll just turn around and go home."

"Not so fast," snapped Underwood. "Way I see it, had you been with the posse and tracked us down, you'd have done your utmost to shoot us, wouldn't you? Since you don't know us, and have no good reason to dislike us, that amounts to cold-blooded murder. Boys, I think we should put Mr. Dawson here on trial for murder."

"One small point," said Frank Jackson. "He hasn't killed any of us yet."

"Okay, attempted murder, then."

"Oh, Jesus," breathed Dawson, breaking out in a cold sweat.

"I recollect telling you to get down off that horse," said Arkansas Johnson. "I don't cotton to repeating myself."

Dawson dismounted, shaking like a man with the ague. He cringed as Underwood urged his horse forward, bent down, and plucked the pistol from Dawson's holster.

"Why, this hogleg looks brand-new," said Underwood. "Have you ever fired this gun?"

"N-no, sir. I'm not much of a shot."

"I am." Underwood performed a deft border roll with the pistol, then slid it under his belt. "That's a handsome saddle you've got there. Must have cost you a pretty penny."

"Take it. Please, take everything. Just—just let me go."

"Oh, I aim to take it. Though I might leave that brand-new rope with you." Underwood reached over and took the coiled rope from the saddle and shook it out. "Know how to make a hangman's knot?" he asked Dawson.

Dawson shook his head, no longer trusting himself to speak without babbling incoherently.

"Well, I do," said Underwood. As he made a noose, he asked his companions, "So what do you think, boys? Is Mr. Dawson guilty of attempted murder or not?"

"He sure acts like he's guilty of something," said Frank Jackson.

"Hang him and be done with it," growled Arkansas Johnson. "Might make others think twice before they ride against us."

Underwood dropped the noose over Dawson's head. Dawson's knees nearly buckled.

Glancing at a growing stain in the crotch of Dawson's trousers, Frank Jackson said, "I believe you've scared him enough, Hank. He just pissed all over himself."

"Yeah, that's enough," said Bass. "Get that rope off him, Hank."

Underwood shrugged—and removed the noose.

"I thought we really were going to hang him," said Arkansas Johnson with a disappointed frown.

"I know you did," said Bass. "Mr. Dawson, you better get going." He threw a thumb over his shoulder. "Better go that way. You'll find Dad Egan and his posse back there."

The outlaws rode away, leading Dawson's horse and leaving the frightened and humiliated man eating their dust.

The gang stopped at noon near Pond Creek to cook up some biscuits and coffee, but just when the biscuits were nearly done, Sheriff Bill Everheart and ten men broke out of some trees and galloped toward the camp, shooting up a storm. Bass and his friends leaped for their horses and made a run for it. The posse chased them for a while, firing constantly. The outlaws vanished into the swampy thickets along Clear Creek and finally shook off the pursuit.

"You know," said Frank Jackson, "I'm thinking about giving myself up just to get a decent meal. I mean, they'd have to feed me in jail, right?" When Bass gave him a disapproving look, Jackson smiled. "Relax, Sam. I'm just kidding around. But those biscuits sure were looking tasty."

That afternoon they met an old farmer driving a rickety spring wagon down the road. The plowpusher informed them that Captain June Peak and his Rangers had just passed him an hour earlier, heading in the direction of Bolivar. Peak had told him that Wise County's sheriff, G. W. Stevens, also had a posse out on the bandits' trail. That made four groups of men looking for the Bass Gang—Peak's Rangers and the posses led by Stevens, Bill Everheart, and Dad Egan. And it didn't look like they were going to quit looking anytime soon, either.

Dad Egan's deputy, Clay Withers, joined up with the Stevens posse, who later met June Peak and his Rangers. This large group of manhunters paused at Salt Creek to water their tired horses and talk things over. It was decided that they would split up into two groups and thoroughly scour the eastern part of the county. June Peak and his Rangers would go one way, the Stevens group would go the other. They had just parted company when Peak heard shooting from down the creek, in the direction the other group had taken. The gunfire was fast and furious. Peak led his men along the creek at a gallop. In less than two minutes the shooting spree had ended; by the time Peak arrived on the scene, the gunfight was over. Clay Withers and Sheriff Stevens stood over the body of a man sprawled face down in the mud at the water's edge. The rest of the posse was searching cautiously through the thick brush nearby.

"We rode right up on them," Withers told Peak. "It was Sam Bass and three other men. This one didn't get away."

"Is it Bass?" asked Peak.

Withers shook his head, slid the toe of his boot under the dead man's shoulder, and flipped the corpse over. Peak could see that the outlaw had been shot squarely in the chest.

"I believe this to be the one they called Arkansas Johnson," said Withers.

Peak nodded. "Fits the description. Who shot him?"

"I have no idea. They were sitting here beside the creek when we came up. Caught them by surprise. Everybody started shooting at once. One of the outlaws made it to the horses, tethered over yonder. Johnson here was hit right away. The other two ducked into the brush on foot. We captured their mounts. I'd say with any luck at all we'll at least catch the pair who ran off in that direction."

Peak ordered his Rangers to assist in the search. Dismounting, he searched the body of Arkansas Johnson. He found thirty-five cents in the dead man's possession, and held the coins in the palm of his hand for Withers to see.

"Not much to show for a life of robbing trains and stagecoaches."

"Then who is going to pay for his burial?" wondered Stevens.

"I believe we're in your county, G.W.," said Withers.

Stevens was chewing tobacco—now he spat a stream of brown juice that splattered on the ground right beside Johnson's corpse.

"Then if it's up to me, I say we bury him right there and call it a job well done."

Peak took Johnson's Bowie knife and Colt pistol and handed the weapons to Clay Withers.

"Don't you want one of these for a souvenir?" asked Withers.

"No," replied Peak. "All I want is for this to be over with so we call all go home."

As they were digging Johnson's grave, the sky opened up and a heavy rain began to fall. Peak noticed how the rain washed the mud from the dead outlaw's pockmarked face. But that didn't count for much, because the hole they were making quickly filled with water—the ground was pretty well saturated from all the rain they had been getting of late. Before long they had given up trying to deepen the grave, and rolled the corpse into it and covered the body with muck.

"Ashes to ashes," said Peak.

Withers said amen to that.

"I wouldn't mind digging two more graves today," said Stevens. "Let's see if we can't find those two that ran off."

They tried, but the weather worsened, and after hours of

fruitless searching they gave up. The two outlaws had slipped through their fingers. Wet and tired and disappointed, the Stevens posse mounted up and turned for home. Clay Withers chose to stay with Peak's Rangers and continue the hunt for the elusive Sam Bass. Catching Bass had become a personal crusade for him.

CHAPTER SEVENTEEN

WHEN MAJOR JOHN B. JONES OF THE TEXAS RANGERS visited the Tyler jail to see Jim Murphy, who had been incarcerated there for the better part of a month, it was no social call. The major was not a sociable fellow to begin with, and he was particularly averse to hobnobbing with lawbreakers. But he had heard an intriguing story, and curiosity had gotten the best of him. Curiosity—and desperation. If what he had heard was true, then there was a fair chance of finally bringing Sam Bass to heel, and that was, after all, the job the governor of Texas had sent him to do. Major Jones would leave no stone unturned, no option unexplored, in pursuit of the successful completion of that task.

Once he had been allowed into the cellblock, Jones asked the jailer, a deputy town marshal, to leave him alone with the prisoner. The Texas Ranger knew how loose-lipped some people could be, and he didn't think what he and Murphy were about to discuss needed to be made public knowledge.

Murphy was a stocky, red-haired man, and he sat slump-shouldered on a cot in the iron cage that had been his home for weeks that seemed more like years. He took one look at Jones and then resumed his disconsolate examination of the cell's scuffed timbered floor. Jones had lawman written all over him and if Murphy had learned one thing in the past few weeks, it was that lawmen were not bearers of good news.

After introducing himself, Jones said, "I'm told that on your way here you told a United States deputy marshal that you had a deal for him. Is that true?"

Murphy looked up at Jones again, curious now. "Could be."

"What was that deal?"

"Why are you asking me? Didn't the deputy marshal tell you?"

"Nope. He told somebody, and that somebody told somebody else, and it worked its way on down the line." Jones didn't bother explaining that the deputy marshal had told U.S. Marshal Lane, who had told a federal district attorney, who had told the Texas Ranger. "That being the case, I want to hear it from the horse's mouth."

Murphy took a cautious look around. The adjacent cell and the one directly opposite were empty. The closest fellow prisoner was two doors down, and sound asleep. Murphy stood up and stepped closer to the strap-iron cell door beyond which stood Jones. He took the added precaution of pitching his voice low.

"I told him I ought to join the Bass Gang and then sell them out."

"I thought you and Sam Bass were good friends, going back a long way."

"We were. We are. I've known Sam ever since he come to Texas." Murphy smiled, remembering. "We used to get drunk together and talk about what big honchos we would be someday."

"Well, you might still be. But not Bass. He chose the wrong road. It's too late for him. Might not be for you, though."

"I don't know that I follow what you're trying to say, Major."

"We'll get to that in a minute. But first I want to know why you would be willing to betray such a good friend as Bass."

"Because I don't want to spend another hour in here. I can't stand being cooped up in here."

"I see. Your father, Henderson Murphy, is an important man in these parts, I understand."

Murphy grimaced. "He won't even come see me. I sent word to him, asked him if he could help me. Maybe get me a good lawyer. He didn't even bother with a reply. I hear he's told others that he isn't surprised I ended up like this. That he always knew I would. Well, I'm not going to end up this way. He'll have to eat crow, my father will."

Jones could almost feel the heat from the rage that simmered right below Jim Murphy's surface. The man had something to prove to his father, and he wanted to prove it so badly that he was willing to play the turncoat and bring down his own friend.

"So are you interested in my offer?" asked Murphy. "You boys must be desperate. I'm told Sam has led everybody a merry chase for some time now."

"He's been lucky. And he's audacious. That's kept him alive this long. But it won't last him for much longer."

"I thought the Rangers always got their man, and no exceptions."

"Oh, we will get him. It's just a matter of time. And I'll do whatever I have to. Even make a deal with the likes of you."

Murphy bristled at the Ranger's contempt, but he didn't let his anger get the better of him.

"How come you boys want Sam so bad, anyway? There are hundreds of desperadoes in Texas. A lot of them are killers. That's one thing Sam will never be. All he's done is rob a few trains. A lot of folks don't see much harm in that."

Jones nodded. "Exactly. And that is what makes Sam Bass so dangerous. He's become a folk hero of sorts to some."

"I'll tell you what it is. People think the railroads and the Reconstruction government up in Austin are in bed together. That they're both just getting rich off Texas sweat.

The governor has staked his career on stopping Sam. You know, Major, I think you could be wrong. You say Sam will never be a big honcho. But it seems to me that that's exactly what he's become already."

"So let's say I accept your offer," said Jones. "How do I know that I can trust you, Murphy? You'll betray your friend Bass. What's to stop you from betraying me, too?"

"I guess you'll just have to take my word for it."

"I don't have to do anything of the sort. I could turn and walk right out of here and let you rot in that cell. In fact, I'm inclined to do just that."

"No, wait," said Murphy, all trace of bluster gone. "I swear, I'll do whatever you need me to do. You have my word on that. Just—just get me out of this place. For God's sake, help me and I'll help you."

Major Jones gazed thoughtfully at Murphy for a long minute—a minute so long from the prisoner's point of view that it made him wonder if time was standing still. Try as he might, Murphy couldn't discern a thing from the Ranger's angular, weathered face. He considered giving voice to further assurances in an effort to persuade Jones. He even considered begging. But he decided against it, not because he was too proud to beg—under those circumstances he would have readily humiliated himself completely to secure release—but rather because his instincts told him that more entreaties might actually work against him. Major Jones wasn't trying to break him. The Ranger just needed to be convinced that Jim Murphy was a man who could be counted on. And a man who had enough backbone to lie to the outlaw leader even if it might cost him his life.

Then Jones gave a curt nod. "Okay. I'll see what I can do to get you free."

"Thank you," gushed Murphy. "You won't regret it. You'll see."

"Yeah, well, you'll regret it plenty if you cross me. You do right by me, and I'll help you in any way that I can. But if you let me down, you'll rue the day you were born."

Jones went immediately to the United States district attorney and persuaded him to order Murphy released on bond. The district attorney arranged for a waiver of the bond payment and put in writing his promise to protect Murphy from any prosecution, state or federal, for past misdeeds—if Murphy proved of use in the capture of Sam Bass. The Texas Ranger took this amnesty paper back to the Tyler jail so that Murphy could see it. But when Murphy reached through the strap iron bars to take the document, Jones pulled it back out of his reach.

"I'll be holding on to this," said the major. "You can have it when you've done your job."

"Whatever you say. So how do we do this?"

"Right now there are only four people who know about our deal. You, me, the district attorney, and June Peak. If you want to stay alive, we had better keep it that way. I don't know whether Sam Bass would shoot you if he knew you were a turncoat, but he might or one of the men riding with him might do it."

Murphy doubted that Bass would kill him if the truth came out. Sam just wasn't a killer, pure and simple. But he didn't tell Jones this because he didn't want to appear as though he were defending Bass. He didn't want to say or do anything that might give Jones the impression that he could not be relied on to betray Bass when the time came to do so.

"This is what you'll do," continued Jones. "First, you go home. Wait for Bass to seek you out. Whatever you do, don't go looking for him."

"Why not?"

"Because he's a smart devil, that one. You go volunteering to join up with him right after you get out of jail and he'll likely know that something is up. No, that dog just won't hunt. Sooner or later he'll hear you're a free man, and he'll show up at your door. He's on the run and hard-pressed, and he's in need of all the help he can get from old friends."

"Okay, and after he's found me, then what?"

"Ride with him if he asks you to."

Murphy fretted at the prospect. "On any given day there are probably a hundred men out there searching for Sam and his gang. Most of them are trigger-happy amateurs. I ride with Sam and I'm likely to get shot to pieces for my trouble. I won't be much good to you dead."

Jones shrugged his indifference to Murphy's fate. "Outlawing is a risky business. So is catching outlaws. Now, if you don't have the stomach for this work just say so, and I'll tear up this here amnesty paper and be on my way."

"No, no," said Murphy hastily. "I'll do whatever I have to. So let's say I start riding with him. What then?"

"You find some way to get word to me or June Peak where his hideout is, or when and where he's going to pull his next job. It's as simple as that."

"I don't see all this as being too simple, but I'll do it. I won't let you down, Major. We'll catch him. Sam's days are numbered."

"They have been from the time he pulled his first robbery," replied the Texas Ranger.

WHEN JIM MURPHY got back to Denton County, he let it be known that the authorities had released him because they lacked evidence to bring him to trial. But the word got out that he had jumped bond, and several prominent newspapers excoriated the Texas Rangers, local law officers, and the United States district attorney for letting Murphy get away with flaunting the law. The newspapers had been giving the lawmen of Texas a hard time for some weeks now due to their failure to capture the elusive Sam Bass. The Rangers were their favorite target, and the criticism had become so intense that the governor himself had sworn that if Bass wasn't caught by the year's end, he would not run for reelection. Murphy was fearful that the critics would sting the likes of Major Jones and June Peak—who had just been promoted to captain—so badly that the Rangers would feel obliged to apprehend him and haul him right back to that Tyler jail cell.

It wasn't until later that Murphy learned, much to his surprise, that the rumor about his bond-jumping had been circulated by Major Jones himself, a clever ploy to garner prominent mention of Jim Murphy's name and current whereabouts in the newspapers. Jones hoped that in this way he could bring to the attention of one Sam Bass the fact that his friend was a free man.

Ten days after his return home, Murphy was sitting on his porch chatting with a neighbor when he looked up to see three horsemen passing down the road in front of his house. It was Bass, accompanied by Frank Jackson and Seaborn Barnes. Murphy nearly stood up and waved—but Bass glanced at him and then looked away as though he had no idea who Murphy was and could not have cared less. Murphy took his cue and made no show of recognizing the riders. The neighbor gave the dusty trio a hard look, though.

"I ain't never seen Sam Bass in the flesh," he said, "but danged if that feller yonder don't fit the description right down to the ground. Jim, you know Bass. Is that him?"

"Who, that man there? Nope, that isn't Sam," said Murphy with absolute conviction. He promptly changed the subject.

After his neighbor had said so long, Murphy saddled up a horse and rode back into the thickets behind his place, heading for a spot near a branch that he knew Bass had used for a campsite in times past. Sure enough, Bass and his two saddle partners were there.

Grinning from ear to ear, Bass greeted Murphy like long-lost kin. "Well, you old jailbird. Heard they put you up in the crossbar hotel for a spell. How did you take to the life of a prisoner?"

"I didn't like it at all. I sure as hell wouldn't recommend it to you, Sam."

Bass shook his head. "No, sir. That's not for me. I'm too accustomed to running wild and free. I know I couldn't tolerate one single day in an iron cage. So I reckon I'll put up a fight when they finally corner me and make sure they don't bring me in while I'm still breathing."

"Sam, why are you still in these parts, anyway? Seems to me you're just asking to get caught."

"I don't want to leave. I've got friends around here. Like you, Jim. Makes life on the outlaw trail right tolerable, sometimes."

"No offense, but knowing you has made life tough for me of late," said Murphy. "Lot of folks won't have anything to do with me anymore. Figure I must be as crooked as a dog's hind leg, and not one to do business with, as a result."

"I'm sorry to hear that, Jim, I really am," replied Bass earnestly. "I led Frank here astray, and now I've muddied up your water. Never meant for that to happen."

"I don't put you at fault. I gave you horses of my own free will. You didn't put a gun to my head."

"He didn't put one to mine, either," said Frank Jackson. "He did one better—showed me saddlebags so full of gold they were about ready to bust at the seams, and told me it was all mine if I wanted it, and that there was a lot more where it came from." Jackson grinned at Bass. "Ol' Satan tempting Eve with that apple can't hold a candle to Honest Eph here."

"Where's Hank Underwood?" asked Murphy.

"He called it quits after that posse jumped us at Salt Creek and killed Arkansas Johnson. He said he knew when the game was up. I think he headed up into the Indian Nations, and I don't reckon we will see him around here again."

"So it's just the three of you now."

"I think the best thing for you, Jim, is to ride with us," said Bass. "We'll make some real money on our next job, and then ride down into Mexico and lay low for a spell. What do you say?"

"Yeah, he keeps telling me I'm going to make so much money I'll be able to buy a hacienda south of the border and live like a king," Jackson said with a laugh.

"Shut your trap, Blockey," said Bass good-naturedly. "I'm trying to corrupt Jim and you're not making it any easier."

"You have another train picked out?" asked Murphy.

"No more trains for me. Figure we'll try a bank on for size."

"What bank?"

"Does it matter?" asked Seab Barnes. "And, if so, why?"

"Well, I'd like to take my money out if it happens to be a bank I do business with."

Bass chuckled. "Come with us, Jim, and you can withdraw your funds and everybody else's, too."

Murphy decided it wasn't safe to push for the identity of the bank. He pretended to give Sam's offer serious consideration.

"Okay, I'll ride with you, Sam," he said. "Give me a couple of days to attend to a few matters."

Bass nodded. "Sounds fair. We'll make camp a mile or so up this creek and wait on you."

Murphy returned to his place. The next morning his breakfast was rudely interrupted by the arrival of Sheriff Bill Everhcart from Grayson County.

"I have heard the strangest story," said the tall, cold-eyed lawman.

"I did not jump bail," replied Murphy. "They let me go for lack of evidence."

"Not the story I mean. I have been told that you're a spy for the Texas Rangers."

"Where the hell did you hear a thing like that?"

"June Peak told me."

Murphy felt like cursing. Captain Peak had let him down, and that surprised him. The more people who knew about his bargain with Major Jones, the more danger he was in. Maybe not from Sam Bass—though he had seen something new in his friend, a hardness, born no doubt of desperate times, that had not been there before. But if Bass didn't kill him for playing the role of Judas, Seab Barnes

most surely would. Nubbins Colt did not think twice about
using his guns.

"Well," drawled Everheart, "I can see by the look on
your face that the story is true. I have a hunch that Bass is
somewhere close by, and I figure you know right where I
can find him. I want you to tell me."

"I only deal with Major Jones or Captain Peak. That was
part of the deal."

"I see." Everheart sat down at the table. He pulled Murphy's plate closer and began eating the breakfast. Between
bites he glanced at Murphy and said, quietly, "You really
do want to reconsider that, Jim. The Rangers aren't going
to be the ones who get Bass, and neither are the Pinkertons,
and neither is Dad Egan. You see, I'm going to be the one.
And you're going to help me."

Murphy didn't ask what Everheart intended to do to him
if he didn't cooperate. He didn't want to know. So he caved
in and admitted that he thought he knew where Sam Bass
could be found. Everheart grinned triumphantly. He stood
up and gave Murphy a hard slap on the back—a little harder than Murphy thought was necessary to demonstrate ca-
maraderie.

"You made the right decision, partner. I'll be back in
the morning bright and early—with a posse of good men—
and we'll formally and forever close the book on the career
of the notorious Sam Bass."

Murphy spent a sleepless night. He was nervous and
jumped at the slightest sound. His fear was that somehow
the outlaws would find out that he was preparing to betray
them—and he half expected to see Seab Barnes step out of
the night shadow, quiet as an Indian, knife or pistol in hand.
He dozed off once or twice and had a dream in which he
and Sam Bass stood, back to back, saddling their horses,
and suddenly Bass said, in a soft and subdued voice, "Jim,
whatever happens, I won't hold it against you." And in his
dream Murphy felt his knees go weak as he realized that
Bass knew the truth and was forgiving him his treachery
even before it happened, as Jesus had forgiven Judas Is-

cariot. He stammered at a weak denial but was cut short when Bass turned to give him a steady, slightly critical look. "Don't say anything, Jim. You might make me mad."

And at that point Murphy woke up in a cold sweat.

The next morning Murphy was saddled up and ready to ride at the crack of dawn, expecting Everheart and his posse to show up early, as promised. But hour after hour crept by—and no Everheart. By noon Murphy had made up his mind that the Grayson County sheriff wasn't coming. Something had happened. Murphy was relieved—and worried, too. Maybe Sam and his saddle partners had been caught or killed. If that had happened, what effect, he wondered, would it have on his amnesty, since he would have played no part in the business? Suddenly Murphy could sit idle no longer. He mounted up and rode to the creek, then followed it north, in search of Sam's camp. A gunshot, close at hand, nearly made him soil his trousers. Then another shot shattered the hot, almost breathless stillness of the woods. Dismounting, Murphy swallowed the big lump of fear in his throat and proceeded on foot, leading his horse. There was a third shot, then a fourth, well spaced out. That puzzled Murphy—it didn't sound like any gunfight he had ever heard.

When he entered the clearing where the outlaws were camped, he saw that Sam Bass and Seab Barnes were engaged in some target shooting, knocking the branches off saplings with bullets fired from their pistols. Frank Jackson was stretched out on his blankets; hands behind his head, he gazed placidly up at the blue sky.

"You boys must be crazy," said Murphy, shaking his head in amazement. "This country is crawling with posses, and here you are firing off your smoke-makers like it's the Fourth of July and you don't have a care in the world."

Bass was wearing his usual infectious grin. "Don't fret, Jim. We're just getting a little practice in. There's likely to be a lot of gunplay in our next job, so it pays to stay sharp."

"You haven't told me a damn thing about the next job, Sam," complained Murphy. "Don't you reckon I have the right to know, seeing as how I'll be riding with you and sticking my neck out?"

"I'll tell you on the road. We're ready to get moving if you are. But first we've got to get us some fast horses and some more ammunition."

"Well, how far are we going to ride?" asked Murphy, hoping to get at least a clue as to the location of the robbery Bass was contemplating.

"Oh, it's a good ways from here," replied Bass. "It would be suicide to try a bank in these parts right now."

"We might be crazy," remarked Jackson laconically, "but we aren't fools."

Murphy didn't know about that. As he rode out of the clearing with Bass and Jackson and Barnes, he felt like the biggest fool in Texas for putting himself in the situation that he was in.

CHAPTER EIGHTEEN

━━◆━━

AFTER STEALING SOME HORSES, SAM BASS AND HIS FRIENDS left Denton County and headed south for Dallas. They stopped in a small town ten miles from the city to have one of the horses shod. As they lounged around in the dusty sunshine in front of the blacksmith shop, a barefoot boy in overalls came up to them carrying a sack of peaches.

"I don't guess you men want to buy some peaches," he said.

Bass studied the farm boy's long face. "Now, why do you say that, kid? We might want some peaches, and then again, we might not."

"On account of I ain't sold a single peach all day. I don't want to be in farming like my pa is. There just ain't no money in it."

"What do you want to be in, then?"

The boy's eyes lit up. "To tell the truth, I have a notion to find Sam Bass and ride with him and go to robbing stagecoaches and express trains and the like. Now, that's the way to make some easy money!"

Hearing this, Frank Jackson had to laugh. "Oh, yes," he said, much amused, "that's easy money, sure enough."

Bass reflected on life on the outlaw trail—the harrowing brushes with the law, the cold camps short of food, the long hours in the saddle, living with the constant fear that around the next bend was the bullet that would end his career. Most of all he thought about Hannah Howard, of a happiness that he would never know. He reached out and took the sack of peaches from the boy.

"I'll buy them all," he said.

"All of them?" asked the boy, astonished and sure that he hadn't heard right.

"Yep." Bass handed him twenty dollars in paper money. "Will that cover it?"

The boy's eyes looked like they were about to pop right out of their sockets. "Twenty dollars!" he gasped. "Mister, I can't take this. Those peaches ain't worth anywhere close to twenty dollars."

"They're worth that much to me. Take my advice, kid, and stick to farming. There's enough money in it to get by, if you're willing to work hard. And it beats being a desperado by a country mile. An outlaw might luck into a big haul, but he can't spend any of the loot the way he wants to because John Law is hounding him like he's a stock-killing lobo. And there's not much glory lying dead in your own blood or rotting away in an iron cage."

The boy peered curiously at Bass. "Are you an outlaw, mister?" he asked.

Bass grinned. "Nope. But I know what I'm talking about. We're Texas Rangers, you see, and we're hunting this feller, Sam Bass. We'll catch him, too."

"My pa says he's all for Bass because Bass is making war on the railroads."

"Bass is just looking out for himself. The only reason he took to robbing trains was that they carried more loot than the stagecoaches he started with."

The boy looked at the paper money clenched in his fist. "My pa wouldn't want me to have this if he knew it came from Texas Rangers on the prowl for Sam Bass."

"Well, just don't tell him who you got it from."

"I know," said Jackson. "Tell him Sam Bass bought the peaches from you. That ought to make him right proud."

The boy laughed. "That's a good one! I might just do that."

The outlaws rode on. That afternoon Bass told the others to continue down the road—he intended to branch off here and would meet up with them a few miles farther on.

"Where is he going?" Murphy asked Jackson after Bass had left them.

Jackson shrugged. "The Henry Collins place, would be my guess. That's right near here. Henry is Joel's older brother, and Sam and Joel were good friends, you know."

True to his word, Bass rejoined them a short while later. Henry Collins was riding with him. As they drew near, Collins gave Jim Murphy a hard and unfriendly look and then spoke to Bass loudly enough for Murphy to hear.

"Sam, you ought to kill the son of a bitch right here and now."

Murphy's blood ran cold in his veins. "Frank," he whispered to Jackson, "did you hear that? What the hell is going on?"

"Don't rightly know. Just keep your nerve and we'll find out."

Bass was looking as grim as Murphy had ever seen him. "What's the matter, Sam?" he asked. "Who's going to get killed, anyway?"

"I think maybe you," replied Bass.

"What are you talking about?" asked Jackson.

"The word is that one of the Murphys has made a deal with the Rangers to give you boys up," announced Henry Collins.

"Where did you hear such nonsense?" asked Murphy. Beads of cold sweat broke out on his brow.

"A cousin of mine is a telegraph operator," said Collins. "He sent a wire to Dallas from the Grayson County sheriff in which the sheriff said a man named Murphy was going to lead Sam Bass in to a trap, and that you boys were headed down this way."

"That would be Bill Everheart," said Jackson.

"Well, it's a damned dirty lie," protested Murphy.

"Why would Everheart make up a story like that?" asked Seaborn Barnes. "I tell you, Sam, I never did trust this feller."

"I know you didn't, Seab."

"I think Henry is right—we need to kill him right now."

Murphy looked at Bass—and saw how close to death he was at that moment.

"Okay," he said. "I did make a deal with a Ranger major named Jones. But I had no intention of keeping up my end of the bargain. I agreed to it just to get out of jail. Sam, you got me into that trouble, coming to me in the first place and using our friendship to get me to help you with horses. Well, they were going to keep me locked up until hell froze over, and I would have made a deal with the devil himself to gain my freedom."

"But you wasn't ever thinking of going through with it," said Bass.

"No, Sam, I wasn't. I swear to you."

"That sounds awful thin to me," said Barnes.

"Not to me," said Jackson. "In Jim's shoes I might have done the same."

Bass mulled it over. Then he shook his head. "Sorry, Jim. Things have gone too desperate to be taking any chances. I think you will have to die."

"The hell you say," snapped Jackson. "I have never bucked you before, Sam, you know that. But this time I have to because you're all the way wrong. Jim is an old friend of yours, and mine. Are you forgetting that? No matter how desperate the times, it ain't no excuse to turn on your friends. Jim has not done a damned thing against us and he don't deserve to be found guilty based just on hearsay."

"Well, he ain't never been no friend of mine," said Seab Barnes, drawing his pistol. "So I guess that leaves me free to do the job."

"You won't kill Jim without killing me first," said Jackson grimly.

"Put that lead-slinger away, Nubbins," Bass told Barnes.

"Blockey means what he says, and I won't see him killed, because he has been with me longer than any of the rest of you."

"If you don't trust Murphy, how can you let him ride with us?" asked Barnes.

"I trust Blockey. So if he vouches for Jim, that will be good enough for me."

"Well, maybe it ain't good enough for me, though," countered Barnes.

"You're free to cut your own trail anytime you get the notion."

"I'm going," said Henry Collins. "I'll say my so-longs to you boys now, as I don't expect to see any of you alive again."

"You should stick with us, Henry," said Bass.

"Nope. My brother and me are going to head out to Arizona, see if we can't make a go of it out there. I'm afraid you're about to the end of your line, Sam. I think you know that as well as I do, too."

Collins shook hands with Bass, Jackson, and Barnes— but not with Murphy—and then rode away.

THE WAY BASS had it figured, a small-town bank would provide them with more loot that any express train. He would pull one last holdup and then slip away to live in high style south of the border. The key was in finding the right bank. Riding west out of Denton County, he and his companions camped near the town of Rockwall. Bass sent Seab Barnes into town to buy some provisions and take a look at the bank there. When Barnes returned, he told Bass that he had seen a gallows.

"A gallows? In Rockwall?"

"Just outside of town. Right out in the middle of nowhere."

Curiosity got the better Bass. He rode back with Nubbins Colt to see the gallows. The structure stood in an open field a bit off the road, and it clearly had been standing for some months now.

"You don't reckon they got this waiting here for us, do you, Sam?" asked Barnes.

"Nope, I don't think that's the case, Nubbins. It has been here for a while."

"Still, if you ask me, it's a bad sign. Maybe we ought to leave Rockwall be and ride on."

"Follow me. I see a farmhouse yonder."

As the two outlaws rode up, an old woman came out of the farmhouse. Squinting suspiciously at Bass and Barnes, she cradled a shotgun like it was a baby.

"If you've come to steal my chickens you had better think twice. You varmints look like a pair if no-account chicken thieves to me."

"We've got no designs on your chickens, ma'am," said Bass. "Just wanting to know the story behind the gallows over there."

"Folks in Rockwall put that up last year. They was all set to hang a feller named Garner, who was tried and found guilty of killing our sheriff. But the night before he was supposed to hang, Garner killed himself. Seems his wife visited him in the jail. She had some bottles of morphine hidden under her clothes. They drank every drop and keeled over dead, the both of them."

Bass glanced at Barnes, then back at the old woman. "And they just left the gallows standing?"

"Yep. They figured they would need one again sooner or later. Besides, it gives people coming into Rockwall with mischief on their mind something to think about."

Riding away, Bass laughed softly. "Well, Nubs, I have to admit, those gallows sure have made me reconsider that bank at Rockwall. Guess those folks were right smart leaving it up."

"So we ride on?"

"The sooner, the better."

The next town they came to was Terrell, located on the Texas & Pacific Railroad some thirty miles east of Dallas. That evening Bass and Jackson rode into town and looked over the bank, but decided it was too poor. The third town,

Kaufman, had no bank at all. Ennis was next, but the bank there looked like a tough nut to crack. Swinging south and westward, they arrived in the vicinity of Waco. Jackson and Murphy rode into town. They ate dinner, visited the barbershop, and took a stroll through the bustling business district. Waco could boast of three banks. Jackson entered one of them and asked the clerk to change a twenty-dollar gold piece. When they got back to camp, Jackson told Bass he had seen a lot of gold and paper money at the bank he had visited. "I think we've found the place we're looking for, Sam," he said.

"I think you should go in and have a look for yourself," Murphy suggested.

Bass agreed. He rode into Waco the following morning, strolled into the bank Jackson had picked out, looked it over, then indulged in a bath and a shave at an emporium down the street before leaving town and rejoining his comrades.

"We've struck pay dirt," he said enthusiastically. "I seen plenty of cattlemen and merchants doing business at that bank. Reckon they've got all their money in there for safekeeping."

"I think we should be clear on an escape route before we go charging in there," said Murphy.

"Don't worry about all of that, Jim," said Jackson. "We'll spook those townsfolk so bad they won't give us any trouble at all."

Murphy spent a sleepless night. He did not want to be party to a bank robbery, but he couldn't see any way out of participating—or any way of notifying June Peak or Major Jones of the gang's intentions.

Bass sent Murphy and Jackson into Waco the next day to buy some provisions. After hitting the bank, they would be on the run for a while and needed plenty of supplies. As they were leaving town with the provisions in big gunnysacks tied to their saddles, Murphy made a desperate play.

"While you were paying the store clerk, Frank, I stepped

outside and saw a Texas Ranger across the street."

Jackson looked at him sharply. "The hell you say."

"I saw him," lied Murphy. "I swear to God."

"A Ranger. Where do you know him from?"

"Tyler, when I was locked up there. He is one of June Peak's men."

"Was he by himself?"

"Nope, there were two others with him. Now, I never seen either one of them before, but my guess is they're Rangers, too."

Jackson cursed. So did Sam Bass when he heard what Jim Murphy had to say.

"I thought for certain we had given them the slip," he said. He thought it over and then, disappointed, admitted that maybe it would be better for them to forget about robbing the Waco bank.

"I know of a bank not far from here," said Murphy. "In a town called Round Rock. That's cattle country, so there's usually plenty of money in the safe there. But I don't think it would be all that hard to crack."

"How do you know so much about it?" asked Bass.

"I used to do a fair amount of business with some of the cattlemen in those parts. I took ten horses out there last year and sold them to a rancher who took me to that bank. I was standing right there when the manager opened the safe. It was full of money, Sam."

Bass nodded. "Okay. Sounds good to me."

"Guess it's a good thing you didn't plug Jim," said Frank Jackson. "Otherwise we might have marched pretty as you please into a Ranger trap in Waco."

"Rangers or not, I'm going into Waco to have me a drink," said Bass. "This here is my last gold double eagle, boys. All that's left of my share of that Union Pacific holdup. I plan to spend it on some good sour mash. Who's going with me?"

Of course, they all were. Murphy didn't mind—after all, the Texas Rangers had just been a fabrication. A brilliant stroke, if he did say so himself, designed to persuade the outlaws against robbing the Waco bank. So Murphy wanted very much to go to town, though it wasn't whiskey he was after. All he needed was a chance to get word to Jones or Peak that the gang was headed for Round Rock. Maybe Bass and Barnes would grow careless—both men had been watching him like a hawk. Perhaps the whiskey would make them that way.

It was pure bravado on Sam's part, this reckless notion of riding into Waco bold as brass just for a drink. You had to admire Bass, thought Murphy, no matter what side of the fence you were standing on—he had gumption to spare. They went into the Ranch Saloon and Bass bought a drink for his friends and the barkeep, paying with the last Wells Fargo double eagle in his possession.

"That's it, then," he told Frank Jackson. "My pockets are full of nothing but dust now. Seven, eight thousand dollars is what I came back to Texas with and I'll be damned if I can remember where I spent any of it. But I don't care. Like they say, you can't take it with you."

"Guess we had better go scare up some more," said Jackson.

"I guess. I recall when I crossed over the Red River with all that money that I thought my career as an outlaw was over with. I was sure wrong about that!"

"You were meant to be a freebooter, Sam. Might as well face facts."

"And what about you, Blockey? What were you meant to be? Not a tinsmith, that's for certain."

"I was meant to sit in a fancy hotel room all day reading the newspaper," replied Jackson, and laughed.

"Yeah, I guess we both should have been born rich."

Murphy decided that he wanted to sample the pleasures of the local cathouse. While Bass, Jackson, and Barnes stayed in the downstairs parlor, flirting with the ladies and singing bawdy tunes around a piano that was as out of tune as they were, Murphy was escorted upstairs by a big-boned, plain-faced redhead. As soon as they were in the upstairs room, the calico queen bent over the footboard of the bed and lifted her skirt and petticoats to expose her bottom.

"Come along, cowboy," she said in a husky, salacious voice. "Let's see how good you can ride me."

Murphy took her by the shoulders and sat her down on the edge of the bed. "I've got one hundred dollars here," he said, waving the greenbacks in her face. "It's yours if you do something for me."

The fallen angel was suspicious. "It must be something pretty strange or downright painful if you're willing to pay all that money for it."

"No, it's nothing like that. My name is Jim Murphy. One of them downstairs is the outlaw, Sam Bass. You've got to get word to Captain June Peak or Major John Jones of the Texas Rangers. Tell them that Bass is planning to rob the bank at Round Rock. You got that? Can you do that for me?"

Her arms coiled slowly like serpents around his neck and she put her face close to his and licked her lips, smiling. "Sure, cowboy. I can do that for you—and a hundred dollars. But only on one condition."

"What's that?"

"That you ride me—hard." She leaned back on the bed, pulling Murphy down on top of her, and wrapped her legs tightly around his waist.

Murphy figured he was crazy to rely on the soiled dove to deliver a message to the Rangers. But what choice did he have? This was the first—and probably be the only—time he would not be accompanied by a member of the gang. When he was done, he buttoned up, paid her the hundred dollars, and made her promise to take his message to the Texas Rangers. Then he went back downstairs to rejoin Sam Bass and the others.

An hour later they were riding down a moonlit road in the direction of Round Rock.

CHAPTER NINETEEN

"THAT MUST HAVE HIT YOU PRETTY HARD," SAID JED BANKS, *"finding out that your friend, Jim Murphy, betrayed you."*

Lying there staring up at the rafters, Sam Bass nodded. Every movement caused him pain—every breath was an ordeal. He reached for the bottle of laudanum the doctor had left for him, and took a sip.

"They told me while I was lying out there in the bush, when we were waiting for the wagon that would bring me here," said Bass. "I wish they hadn't told me. I would have rather died not knowing the truth."

"Are you saying you're sorry you didn't listen to your instincts and kill him when you had the chance?"

Waiting eagerly for the laudanum to take hold and ease the aching pain that coursed through his whole body, Bass wondered what day it was. How long had he been laid up in this place? Maybe a week, maybe only a couple of days—time didn't seem to matter much anymore because he had run out of time.

"Naw," he said at last, "I don't really hold a grudge against Jim. Maybe I would have if Blockey had gotten killed. But Blockey got away, didn't he?"

"Yes, Frank Jackson got away. But you didn't. And Sea-born Barnes got his head shot off."

"Well, Nubbins and I were born to meet a bad end, you

know." Bass smiled. "If it hadn't been here and now it would have happened somewhere else, and soon. With or without Jim Murphy we were going to die. I don't know how a person could do that, though—turn on his pards."

"Seems to me he did it because he couldn't stand the thought of spending months, maybe years, in a cell."

Bass nodded. "That's a fearsome thing. But even so, a man has got to stand for something. I don't rightly know how Jim is going to live with what he's done. I don't think I could. Is he here, in Round Rock? Jim, I mean. Have you talked to him?"

"Yes, I talked to him briefly. He told me he was afraid to go home. Said that you still had a lot of friends in Denton County, and when word got out that he had turned on you, his life wouldn't be worth a plugged nickel."

Sam Bass suddenly went rigid, his fingers clawing at the blanket that covered him.

"Are you all right, Sam?" asked the newspaperman.

Bass smiled wanly. "Yes, yes I'm fine. Just couldn't catch my breath for a minute, and everything was getting kind of dark."

"Maybe you should rest for a while before we continue."

"No. The story is almost told. Let's finish it. . . ."

They rode south through the arid hill country of dust and rock and cactus and live oak. Crossing the shallow, stony Lampasas River, they pressed on across a prairie seared by the summer sun and finally reached Georgetown, a dozen miles from their destination. Bass rode straight into town. He felt fairly safe this far removed from his old stomping grounds around Denton. In recent weeks he had grown a beard, cognizant of the fact that all the flyers out on him described him as being clean-shaven, with a boyish expression.

Williamson County's deputy sheriff, Milt Tucker, happened to be in Georgetown on the day the outlaws arrived. He spotted them riding down the center of the street, two by two, and melted back into a mercantile's doorway so that he could watched them without being conspicuous about it. The four hardcases dismounted in front of a saloon and Tucker took note of the way they made long, cautious surveys of the street. Tucker had been lawdogging all his life. He didn't know anything else. And he had seen more than his share of outlaws.

When the four suspicious-looking strangers entered the saloon, Tucker hurried along to the town marshal's office. He found Joe Chamberlain taking his noonday siesta.

"Joe, we've got some bad company. Come on—you can sleep later."

Chamberlain was groggy and slow to comprehend. He sat up on the bunk in the spare cell where he had been napping. "What do you mean, you got company, Milt?"

"Four men just rode into town. They're desperadoes or I'll eat my hat. You need to come and have a look at them."

Chamberlain reluctantly got to his feet, strapped on his holster, and took a sawed-off shotgun from the gun rack by the door. He followed Tucker down the street until they stood in the shade of an alley across from the saloon Bass and his friends had entered moments before.

"Well, hell, let's go find out what they have to say for themselves," said Chamberlain crossly. It was hot and he was sleepy and he didn't feel like standing around outside all afternoon.

"No," said Tucker, "give those boys some space."

Chamberlain grimaced. But he didn't argue with Tucker. Milt had made law enforcement a career. Chamberlain, on the other hand, had sought and won the sheriff's job merely as a stepping-stone to better things. So he bowed to Tucker's experience in these matters—and waited for what seemed like an eternity until the four men emerged from the saloon. They stood around on the boardwalk for a minute or two, taking the measure of the town, and Chamberlain realized that Tucker had been right. They were hardcases, all right. No question about it.

"Who are they?" he asked the deputy sheriff

Tucker shook his head. "I don't know them. Check your flyers, Joe, and I'll go through mine."

The lawmen watched as Frank Jackson and Jim Murphy entered the store/post office adjacent to the saloon. A couple of minutes later, Jackson came out eating tomatoes from a tin. He rejoined Bass and Barnes, who still loitered in front of the watering hole. Then Bass went into the store and came out with Murphy in tow. The outlaws mounted up and rode down the street, heading out of town. While Chamberlain returned to his office to look through a stack of recent wanted posters, Tucker crossed the street and went into the store.

"Afternoon, Bill," Tucker said to the bespectacled clerk. "I'm interested in the men who were just here."

"Rough-looking bunch," said the clerk. "Thought they were robbers, for a minute. But damned if they ain't Texas Rangers."

"Rangers? Why do you say so?"

"Well, one of them posted a letter. Here, I'll show you." Bill handed Tucker an envelope addressed, *Major J. B. Jones, Texas Rangers, Austin, Texas.*

"Which one gave this to you?"

"The big fella with the red hair. Said it needed to get to Austin in a hurry. I told him it would be on the southbound stage tonight and get where it was supposed to by tomorrow evening."

"Hmmm," said Tucker, turning the letter over and over in his hands.

"He also said it was a good thing Sam Bass was finished robbing stagecoaches," said Bill.

"He said that, did he?"

"Yep. Thing is, the redheaded one looked mighty nervous, and when the bearded one came in and asked what was taking him so long, the redheaded man said he was trying to talk me out of my newspaper. Well, he hadn't been doing anything of the kind, but the look he gave me made me see that I'd better play along. So I said that was true and that I hadn't finished with the newspaper but seeing as how they were in a hurry he could go ahead and have it."

"They call each other by name?"

"Not that I recollect, no."

"I'm going to open this letter, Bill."

The clerk let out a low whistle. "There'll be hell to pay if you tamper with the mail—especially Ranger mail."

"I know. But I have no choice. And my gut hunch is that those boys weren't Texas Rangers."

"You open that letter, Milt, you're on your own, that's all I've got to say."

Tucker nodded, looked again at the letter, hesitated, then tore it open.

A few minutes later he showed up in Chamberlain's office again. The town marshal had just propped his feet up on the corner of the desk and gotten comfortable. "Now what?" he asked, exasperated.

"They're making for Round Rock," said Tucker. "Sam Bass and his gang. They plan to rob the bank there."

THERE WERE ACTUALLY two Round Rocks—the Old Town located down on Brushy Creek and the new one a little less than a mile to the southwest, which had sprung up around the station on the Great Northern line. Old Town was a quiet, sleepy place, but the new Round Rock thrived, located as it was on the edge of the raw frontier. Many farmers and ranchers did business in the new Round Rock, buying goods shipped in on the iron road and moving their stock and produce east by the same means.

Bass and his boys bought feed for their horses at a store in Old Town and then rode along the San Saba Road two miles before making camp. The next day they rode into the new Round Rock, Bass and Jackson together, while Barnes, accompanied by Murphy, entered the town by a separate route. They all got a good look at the bank and the layout of the town, then met back at the camp.

"I think you're right, Jim," said Bass. "That looks like a fat bank to me, judging by its clientele."

"And it's a corner building, near the edge of town, two

blocks from the main square," said Jackson. "That all works in our favor, if you ask me."

"I told Jim it was too bad our horses weren't fresh," said Barnes, "or we could have gone ahead and taken the bank today. We could always steal us some getaway horses."

"That's not a good idea," said Murphy. "Horse-stealing would stir up the town. I say let sleeping dogs lie."

"Jim is right," said Bass. "We'll just have to let our horses rest for a few days. What's today, Blockey?"

"It's Tuesday, Sam. I think it is, anyway."

"We'll hit the bank on Saturday. Until then, if anybody asks any questions, we're cattle buyers."

They moved their camp away from the well-traveled San Saba Road, settling for a spot near a graveyard shaded by a grove of ancient oak trees and located a half mile to the north of Old Town. A shantytown at the edge of the grove was home to about two dozen black people. Though he had used up all his gold double eagles, Bass still had a roll of banknotes in his possession, so he hired a young black woman named Mary to cook for them. He told Mary and others in the shantytown that he and his companions had been hired by the United States Army to recover runaway government mules.

The others looked to Bass to plan the robbery, so after giving it one whole day of study, Sam laid out the scheme for them. He and Seab Barnes would walk in first. Bass would tell the bank clerk that he wanted to exchange all his paper money for gold or silver. When the clerk opened the safe to get the coin, Bass would draw his pistols and keep everyone covered while Barnes went over the counter and put the contents of the safe in a gunnysack he would bring concealed under his duster. Frank Jackson would stand with the horses at the corner while Murphy would linger near the bank's front door. If anyone went inside while the holdup was in progress, Murphy would follow right behind and get the drop on them. If there was no trouble, they would mount up and ride out of Round Rock together. If there was trouble, however, they would split up, each man going in a different direction, to meet up later, if possible, at the old graveyard. In that scenario Bass would be responsible for carrying the loot out.

One of the shantytown residents brought them a newspaper of recent vintage, and Bass learned that two of the men who had been with him on the Mesquite train robbery, Sam Pipes and Al Herndon, had been found guilty of robbing the United States mail in an Austin trial, and sentenced to life in prison. Billy Scott had identified both men as part of the Bass Gang.

"That feller Scott has an awful big mouth," commented Frank Jackson. "It's too bad about Sam and Al. They were good men."

"They say a Ranger name of Major Jones pulled a bluff on Scott and got him to sing," said Bass. "Life in prison." He shook his head. "Reckon it might make that go a little easier for Pipes and Herndon if they knew that Billy Scott had gotten his just reward for turning them in."

"You mean we should kill Scott?" asked Jackson, surprised.

"That's exactly what I mean."

"Never thought I'd hear you say such a thing, Sam."

"Hell, I'll be glad to do it if you're too squeamish," said Nubbins Colt. "Don't bother me at all."

"Yes, you were the one itching to plug Jim," said Jackson. "Now aren't you glad you didn't?"

Barnes shrugged bony shoulders. "Guess I was wrong about Murphy. But there's no question that Billy Scott turned on Al and Sam Pipes."

Jim Murphy smiled halfheartedly, wondering if any of his messages had gotten through to the Texas Rangers headquarters in Austin. He had a feeling that the game was almost over. In a few days either he would be dead or Sam Bass would be.

ON WEDNESDAY AFTERNOON, Major Jones received word from Jim Murphy in a most unexpected way.

When he rode up to Rangers headquarters in Austin, a

nondescript adobe structure on Commerce Street, several men were lounging around in front and seemed amused to see him. One of them, a corporal, walked out to take the major's horse as Jones dismounted.

"Someone here to see you, Major," said the corporal. "She says she has something to give you." The man was having a hard time suppressing a grin.

"Who is she?"

"Won't say. Will only talk to you."

Jones sighed, wondering if he was about to be the brunt of some practical joke. He went to the office and found a big-boned redheaded woman in a dress that for all its satin and lace looked a little tawdry. A plumed hat and a parasol completed her outfit. In a glance Jones could tell what she was.

"I'm Major Jones," he said tersely, "and I want to know who you are and who put you up to this."

"You can call me Spanish Red, and a man named Jim Murphy sent me to find you."

"Murphy!" The major's attitude abruptly changed. "I'm sorry if I kept you waiting."

"Oh, it doesn't matter, though usually it's the man who has to wait for me." She grinned. "But Murphy paid me well to deliver a message to you. Besides, it was a good excuse to get out of Waco for a spell. Austin strikes me as a nice town with a lot of opportunity for a woman like me. Maybe I'll go into business here. What do you think? Are you a married man, Major? Happily married, that is."

"I was. Comanches turned me into a widower."

"Oh, I am sorry. I didn't mean to make light—"

"Red, I want to know what Jim Murphy told you and I want to know right now."

"He said that Sam Bass is going to rob the bank at Round Rock."

"When did he tell you this?"

"Three days ago."

Two long quick strides took Jones to the door, which he

threw violently open before bellowing for the corporal. The man came running.

"Vern, you ride to Lampasas. Lieutenant Reynolds and E Company are up there now. Tell Reynolds to bring a squad of men and meet me in Round Rock."

"Lampasas. That's eighty miles, Major. How quick do you want me there?"

"Kill as many horses as you have to."

"Yes, sir." Vern glanced past Jones and couldn't help but grin boyishly at Spanish Red. "It was a real pleasure to meet you, miss," he said, touching the brim of his hat.

"We'll make sure that it's a real pleasure next time, too," she replied.

"You can get acquainted with the lady later, Corporal," said Jones dryly.

Vernon Wilson took off at a dead run without saying another word.

Spanish Red stood to go. "Well, unless you need me for something else, Major . . ." She twitched her hips in invitation.

"I'm afraid you're not going anywhere just yet, ma'am," said Jones. "You will be our guest here until I'm sure your story is on the level."

Spanish Red feigned indignation. "You don't trust me?" She pouted.

"I don't trust Sam Bass. He's a slick customer, that boy is."

"Oh, I see. You think I'm part of a scheme dreamed up by this Bass feller?"

Jones answered with a shrug.

"Do you think I'll be safe in your keeping, Major? In the middle of all these Texas Rangers?"

"Only a few of them here. That's why I had to send Vern to find Lieutenant Reynolds. But I'm not worried about you. It's them I'm worried about!"

Spanish Red just laughed and extended her arms. "Put the chains on me, Major. Make me your slave."

Jones just shook his head, fiercely repressing a smile. In

spite of himself he liked Spanish Red. He yelled out the door to fetch another Ranger.

"Luke, I want you to keep this woman in custody until you hear from me," said Jones, grabbing some extra ammunition and a pair of field glasses out of his desk.

"Yes, sir, Major."

"And God help you," added Jones, clapping a somewhat mystified Luke on the shoulder as he strode out of the office.

VERNON WILSON SPENT two horses getting from Austin to Lampasas. He had ridden a stint for the Pony Express before the war—he had been fourteen years old, but had told them he was older—and of course Major Jones had taken that into account when he'd handed out this assignment. Jones knew everything about the men in his command, their strengths and their weaknesses. That, thought Vern, was what made him an excellent leader.

Vernon knew the precise moment when his first horse went windbroke on him, and, pulling the spare mount up alongside, the young, lithe Ranger grabbed the saddle horn of the second pony's hull with both hands and let the first horse run out from under him, then executed a deft running mount to swing up into the fresh saddle pretty as you please. It reminded him of the countless times he had approached a Pony Express way station at a flat-out gallop, making a running dismount, swinging the saddlebags carrying the mail onto a fresh horse held by the station's hostler, and laying his quirt along the new mount's flanks to get it moving even before he was in the saddle. Now, as then, he could do these things in his sleep.

He was never at less than a gallop the whole eighty miles from Austin to Lampasas, and when he reached the latter town his second horse died under him. Vern jumped clear as the animal went down, brushed himself off, and strolled into the nearest saloon to find out where Lieutenant Reynolds and E Company were to be found, leaving the dead horse in the middle of the street for the locals to gawk at.

Ten minutes later he was the westbound stage, having learned that the Rangers had ridden to San Saba that morning. Reaching San Saba, Vern rented a horse and rode three miles upriver to Reynolds's camp. The trek from Austin had taken him a little more than six hours.

Reynolds was ill. He summoned Sergeant C. L. Neville and told him to pick eight of the best shots and eight of the fastest horses in the company and report back in ten minutes. In a half hour Neville and his squad were on their way to Round Rock. Reynolds followed in a wagon, with the exhausted Vern sleeping soundly in the back.

In Austin, Jones could scare up only three other Rangers—these he dispatched to Round Rock. He found an old friend, Maurice Moore, an ex-Ranger turned Travis County deputy sheriff, and told Moore what was afoot.

"You want to come along, you're welcome," said Jones.

"Sounds like good sport," said Moore. "It'll be like the good old days."

"I don't remember them being all that good, but if you say so."

Together they boarded the afternoon train that would put them in Round Rock that night.

CHAPTER TWENTY

By Thursday morning there were thirteen Texas Rangers—and one ex-Ranger, Maurice Moore—in Round Rock. Jones made camp along Brushy Creek between Old Town and the new one.

"After this," he told his men, "I don't want to see more than two of you together again. Maurice, you'll stick with me. The rest of you will pair up. I want three pair out scouting the countryside today. The other three pair on patrol in Round Rock, keeping an eye on the bank. Don't be conspicuous. Don't tell anyone who you are. And I mean no one. If the governor himself shows up and asks you what the hell you're doing, you just tell him you're an out-of-work cowboy, and ask him if he'll buy you a drink since he's obviously got money in his pocket."

The Rangers laughed.

"There is one man in Round Rock that we should tell," said Moore. "Cage Grimes lives here now with his family."

"You're right. I'd forgotten. Cage is a damned good man." Both Grimes and Moore had ridden with Jones on many a campaign against Comanche raiders, cattle theft rings, and border bandits.

Jones and Moore rode into Round Round and hunted up Grimes. When they told him their purpose, Grimes immediately bought in, much to the obvious dismay of his wife.

Her reaction gave Jones pause to reconsider.

"Maybe you ought to stay clear of this one, Cage," he said. "You've got a wife and three children to take care of and I would hate to see anything happen to you."

Grimes laughed softly. "I rode with you twelve years, John, and never even got scratched."

Jones let it go—he knew how futile it would be to try to talk Cage Grimes out of something once he had made up his mind.

Thursday passed, then Friday, with no sign of the outlaws. The scouts found no trace of them, while the patrols in town spotted nothing to arouse their suspicions. Jones wondered if Jim Murphy had misled him. Or maybe Sam Bass had changed his mind. It was even possible that Bass had been here and found out that Texas Rangers were looking for him and slipped away unnoticed.

In fact, Bass had come to Round Rock on Thursday. He strolled the main street like he owned the town. His instincts alerted him that something was wrong. He saw two Ranger patrols. Though he wasn't sure who the four men were—they looked like ordinary cowboys—he could not shake the feeling that there was something menacing beneath the surface, something he could not see. He returned to camp just about convinced that he ought to call the whole thing off.

"I think you're getting a case of nerves, Sam," said Murphy. "It's all this sitting around waiting. Tell you what. Me and Frank will go in tomorrow morning and take a look around."

Bass agreed to that. Murphy and Jackson returned around noon the following day, and both men reported seeing nothing out of the ordinary. That made Bass feel better. "Maybe I'm getting too old for this kind of work," he said, and they all laughed. It was decided that they would all go back into town later that afternoon and buy some tobacco and have one more look at the bank. As they rode in, Murphy suggested that he swing through Old Town and see if anything unusual was going on there. "I'll meet up with you in Round Rock," he promised. Bass just nodded, and Murphy went his separate way.

Though he had not seen a familiar face in Round Rock, Murphy wondered if Bass was right—if indeed there were Rangers in town. If so, he did not want to ride in with the rest of the gang. He intended to ask around in Old Town. Surely by now at least one of his messages had reached Jones in Austin, and surely by now the major had sent his men to Round Rock. Were the Rangers here? Until he found out, Murphy figured it would be safer not to be seen in public with Sam Bass.

The day was a hot one, and the dusty streets of Round Rock were quiet. As Bass rode into town flanked by Frank Jackson and Seab Barnes, they saw very little activity. A spring wagon was parked in front of a hardware store and a farmer and his young son of about ten years were loading the bed with lumber and barbed wire. Across the street at the livery stable a young man was unloading a hay wagon. Bass led the way into an alley off the main street and dismounted. They tethered their horses and crossed over to a stone building that housed Henry Koppel's general store. As they neared the store, Bass spotted a man standing several buildings away down the street, in the shade of the boardwalk fronting a barbershop. The man was looking straight at them. But Bass didn't let that worry him. He had been in Round Rock several times already, and always without incident. Leading the way into the general store, he sauntered up to the counter and asked the clerk for some Union Leader tobacco.

The man in front of the barbershop was Maurice Moore, and he was very curious about the three men who had just entered Koppel's store. Since he was a stranger to Round Rock himself, he could not be sure that the three were actually newcomers—for all he knew, they might be cowboys in town on liberty from a nearby cattle spread. But as soon as they disappeared inside the store, Moore began walking up the street with easy, casual strides. He spotted Cage Grimes coming around a corner. Grimes paused to speak to a boy standing beside a wagon in front of the hardware store. Moore quickened his step, quartering across the street to approach Grimes. He found himself wishing that John Jones was available—but the major had ridden to the Ranger camp to check with the scouts.

"Hello, Dock," Grimes greeted the farm boy. "What are you doing out here? Where's your pa?"

"He's inside the store," replied Dock, fidgeting with excitement. "I think he's going to buy me a jackknife!"

"Well, what do you know. Reckon you're old enough. Every boy needs a good knife." Grimes looked up to see Moore coming closer.

"Three men just went into Koppel's store," Moore told him calmly. "I'm wondering if they're from around here."

"If they are, I'll know them," replied Grimes. "I'll go over and see."

"I'll come along, just in case."

"You a little edgy, hoss? You used to be the coolest hand in the company."

Moore smiled dryly. "Yeah, well, I lived long enough to know better. I don't know—I just got a funny feeling at the base of my spine when I saw those three jaspers."

Grimes tousled Dock's hair and turned his steps toward the general store, with Moore falling in alongside. When the two ex-Rangers reached their destination, Moore held up just outside the door while Grimes strolled inside. Bass and Jackson and Barnes stood at the counter with their backs to him.

"Howdy, boys," said Grimes. "Are you all heeled? If so, you'll have to check your artillery at the town marshal's office while you're here."

"Yes, I'm heeled," said Nubbins Colt—turning with his pistol in hand.

"Hold up, now," rasped Grimes, taking one step back, his hand dropping to the pistol at his side.

Seeing this, both Bass and Jackson drew their guns. All three outlaws fired almost simultaneously. The impact of the bullets sent Grimes reeling backward. His lifeless body flopped across the threshold at Moore's feet. The gun was still in its holster.

Moore drew his pistol and, shouting at the store clerk to get the hell down, began firing into the store. The interior was quickly filled with an acrid, blinding pall of gunsmoke. Moore dauntlessly moved into it. All that the combatants could see of one another were dark shapes illuminated momentarily by muzzle flash. Bass felt his right hand go numb. He held it up close to his hand. His finger was still wrapped around the trigger of his six-shooter, but a bullet had sheared away his middle and ring fingers. He took the gun into his left hand and emptied it in the general direction of Moore, then stumbled toward the door. Frank Jackson grabbed him by the arm and led him out. Barnes followed, pausing to fire twice more into the store, and stumbling over the body of Cage Grimes on the way out.

Moore went after them. Suddenly feeling faint, he leaned against the doorframe and looked at the blood on the front of his shirt and coat. He had been hit, and the bullet had passed clean through his left shoulder.

The outlaws were heading across the street toward the alleys where their horses were located, but as Moore watched, three Texas Rangers emerged from opposite ends of the street, blazing away at the trio. A one-armed citizen of Round Rock named J. F. Tubbs took the gun from Cage Grimes's holster and started shooting, too. Moore reloaded his pistol and joined in—and for a moment Bass and his friends faltered in the middle of the street, fired on from all sides, and uncertain which way to go.

Major Jones rounded a corner onto the main street, quickly surveyed the situation, and, firing his pistol on the run, moved to join Moore in front of Koppel's store. He grabbed Moore by the arm and sat him down with his back to the wall.

"You've got a hole in you, amigo," said Jones. "Just have a rest. You've done more than enough. We'll finish up here."

Moore was too weak to do anything but nod.

Jones turned to see that the three outlaws had made it to the alley across the street. The three Rangers—Connor, Harrall, and Ware—ran to the mouth of the alley and fired into it. Bass was halfway down the alley, nearly to the horses, when he was hit again, the bullet entering an inch to the left of his spine and exiting a few inches left of his navel, perforating a kidney. Seab Barnes spun around to shoot at the Rangers, but the hammer of his gun fell on an empty chamber. Ranger Ware took aim and shot Nubbins Colt right between the eyes.

Firing at the Rangers with the pistol in his right hand, Frank Jackson used his left to help Bass into his saddle. Then he mounted his own horse and together they rode out the back end of the alley, stirrup to stirrup. Jackson held on to his wounded friend to keep him from falling and sent one last bullet back at the Rangers.

As Jones crossed the street, Ware turned to shout that one of the robbers was dead and two were getting away, though one of them was badly wounded.

"Go after them," said Jones tersely, and went back to Koppel's store to confirm his worst fears. Cage Grimes's wife was now a widow.

. . . I am damned sorry about that man Grimes," Bass told Jed Banks, the Galveston newspaperman. "It bothers me to think of his wife and children alone in the world now."

Banks solemnly closed his notebook. He felt sick to his stomach and he didn't know precisely why. He thought it might have something to do with the way Bass and his friends had gunned down Cage Grimes. That had struck him as out of character, at least where Bass and Jackson were concerned. Throughout the narrative he had found himself at times sympathizing with Bass, but now that sympathy was gone.

"Why did you do it, Sam? Why did you just turn around and start shooting like that? You seemed so dead-set against killing anyone. You went to great lengths to prevent anyone from getting hurt during the commission of your

crimes. There were times when men were shooting at you, shooting to kill, and all you did was shoot over their heads to discourage them. But that day in Koppel's store . . ."

"I don't know. I guess maybe it was because of the way things had been going lately. All of a sudden things had gotten a lot more serious. It's hard to explain and I don't reckon I'm making any sense. I don't have a way with words like you do, Jed."

"Well, try," said Banks. "Try to help me understand. It's important."

"When I first started out robbing stagecoaches in the Black Hills, it was kind of a lark. It was a game, really. Fun in a lot of ways, except for that one time when the stage driver got killed. Same goes for down here in Texas, at first. But then the railroads and the Rangers got serious. They hunted us hard and just never seemed to quit. It wasn't a game anymore. The Rangers, they weren't going to take great pains to bring us in alive, you know. No, sir, they were going to kill us. That was their job. That's what Texas Rangers do. So at some point we started to play for keeps, too. I think maybe I knew that when Arkansas Johnson got killed."

"And you really would have killed Jim Murphy, had you known the truth?"

Bass nodded. "Maybe so."

Banks sat there a moment, watching Bass. In the last few hours he had noticed that the mortally wounded outlaw would seem to drift away more and more often. Sam's breathing would become very shallow and his eyes would lose their focus. At first these spells were of short duration and happened infrequently. They were coming all the time now. Banks didn't need a doctor to tell him that Sam Bass had very little time left.

"Sam," he said softly, "is there anything you'd like to tell me?"

Bass smiled. "Are you really going to write a book about me?"

"Yes, I am."

"You reckon anybody will even want to read such a book?"

"I believe that a lot of people will want to read it, yes."

"Imagine that. Makes no sense to me. I mean, I'm just a farm boy from Indiana who wanted to be a Texas cowboy."

Jed Banks stood up, then leaned down to lay a hand on Sam's arm. He couldn't shake the feeling that he would not see the famous outlaw alive again.

"Good-bye, Sam."

"So long, Jed. Thanks for keeping me company. This dying can sure be a lonely business, can't it?"

JED BANKS WAS in desperate need of a drink, feeling more than a trifle overwrought after parting company with Sam Bass for what he knew would be the last time. He felt as though he had known Sam all his life, though it had only been yesterday that he had first laid eyes on the notorious robber.

Heading for the nearest saloon, the Galveston newspaperman bellied up to the bar and ordered a whiskey. He knocked the drink back, gasped as the liquid fire engulfed him—and immediately felt better about things. The aproned barkeep was pouring him another stiff shot when Major John B. Jones walked in. The Texas Ranger joined Banks at the mahogany. Banks could not read any emotion on the craggy dark stone of the major's face. The cold gray eyes betrayed nothing as they fastened on the young correspondent.

"Know who I am?" asked Jones.

"Yes, I do. You're Major Jones. Can I buy you a drink?"

"No, thanks. I always pay my own way." Jones flicked some hard money on the bar and the man behind it produced a shot glass and a bottle and then walked away so that he would be out of earshot. Banks surmised that the barkeep had waited on Jones before and knew what was expected of him. The saloon was pretty empty—three men played cards at a table in the back. So there was no one near at hand.

"I hear you've been spending a lot of time with Bass," said Jones.

"That's true. But don't worry, Major, I'm not part of a scheme to break him out." Banks chuckled. He meant it as a joke, but Jones did not look the least bit amused.

"Not at all worried about that," replied the Ranger. "I know Sam Bass isn't going anywhere—except boot hill."

"He has told me his life's story," said Banks, "and I intend to write a book about him."

"A book," said Jones, as though he couldn't fathom why anyone would waste his time in such a useless pursuit.

"Yes, sir. A book about Sam Bass, I think, will be very well received. A great many people are interested in what made him do the things he did. He's even, I daresay, a hero to some."

"A hero," said Jones. The corners of his hard, grim mouth turned down. "So that's the kind of book you aim to write, is it?"

"I intend to write the true story. I will not embellish it. I don't have to. It is exciting enough as is."

"The truth—according to Sam Bass?"

"Well . . . yes."

"I'll tell you the truth about Sam Bass," said Jones curtly. "He was lawbreaker. A no-account who didn't have what it takes to work hard and make something of himself. So he took the easy way out. He started stealing. He thought that was the road to fame and fortune. Sam Bass was a nobody who used a gun to make people sit up and take notice of him. I've seen it before, many's the time."

Jones paused to pour himself a shot.

"You want to put the truth in that book of yours, Mr. Banks? Then you should write this—that Sam Bass died young and died badly because he didn't have the grit to live by the rules."

The Texas Ranger knocked back the whiskey, put the glass down, and gave Jed Banks one last speculative look.

Then, to the newspaperman's surprise, Jones smiled. It was a rather cold, thin smile, but it was something.

"And when you don't play by the rules," added Jones, "bad things are guaranteed to happen to you."

He turned on his heel and left the saloon.

Banks remembered to start breathing again. He drank his second shot in a hurry. The bartender returned, picked up the bottle, and refilled the newspaperman's glass, a sympathetic look on his face.

"That Ranger, he's a hard man," said the barkeep. "Sam Bass didn't stand a chance against the likes of him."

"No," said Banks. "No, he sure didn't."

EPILOGUE

JED BANKS WAS WALKING OUT OF THE SALOON, FORTIFIED BY several shots of whiskey, when he heard the news he'd been dreading. A boy was scampering up the dusty street from the direction of the Hart House, where Bass had been kept, shouting at the top of his lungs that the outlaw leader was dead. Feeling empty inside, Banks headed for the Hart House, and intercepted Dr. Cochran as the physician emerged into the afternoon sunlight, his face pale and drawn.

"Is it true?" asked the newspaperman.

The doctor nodded wearily. "You know, I've seen many people die in thirty years of practice, and I still can't get used to it."

"Did he say anything? Any last words?"

"I asked him if he wanted to make a statement. He just said, 'Let me go.' He was gone about twenty minutes later. He said the world was bobbing around him, and then he drew his last breath. He died at three fifty-eight."

"Sunday, July twenty-first, 1878," murmured Banks. "There's something about this date, I can't quite put my finger on it."

Cochran shrugged and moved on, shouldering through the crowd that was beginning to gather around the Hart House.

When Major Jones received the news, he sent a telegram to Austin and asked if the governor wanted the body of the notorious outlaw to be brought to the state capital. The answer came back promptly: No, just bury him. Jones figured that was the smart thing to do. Bass was still a hero to some in Texas, and to put his body on display would reflect poorly on the authorities.

Jones rode to the Ranger camp and gathered his men together. "Some of you may think we've done the job we came here to do," he said. "But the fact remains that there is still one member of the Bass Gang running free. That's Frank Jackson."

"I reckon he's long gone by now," said one of the Rangers.

"Don't be so sure. Jackson and Bass were best of friends. It might be that Jackson is hanging around these parts waiting to hear some word about Bass. But when he finds out Bass is dead, then I reckon he will move on. So now is our chance to find him. I want everybody in the saddle in ten minutes."

Though part of him wanted to hop a train for Galveston and home, Jed Banks lingered in Round Rock to attend the funeral of Sam Bass. While a coroner's inquest was conducted, a number of people gathered for an impromptu wake for the slain outlaw at one of the local saloons. Meanwhile, a cabinetmaker worked late into the night fashioning a coffin for the dead man. That night Banks found Jim Murphy, sitting in a chair on the front porch of the hotel.

"How do you feel now that Bass is dead?" asked the reporter.

Murphy gave him a suspicious look. "How am I supposed to feel?"

"I don't know. Remorseful, maybe. After all, he was your friend, wasn't he?"

"I guess he was. But I wasn't much of a friend to him, when all was said and done."

"You did what you felt you had to do."

Murphy smiled thinly. "You can't fool me. You think

I'm lower than a snake's belly because I betrayed him."

Banks shrugged. "Not my place to judge. I reckon there are some who think of you that way. Others will call you a hero. Say it was a brave thing you did, infiltrating a gang of desperadoes to get the goods on them. I guess in the end it doesn't matter what anyone thinks. Only thing that really matters is whether you can live with what you've done."

"Well, it's all over now," said Murphy, grimly staring at the toes of his boots.

"The Rangers are out looking for Frank Jackson. You think Frank is still around these parts?"

"I have no idea. But I hope they don't catch him. He's a good man."

"Yes, and he saved your life when Seaborn Barnes wanted to put you six feet under."

Murphy didn't say anything.

"Did you know that today was Sam's birthday?" asked Banks. "I knew the date was familiar, and I checked my notes. He was born on July twenty-first, twenty-seven years ago."

Murphy glanced bleakly at him. "No, I didn't know that," he said, and it was obvious he wished he was still ignorant of the fact.

Banks nodded. "Yes, he died young, but then I guess that's a chance you take when you ride the outlaw trail."

"Sam was never bashful about taking chances."

The sound of revelry from the saloon down the street intruded on the silence that fell between them. It seemed to make Murphy too uncomfortable to sit still; he stood up abruptly, looked around like a man who had lost his way, then turned to the door of the hotel.

"Funeral's in the morning," said Banks. "Will you be there?"

Murphy just shook his head. Shoulders hunched, he went inside.

Early the following morning, the body of Sam Bass was placed in the coffin and loaded into a wagon by several black men who had come from the shantytown at the edge of the old oak grove to serve as pallbearers. Over the weekend Banks had attended two other funerals—one for Cage Grimes in which nearly the entire community had appeared to give its last respects, and then the one for Seaborn Barnes, which had been attended by no one. Banks was curious to note that quite a few people were present for the burial of Sam Bass. Round Rock's Methodist preacher said a few words over the grave, but there was no hymn-singing, and there were no tears shed. The coffin was lowered into the ground and then covered up with red clay by the pallbearers as the rest of the people drifted away. Banks stayed behind, watching the black men work. One of them began to sing to the rhythm of his spadework, "Rock of Ages, cleft for me . . ." The others joined in. Though he wasn't sure why, Banks was gladdened that someone was singing over the body of Sam Bass.

Their work done, the black men shouldered their shovels and moved away, leaving Banks alone in the cemetery. The newspaperman found some shade under an oak tree beyond the stone perimeter wall and waited.

The sultry heat of a Texas summer day conspired with his exhaustion, and Banks dozed off about noon—only to be awakened by the distinctive and very unnerving sound of a six-shooter's hammer being cocked. The blazing sun seemed to be balanced on the shoulder of the man who loomed over him, and he squinted to make out the other's features.

"Are you a Pinkerton man?" asked the man with the gun, his drawl deceptively soft. Banks wasn't fooled; he knew this was serious. "Or maybe a railroad detective? I don't take you for a Ranger."

"I'm none of those things," said Banks, trying to remain calm. "I'm a newspaper reporter."

"Are you, now."

"Yes, I am. And who are you?"

"I bet you'd like to know."

Banks slowly got to his feet. "You're Frank Jackson, aren't you?"

Jackson looked around, suspecting a trap. "What if I am?"

"I thought you might show up."

"Funny that it didn't occur to anybody else."

"I guess nobody thought you'd be foolhardy enough to try it. But I thought you might. Just to pay your last respects."

Jackson peered speculatively at the newspaperman. "You don't appear to be heeled. Maybe you are what you say you are."

"I am. I've been with Sam Bass for the last two days. He has been talking to me. I'm going to write his story."

Jackson holstered his gun, glanced at the fresh graves along the western wall of the cemetery. Neither grave had a tombstone. "I reckon that's where Sam and Nubbins Colt are laid out. Which is which?"

Banks showed him. Jackson took off his hat and stood for a moment, hipshot, at the foot of Sam Bass's grave, head bowed. Banks maintained a respectful distance, waiting until Jackson was finished. After a few moments, the outlaw knelt and picked up a handful of the red clay that covered his friend's final resting place.

"He always said he didn't want to grow old," said Jackson, more to himself than to Banks. "Guess that was a good thing, too, as there wasn't much chance of it."

"They've written a ballad about him. Did you know that?"

Jackson stood up. "No, I didn't."

"I have it right here. The newspaper printed it yesterday." Banks handed over the clipping. Jackson read:

Sam Bass was born in Indiana, it was his native home;
And at the age of seventeen young Sam began to
    roam.
Sam first came out to Texas, a cowboy for to be.
A kinder-hearted fellow you seldom ever see.

He made a deal in race stock—one called the Denton
  Mare.
He matched her in scrub races and took her to the fair.
Sam used to coin the money and spent it just as free.
He always drank good whiskey, wherever he might be.

Sam left the Collins ranch in the merry month of May
With a herd of Texas cattle, the Black Hills for to see.
Sold out at Custer City and then got on a spree.
A jollier set of cowboys you seldom ever see.

On their way back to Texas they robbed the UP train,
And then split up in couples and started out again.
Joel Collins and his partner were overtaken soon;
With all their stolen money, they had to meet their
  doom.

Sam made it back to Texas, all right side up with care.
Rode into the town of Denton, with all his friends to
  share.
Sam's life was short in Texas   three robberies did he
  do;
He robbed all the passengers, mail and express cars,
  too.

Sam had four companions, each a bold and daring lad—
Underwood and Jackson, and Barnes, all galahads.
Four of the boldest cowboys the ranges ever knew.
They whipped the Texas Rangers and ran the boys in
  blue.

Jim Murphy was arrested and then released on bail;
He jumped his bond at Tyler and took the train to
  Terrell.
But Major Jones had posted Jim and that was all a stall.
'Twas only a plan to capture Sam before the coming fall.

Sam met his fate at Round Rock, July, the twenty-first;
They pierced poor Sam with rifle balls and emptied out
   his purse.
Poor Sam he is a corpse and six foot under clay,
And Jackson's in the bushes, trying to get away.

Jim had used Sam's money and didn't want to pay.
He thought his only chance was to give poor Sam away.
He sold out Sam and Barnes and left their friends to
   mourn—
Oh what a scorching Jim will get when Gabriel blows
   his horn.

And so he sold out Sam and Barnes and left their friends
   to mourn.
Oh what a scorching Jim will get when Gabriel blows
   his horn!
Perhaps he's got to heaven, there's none of us can say;
But if I'm right in my surmise, he's gone the other way.

Smiling faintly, Jackson returned the clipping to the
newspaperman.

"Did you write that?" he asked.

"No, not me. I don't really know who wrote it, to tell
you the truth."

"Well, whoever it was, he got a few facts twisted. I don't
recall ever running into soldiers in blue. We had just about
everybody else after us, though. And I heard it was ol' Clay
Withers, Dad Egan's deputy, who shot Arkansas Johnson,
not a Texas Ranger. But I ain't surprised the Rangers would
take credit for it."

"What are you going to do now?" asked Banks.

"Hell, I don't know. Just ride away. Reckon there'll be
a hole in the ground for me before long."

"Tell me, do you regret ever having followed Sam
Bass?"

Jackson pulled on his earlobe, thinking that one over. "Why, yes, I guess I do. I'm sorry we all went the way we did. One thing about that ballad—all that talk about 'poor Sam' this and 'poor Sam' that. Nobody should feel sorry for Honest Eph. He plowed his own row. He took a big chance when he took all those cows to Nebraska with Joel Collins, and threw away the profits he made on their sale instead of redeeming the notes he signed down here. That put him in a bind, and he made a mistake thinking he could rob his way out of it. And I made a mistake going off to San Antonio with him. But what's done is done. Can't cry over spilt milk. Or spilled blood, either."

Banks nodded. "Good luck to you, Mr. Jackson."

The outlaw turned to his horse and stepped up into the saddle. "You write a good book, mister," he told Banks. "An honest book. Don't spruce it all up the way the feller who wrote that ballad did. Sam was a good friend, but he went bad, and I went bad right along with him, and the trail we rode always ends right here." He pointed at the graves, then whipped his horse around and vanished into the oak grove.

AUTHOR'S NOTE

FOR THE MOST PART, THE EVENTS DESCRIBED IN THIS BOOK AC-
tually occurred. There are two entirely fictional segments—
the Delia/Penrose episode and that involving the character
Hannah Howard. The Sam Bass of legend had quite a rep
utation as a frontier Casanova; however, my impression after studying the historical record is that he was far too shy
to make much headway with the ladies. And, of course,
once he had embarked on his life of crime, he had precious
little spare time to dedicate to romantic pursuits. That being
said, there is evidence to sustain a part of the Bass legend:
that a dark-haired woman arrived in Round Rock some
months after the outlaw had been laid to rest, and that it
was she who had erected a headstone over his grave. That
stone was soon dispensed with by souvenir hunters; in 1920
a local monument maker placed a concrete slab over the
side-by-side graves of Bass and Seaborn Barnes. No one
knew the dark-haired woman's identity; it was suspected
that she might be one of Sam's sisters from up north. But
who knows?

A third fictional element is represented by the character
of Jed Banks; while there was a Galveston newspaperman
on the scene in Round Rock those fateful summer days in
1878, he did not to my knowledge extensively interview or
write a book about the mortally wounded outlaw.

It's safe to say that Sam Bass is the Lone Star State's favorite nineteenth century desperado. That he was not as sanguinary as Clay Allison and John Wesley Hardin and Bill Longley probably contributes a great deal to his standing in that regard. Myth has painted him as a Robin Hood, who shared his stolen loot freely with those in need, and of course it didn't hurt that his favorite targets were the railroads, which were perceived by many as a heartless octopus that stretched its tentacles throughout the land and bled the people dry with exorbitant freight rates, raising the cost to farmers and ranchers of shipping the product of their labors to market while causing the rise in price of merchandise in great demand on the frontier with their high transport rates. Again, the historical record does not seem to bear this out; Bass did not go out of his way to share his stolen gold. To the extent that he did, it was to purchase the assistance—or silence—of the local folk. One must bear in mind that as a youth Sam Bass had been fascinated by the careers of the Reno brothers, that prototypical outlaw gang of antebellum Indiana, and had followed their escapades closely. The Reno brothers had understood the concept of "buying" the support of the locals, just as the James brothers of Missouri understood it. In that sense the successful guerrilla fighter and the wise outlaw rider utilized the same technique.

Sam Bass met his end on July 21, 1878—his twenty-seventh birthday—but the legend lived on. A wax figure of the famous outlaw was created and carried from town to town on the Texas frontier for some time thereafter. The residents of the shantytown near Round Rock swore that the ghost of Sam Bass rode through the old oak grove late at night. Texas cowboys adopted Bass as one of their own, although it seems Bass never did amount to much as a cowboy in real life; according to cowboy and manhunter Charley Siringo—and he would know—Sam was "the hero of more cowboys than any other bad man." A number of "penny dreadfuls" purporting to tell the true story of Sam Bass sold quite well in subsequent years. And, as happened in the case of many slain desperadoes, a vast quantity of six-guns and rifles appeared which were passed off as the personal artillery of the legendary Sam Bass. One verifiable artifact is a cartridge belt taken from Bass when he was captured—it ended up at the University of Texas library. The Sam Bass Café opened for business in Round Rock across the street from Koppel's Store within a year of the shootout that claimed the lives of Cage Grimes, Seaborn Barnes, and Bass. Meanwhile, Henry Koppel never bothered repairing the bullet holes in his store that were the result of the shooting spree that had occurred therein; a shrewd businessman, he knew how good for business those battle scars really were.

The recounting of the Round Rock shootout in this book is taken from the testimony of the intrepid Travis County Deputy Sheriff Maurice Moore, who stated:

About 4 p.m. I was standing in front of Smith's livery stable and three men passed up the street. Smith remarked to me, "There go three strangers." I noticed them carefully and thought one of them had a six shooter under his coat. The others were carrying saddlebags. They looked at me rather hard and then went across the street into the store. I walked up the street to where Grimes was standing, and remarked to him, "I think one of those men has a six shooter on." Grimes remarked that he would go and see. We walked across the street and went into the store. Not wishing to let them know I was watching them, I stood up inside the store door[way] with my hands in my pockets, whistling. Grimes approached them carelessly and asked one if he had not a six shooter. They all three replied, yes, and at the same instant two of them shot Grimes and one shot me.

"After I had fired my first shot I could not see the men on account of the smoke. They continued shooting and so did I until I fired five shots. As they passed out [of the store] I saw one man bleeding from the arm and side; I then leaned against the store door, feeling faint and sick, and recovering myself, I started on and fired the remaining shot at them. . . .

The rangers hearing the firing came upon the scene and fired upon the robbers as they retreated. Major Jones reached the place in time to engage in the fusillade. The whole village was thrown into a tumult of excitement, and the citizens who could procure arms joined in the affray. The robbers . . . firing back at every opportunity, retreated down an alley towards their horses. Early in the engagement Bass had received a shot through the hand, and as they retreated down the alley a ranger, George Harrall, shot him in the back, inflicting a mortal wound. He, however, reached and mounted his horse. Barnes was shot by George Ware, a ranger, through the head, just as he mounted his horse, and fell dead on the spot. Jackson and Bass rode off together.

What became of Jim Murphy, Frank Jackson, and other key players in this tale? Frank Jackson, or so the story goes, showed up briefly back in Denton County after the Round Rock shootout, then disappeared from Texas, never to return. According to Charley Siringo, Jackson went to Montana and became a successful cattle rancher. Others say he became a peace officer somewhere out West. Hank Underwood was never seen again, after leaving the Bass Gang in the aftermath of the Salt Creek fight, which claimed the life of his friend, Arkansas Johnson. As for Jim Murphy, the indictment against him was dismissed by the United States attorney, as promised. Murphy tried to make a go of it in Denton, but many of his neighbors had nothing but contempt for the man who had turned on Sam Bass. There were constant threats against his life, to the extent that at one point Jim Murphy had to take up residence in the county jail just to get a good night's sleep. A year after the Round Rock fight, Murphy accidentally swallowed a poison, atropine. He died in agony.

Tom Nixon, who had been one of the robbers of the Union Pacific Number Four Express at Big Springs, Nebraska, made his way home to Canada with his share of the stolen loot and was never heard from again. Jack Davis, who had accompanied Sam Bass to Texas after the UP robbery, made it to New Orleans and then took a ship to South America, where he lived out his years. Sam Pipes and Albert Herndon, who were turned in by Billy Scott and sentenced to life in prison, were pardoned by Governor Grover Cleveland as a reward for their work as volunteer nurses on a plague ship in New York harbor. Joel Collins's brothers, Henry and Billy, met violent ends; Henry was killed by a peace officer in Texas, as was Billy, who died of wounds received in a shootout with a Dallas deputy sheriff who had trailed him all the way north to the Canada border. The deputy sheriff also died of his wounds.

The most persistent of the legends that surround the short and violent life of Sam Bass is that of buried gold. Many a treasure hunter has combed the numerous alleged Bass hideouts in the thickets and caves of north-central Texas. Thirty thousand dollars of Bass loot is buried somewhere in Montague County, north of Denton, or so the legend goes. An interesting episode is related by a farmer named Henry Chapman, who claimed, six months after Sam Bass died at Round Rock, to have been traveling by mule through a thicket near Salt Creek when he happened upon a mound of dirt. At first Chapman thought that a body had been buried there, but curiosity got the better of him and he excavated the site, to find a wooden box filled with gold and silver coin. Since this was quite near the site where the Bass Gang had been surprised by the posse that took Arkansas Johnson's life, Chapman supposed that this was the hidden Bass treasure. The stunned farmer was in the process of filling a sack with this "hard money" when he looked up to see a half dozen rough-looking hombres approaching through the timber. Assuming these men were outlaw cronies of Sam Bass come to claim the gold, Chapman fled for his life. When he returned to the scene some time later with reinforcements, the box was gone. The identity of the six hardcases who frightened Henry Chapman away has so far eluded historians—if, indeed, the story has any truth to it at all.

Before long there were any number of maps circulating that were purported to show the location of the Bass treasure. Near the turn of the century a man named Hamilton, who resided in Round Rock, obtained one such map during a trip to Mexico. Hamilton brought the map back home and enlisted the aid of two friends. The X on the map led them to an old oak tree on the Liberty Road—a tree which they made short work of with their axes, laboring in the middle of the night by lantern light. All they found, to their great dismay, was a single rusty nail. That is all that anyone who has ever hunted for the Bass treasure has ever found. Still, the legend of a hidden cache of gold lingers on. Not too many years ago it was said that a map had been discovered that revealed the place where Bass had hidden *two hundred thousand* dollars' worth of gold bullion on the banks of the Trinity River. Bass never had anything close to that much stolen loot in his possession, but treasure hunters need be eternal optimists; for several weeks feverish work was done and vast excavations made on the banks of the river. Needless to say, it was all for naught.

So who was Sam Bass, really? He was a dark-haired, dark-eyed young man of slight build who stood five feet eight inches tall. He was charismatic, illiterate, charming, a good friend, reckless and daring in his ways, who thought, in his own words, that he "had the world by the tail with a downward pull," who did not have much success in his chosen vocation as bandit, and who met the fate that so many meet when they walk on the wrong side of the law.

THE AUTHOR IS indebted to the following sources: *A Sketch of Sam Bass, the Bandit,* by Charles L. Martin (Norman: University of Oklahoma Press, 1956), *Sam Bass,* by Wayne Gard (New York: Houghton Mifflin, 1936), and *Life and Adventures of Sam Bass* (Dallas: Dallas Commercial Steam Print, 1878).